PLACES & STORIES

ALSO BY WILLIAM BRIDGES

Poetry

Common Places

Weedpatch or Jericho?

The Arafura Sea

The Perfect Country of Words

Eye

The Landscape Deeper In:
Selected Poems, 1974-2004

Other

Dear Viola: Reporting, Writing and Editing
for the Student Journalist

Under the Heaven Tree: An Indiana Childhood

Five-Mountain Morning: A Memoir

A Fine Smirr of Rain: Variations on a Theme

"Places & Stories," by William Bridges. ISBN 978-1-60264-137-2.

Published 2008 by Virtualbookworm.com Publishing Inc., P.O. Box 9949, College Station, TX 77842, US. ©2008, William Bridges. All rights reserved. No part of this publication may be reproduced, stored in a retrieval system, or transmitted in any form or by any means, electronic, mechanical, recording or otherwise, without the prior written permission of William Bridges.

Manufactured in the United States of America.

PLACES
&stories
WILLIAM BRIDGES

CONTENTS

PLACES & STORIES

STORIES

To Karen

Companion through the world

Credits

The short story, *Willie & Walter*, first appeared in *The Flexible Writer* (4th ed.) by Susanna Rich (Addison, Wesley, Longman, 2003). Three pieces, "River Days," "Cherry Delight," and the opening section of "The First Americans," appeared in *Outdoor Indiana* magazine. The poem "The Photographs of Martin Chambi" appeared in the author's chapbook *Eye*, published by Pleasure Boat Studio, Bainbridge Island, Wash. A part of "Lost Villages and a Train Wreck" was published in the *Nostalgia News* magazine of the Johnson County (Ind.) Historical Society. "The Mesozoic Monster" and "Going to Saba" appeared in Franklin College publications. An earlier version of "Liebe zu München" appeared in the author's memoir *Five-Mountain Morning*.

A Note on Spellings

All English spellings of Chinese names are approximations. For ease of pronunciation, I have done my own anglicizing. Thus in the opening essay the more common spelling, Chunghsiao Road, is rendered as Chungshau, and several other place names are spelled in ways that may be unfamiliar to adherents of different spelling systems.

Of Places and Stories

A CALIFORNIA FRIEND, just back from a tour of upstate New York and Quebec, writes winningly about the trip, then adds: "The thread that connected it all was the season—leaves aglow, burnished to amber, gold, citron, flame, crimson." I had been searching for the word *citron* to describe the translucence of a tree outside my door, and there it was.

His description also recalled dimly a science-fiction story about time travelers who visit the great places and seasons of Earth. The reader never meets them—they are seen once at a distance, in an English high autumn of the 13th century, their robes and gaily caparisoned horses disappearing around the bend of a leafy road.

A phrase, "the weather of travel," came into my head. We've grown used to being insulated from the real atmospherics of the places we travel to see. Industries are built on assuring us that we can go someplace without really being there. But one can go in other ways. My Uncle Stephen, an artist, found a home in Venice and went there nearly every year. My wife and I find a deep pleasure in returning to Inverness in Scotland—there are not many "sights" and we've long since seen them. But we still settle happily into this beautiful small city with its friendly people and views of the River Ness.

One can journey this way close to home, too. After much travel, I live now in the town where I was a small child. Every day or two I walk past the house from which I set out on my tricycle at age three, when the traversable world ended half a block from

1

home. I step thoughtfully over the boundary curb, and feel the returning circle of time bringing me back into a loved landscape.

When I began assembling *Places & Stories*, it was mostly with the thought of bringing together "travel" pieces and fiction that I wanted to see in print, in one place. But the work is always wiser than the maker of it. I see now that many of the "stories" are also about journeys of some sort—literally in some cases, psychically in others. Maybe most stories are this way. And some of these stories are also evocations of place. In particular, "I Think I See My True Love Coming" is a valentine to the Phillips Collection in Washington, D.C., which I once visited almost daily for 10 weeks.

Interwoven with both places and stories are people. I would like to have mentioned more of them, but some were glimpsed too fleetingly, at least for non-fiction. What became of the consumptive French boy on the train from Chartres, who spoke with his hand always over his mouth? Or of M.V. Bodnarescu, a Romanian mathematician who could read only the precise journalism of the *Neue Züricher Zeitung*. "My work has distorted me," he said. Or of Grace Morgan, whom I have given her real name in the mostly fictional opening "story." Or the couple who ran a small-town bus station, and took me into their kitchen for warm pie on winter days.

> *The building is still there. A travel agent's*
> *fantasies fill the window. I don't go*
> *anyplace. Oh friends, kind friends,*
> *where, where? You are not even a name now.*

PLACES

& stories

WILLIAM BRIDGES

The paving stones of Taipei: Chungshau Road East

THE WINGS OF THE MORNING

A JOURNAL OF TAIPEI begins this January morning with sidewalk paving tiles—millions of them, all over the city. Each about a foot square, incised with a large circular design, other arcs intersecting on each side, like the ripples when several stones are thrown into a pond. Bright red or red-orange when freshly laid, but wearing quickly to gray, with a lingering hint of old rose.

The design is sometimes almost worn away. Many are crushed and broken, and others unstable. "Clams," my coworker Sam calls these, because on a rainy day you can step wrong and send a squirt of water up your pants leg. Very cheap, fragile, but endlessly renewed.

It takes just half an hour to walk from my apartment, west along Chungshau Road, to my work as an editor at the Government Information Office. I've been here five months, and it's all beginning to seem ordinary, which is one reason for this haphazard journal. I don't ever want to stop *looking*. Especially at faces, which are not paving tiles but wonderfully individual and often beautiful. My observations amuse Bob Irick, an old China hand, who says he never observes anything anymore, even when he wants to.

My morning walk into work takes me across seven major intersections—with Chien-kwo, Syinsheng, Chinshan, Hangchow, Shaushing, Linshen, and Tientsin, next to the Lai-Lai Hotel, where I once lived for a week as a VIP guest of the government.

5

Now I work for the government, and peer into the breakfast-room window, at new VIPs drinking their morning coffee.

Seven crossings, but six long blocks, each with its own flavor. The vinegar-works block is almost rural. Then comes the busy block with the 7-11 variety store, followed by a shady stretch with the "golden tower" office building and a firehouse, before the bustle of Hangchow crossing. After that the blocks get more commercial and less interesting, but there's still a pastry shop, the Konica photo store, the "cave" (more on that later), a Buddhist temple, and the Lai-Lai.

At Hangchow crossing, the scream and groan of bus brakes. I wrote a poem about a key embedded in the asphalt here, and I see today there is also a cheap jewelry heart next to it. A key and a heart, in the center of Taipei. Near the 7-11 a youth lounges on a motorscooter and sucks a carton of fruit juice. At a food stall a cook stands on the sidewalk, frying fritters on a grill.

January 28: When you walk in Taipei these days, you walk on iron plates over abysses. These are seemingly bottomless excavations for a subway and related operations—underground malls, parking garages. Sometimes, looking through cracks in the plates, you see work lights in the depths, like distant galaxies. Drivers occasionally fall into these black holes.

A hint of spring today, with soft clouds and the sky darkening toward the city center. The trees are tipped with green. Last fall, a girl sold betel nuts near Syinsheng crossing. Then she disappeared for months, but today she's back, a mystery. An old man is out in a chair by the firehouse, taking the air. He, too, was gone during the "cold" months, but now—like a figure in a barometer—he's come out again into the sunshine. Leucadendron trees (Melaleuca leucadendron) are everywhere, with peeling bark like old bundles of examination papers. Many have "ratoons," a word I learned yesterday for a fresh sprout coming up from the root, a promise of renewal.

January 29: Walked north to the Chungshan Theater today to see *Farewell, My Concubine* for the second time. Realized that what I went to see was the betrayal scene and Juxien's absolutely blank expression as she realizes that her husband has denounced her to the Red Guards. I focused on her, I think, because she was the one who just wanted to live an ordinary life, as I also do. Bob Irick says the Chinese are extraordinarily selfish, even in family relationships. No tradition of self-sacrifice at all. But Bob has to admit he thinks well of the young AIDS activist here who demonstrates by taping condoms all over his body.

I walk home from the theater along Sungchiang, a new street to me but paved with the tiles that are the city's underlying pattern. I cross a long footbridge, then go down some shady steps and under microcarpa trees to the corner of Syinsheng and Chungshau, and then home.

January 31: A study of hair barrettes on the walk into work today. A woman at Chien-kwo wore one with a lurid heart design. A lot of this good-natured kitsch in Taiwan. All kinds of fashion on the street—a woman in brown slacks with a matching checked jacket. Some fairly stylish business outfits, but a lot of jeans, leggings, nondescript slacks and blouses—Taipei going to work on a Monday morning and not much concerned about how it looks. Gritty (although this was a pleasant, half-sunny morning with some mackerel clouds).

I passed again the woman with the terrible bruise under her right eye. Thought a week ago that someone had hit her, but it begins to look like a permanent discoloration. The betel-nut girl is out today, squatting on the pavement, and so is my Old Man Barometer, one sandal on and one off, as he reads the paper. An unfailing indicator of Taipei weather.

Some of us went to Bob Irick's for supper last night. His apartment reminded me of my Uncle Bill's in New York—some beautiful art and tasteful furnishings, but lost in the ruck of an old man's poor housekeeping. I want to get rid of everything I own—let me live a clean, spare old age, without junk (or paper, especially paper).

February 2: Clearing my mind. I can be happy and supported anywhere.

Though I take the wings of the morning and dwell in the uttermost parts of the sea . . . .

February 4: Karen arrives tonight for a month. This "diary" goes on hold.

March 24: A beautiful sunny spring morning. An old man exercises in the courtyard. At Chien-kwo, a plumber passes with a dozen lengths of water pipe over his shoulder. Destruction and rebuilding are endless in Taipei. At Syinsheng crossing, there's a new and temporary wooden footbridge over an excavation in the street. Fun to watch pedestrians start to walk around the construction, then change course when they realize there's a <u>bridge</u>! What is this project anyway? Stormwater diversion, maybe?

Badly shattered paving stones near the corner of Linshen. A metaphor for Taipei—old things, continually broken up, replaced.

April 12: Another going-to-work morning. Lots of motor-scooterists, some with black, insect-like helmets. A woman goes by in a coolie hat, pulling a cart with junk and a *myanbei*, or quilt. The little bridge at Syinsheng is still in place, but the construction seems nearly done. Today there's a new high-rise on the horizon, with a construction crane. When did that happen?

Some sun comes out as I cross Chinshan, shedding a pale light on the paving tiles. By the firehouse with its miniature red truck there's a teahouse I've never noticed, barely wide enough for a door and a sign with antique letters, indecipherable. Waking up in Taipei is like waking every morning in a new city.

A beautiful girl goes by on a scooter, twisting a lock of hair around her finger. My Old Man Barometer is barefoot today, even though the weather is only *mamahuhu*—so-so. (Venny, at work, was surprised I knew that word.)

April 15:

In whom we live and move and have our being . . . .

Brown air at the west end of Chungshau this morning. Bricks and sand are piled next to the 7-11, which is being renovated into—what? A monk runs toward me at the corner of Shaushing, with very unmonklike urgency, across the poor tortured Taipei paving tiles.

Am thinking of my childhood friend Lee, whose grandparents were missionaries in China and who came home on the Swedish repatriation ship *Gripsholm* in World War II. Lee gave me a fragment of a chocolate bar from the ship, a dark and bitter relic.

April 21: The little bridge at Syinsheng is gone and the street repaved. A street cobbler with no business is almost asleep. A butterfly—white wings with black spots—hovers above a broken sidewalk tile. A dog waits nearby, tied to a scooter.

April 22: The butterfly is there again today, on the same tile.

April 30: Taipei is forever changing, forever temporary. A lifesize papier-mâché horse was on the sidewalk yesterday, but is gone today. The barbed wire frames that surrounded my office during recent rioting have been moved to a side street—but are still at the ready. A chair in the street holds a parking place for someone. Every day the flood of motorscooters at Syinsheng presses forward against the changing of the light.

Whatever is replacing the 7-11 will have much fancy interior woodwork, with cove and ogive molding and a tiled entrance.

May 5: Pools of water and moist paving tiles, washed clean by yesterday's "plum rain." An older woman walks ahead of me carrying a flowered parasol. At Syinsheng she overtakes a stoical young man and takes his arm to cross the street. The young man then walks ahead and repeats the pattern at the next corner. A mother and her retarded son, perhaps?

A puff of black smoke from the subway hole, like news from an oracle.

Our church has been praying for Celine, who makes amazing artificial flowers, but who is losing her eyesight and may not be able to work much longer.

May 6: Went out, in a better mind, into the glorious morning, past the sunlit and wind-ruffled gum trees in the courtyard. Fell in behind the same mother and son (if they are) of yesterday, wearing the same clothes, following the same pattern. Doors are open on Chungshan, revealing interiors where "garbage slinks south along the fence," in a line by my poet friend, Mike O'Connor. The vinegar works are fragrant today.

A tall and beautiful Chinese girl waits for a bus. I wrote a poem describing "long-legged" Chinese women, but Sam and another office friend, Jon, who have first-hand knowledge, set me straight. Waists are long but legs short, a fact artfully concealed by clothing. I see a lot of low-slung women now.

Have wondered for months about a dark and ambiguous store just before I turn off for work. I've thought of it as "the cave," in fantasy an opium den, but when I finally went in today, it turned out to be just a meat and produce market.

May 7: A motorscooter is taking off from "the cave" with several hundred eggs loose in a crate. Will they make it unbroken to their destination?

Sam tells me at work today that his Chinese name means "barbarian who plays the flute." Sure, Sam.

May 8: I always think, starting out, that there won't be anything new today, and then there is. This time it's a big pile of rubble near the bus stop. All we walkers become adept at missing the obstacles, like the metal duct at Chinshan, which fills and is almost hidden on rainy days.

And people. Today the old ladies' exercise group is in the courtyard, a girl in a short leopard dress crosses the street, another girl carries lilies at the bus stop, a workman washes the windshield of his truck. A car goes by, full of plants, with a tree sticking out of the trunk. What's going on here?

May 11:

Let not your heart be troubled . . . .

Susan, a colleague, says I should wear a mask against the pollution. Oh, not yet, I think. A girl goes by with no mask but her hand over her mouth. Does that do any good?

The girl selling betel nuts is back today, after more months of absence. Why is she there for only a day or two every three months? Who is she, anyway? We say good morning to each other, as usual.

Workmen are sitting outside the old 7-11, which doesn't seem to be metamorphosing into much of anything these days.

May 12: The sounds of Taipei. A constant, low roar of traffic, but surprisingly few horns. An occasional short blast, but even in a jam drivers just beep—no sustained blowing. Because of the cramped driving conditions, side mirrors are on flexible stalks. As I rode with Jon on his scooter the other day, the traffic converged around us and he reached out, pushed a mirror out of the way, and we scooted through.

Packing crates block the sidewalk outside a store specializing in large Buddhas and other statues—a Buddha boutique! Next to the crates is an elephant, carved out of a tree trunk. Outside the National Police Headquarters on Chungshau, a white dog is asleep on the sidewalk—or dead, it's hard to tell. Asleep, I think, since Taipei mutts can and do sleep anywhere.

I walk into the office behind Bob Irick, who is dapper in suit, briefcase, and rolled umbrella. I tell him he looks like a diplomat, and he replies, "The umbrella is to keep it from raining."

May 13: To the American Library last night to check out a book of John Haines's poems. Walked home with Jupiter sailing on a rack of clouds in a mauve sky.

May 14: It is HOT! An old woman cycles by with a large and beautifully packed load on the back of her bike—what care went into this! A little altar to the gods has been erected just beyond Chien-kwo, with a toy stove and a tremendous smell of garlic nearby. All there is today.

May 17: A girl waits for the light at Syinsheng, giving her long black hair a quick comb. Another girl, wearing a big hand-kerchief as a pollution mask, looks as if she's on her way to a holdup. Faces of Taipei: Expressionless this morning. Going to work, but not liking it much.

Work on the former 7-11 has resumed. This is beginning to look like a florist or some other classy boutique. A big glass-fronted fridge for flowers has been installed.

The tiny teahouse with the antique sign has been identified as the Celestial Clouds, or more probably the Ancient Rain Café.

May 20: Counting the time in Washington, D.C., and here, I've been gone from home a year today. Or is this home now?

May 21: A little blue flatbed truck passes. One zipped around our church bus on the way back from an outing at Ilan last Sunday, and Madeline (the South African) exclaimed, "Cheeky blue truck!" They'll be cheeky blue trucks from now on.

THE WINGS OF THE MORNING

My continuing conversation with the betel-nut salesgirl hunkered on the sidewalk is extended today, in English, to "Good morning, how are you?" and "Fine, thank you." A girl passes in a Snoopy the Beagle T-shirt, which is not so bad, but at one level this society is afflicted with terminal cuteness. My local café is the Baby Doll. I've seen enough chirpy cartoon figures to last a lifetime. And also enough motorscooter tail flaps with the puckered-up pig warning, "No Kiss."

I keep seeing the older woman with the flowered umbrella and her grown son, who walks ahead and then waits dumbly for her to catch up. My Old Man Barometer is out reading his paper this morning, in sandals. Some large sinkholes have appeared in the sidewalk near him—the red paving stones are badly broken. Walk around.

May 24: An earthquake shook the apartment last night and a second, milder one hit today while some of us were eating lunch in McDonald's. The chandeliers swayed, but business went on as usual.

May 25: On Jenai Boulevard last night—wonderful summer evening, with strollers, lights. To be remembered.

Hot, hazy morning, with no mountains visible. For a while, there were metal plates over the street project at Syinsheng, but now the plates have been asphalted over, which seems odd. Someone has the asphalt concession? A big yawn from a woman at a food stall. Taipei is not fully awake yet. No betel-nut girl now for several days.

June 3: The mother and son again. He walks 50 paces ahead, carrying her bag.

A city in constant flux, the smash and grab of atoms. The former 7-11 has revealed itself as Debbie's Station, the boutique of all time, with pottery, flowers, a lending library, a food stand, and knick-knacks of every description.

A parked motorscooter shouts its painted slogan: "It's New! It's Only! It's Now!" A woman goes by on the rear of another scooter, bare legs spread around the driver, almost an act of love.

June 6: A major earthquake last night, 6.2, centered near Ilan. My top-floor apartment rolled, but no damage was done. I crouched, as instructed, in the steel-framed doorway until it passed. The mother and son are back this morning, but today he is smiling at her, after months of impassiveness.

June 16: Always out of the crowd, single faces. From the landing this morning, across an areaway, someone in a motorcycle helmet looked out a window for a moment. As I walked home with Sam yesterday, a smiling woman—in her 40s maybe—greeted him. When she had passed, he said something disparaging. "Oh, Sam, you're missing her!" I thought.

June 17: A sun-washed morning after rain. Light-dappled paving tiles, pools of water. Beautiful. Soft voices on the elevator this morning

June 21: Since I had left home early, there was time for a walk through the little park at Chinshan, behind the "golden tower." A black cat crossed my path and also a monk with shaved head, gray gown, satchel. (They wear trousers underneath, I saw recently when a sloppily buttoned one passed me.)

June 23: A long conversation in the Blues Café last night with Mike O'Connor, about trying to record everything—on a train trip when I was a child, and now walking each day down Chungshau. To what purpose? Mike spoke of his own exhaustion after trying to photograph every bit of one strip of industrial Taipei.

We talked about the people, not only the torrent of them, but the thought of the whole history and future of each one. "Ideally," Mike said, "there would just be me."

THE WINGS OF THE MORNING

In a village where he lived, a woman—either very friendly or the resident idiot—used to greet him warmly each day, until he came by one day with his Chinese wife. "Here I was with a daughter of the Empire," he said, and after that the villager was cool to him—which made perfect sense to me. It's as if the betel-nut girl should introduce me to her brother or sister some morning—not just the two of us alone in the world anymore.

Ideally, you have to stop somewhere. "Ideally, there would just be me."

June 25: At Chien-kwo, pedestrians tramp blithely through fresh cement, leaving ragged footprints.

No psychic action this morning at the Hangchow crossing, next to the key and heart in the pavement. A cab goes by with an (apparently) aboriginal woman in the back seat, tiny white triangles painted on her cheekbones.

June 27: Sounds of Taipei: Other than traffic, the main one has been cicadas, which are loud in all the trees today.

June 28: A motorscooter delivers a bag of carrots and celery to a doorstep. Another scooter rider at a drive-up phone, mouth and motor both running.

July 2: Hot, sunny morning, but with enough light breeze to make it bearable—so far. The radio predicts this will continue through next week, but who knows? Pre-typhoon weather, maybe? Anyway, I've gone into summer mode—no more necktie into work. It goes in the briefcase and goes on after I've arrived. (I know, why wear one at all? It's just part of the persona. At least I use a tiebar, and don't sew mine to my shirt, as Sam does.)

Like Venice, Taipei gets smellier as the summer progresses—human smells, food smells, road smells, fumes from the vinegar works, a real stew. A bicycle rider goes by, face mask on, eyes almost closed, oblivious.

Two days ago, the betel-nut girl inexplicably returned and said hello. Today, just as inexplicably, she's gone. Big mystery of Taipei. I think she's in an institution and just comes home occasionally to visit and sell betel nuts.

A woman is looking around and writing things in a notebook. And I am writing in my notebook about her writing in her notebook. What an incestuous business this is!

Jon and I finally visited the Ancient Rain teahouse. The rooms next to it are being remodeled, and there was some noise from that side while we ate. "Someone trying to break in from another dimension," Jon said.

My Old Man Barometer is out, feet half out of his slippers. But facing the other way today, a big change.

July 4: There's a new consignment of statuary in front of the Buddha Boutique. Out to supper last night, with one star shining among the departing rain clouds.

Celine's eyes were worse Sunday, and one was bandaged. But she had made green roses for the altar.

He knoweth our frame; he remembereth that we are dust . . . .

Strangeness this morning at the corner of Chien-kwo—a man in an actual pith helmet, a topi. A woman in a candy-striped hat and shades. A bike-truck loaded with household goods, husband pedaling, wife on behind. The woman with the coolie hat goes by on her bike, loaded today with textiles. The street cobbler is carving a new heel with his knife.

July 11: Typhoon Tim roared through last night, after several days of brilliant blue "pre-typhoon" weather. This morning the streets are littered with shards of broken plastic signs. No wonder everyone is told to stay inside—going out would be like walking into a blizzard of knives.

July 14: The betel-nut girl is back. "Hello, how are you?" she says. "Fine," I reply. Ahead of us, a woman pauses, looks back sharply, and walks on, over the broken tiles of Taipei.

[1993]

A sunny morning in the biergarten of the Victualienmarkt, the farmers' market in the heart of Munich.

LIEBE ZU MÜNCHEN

KLAUS LORENZEN, my Army buddy and deserter from the Hitler Youth, could never understand my love for Munich. To Klaus, whose home was Flensburg near the Danish border, the Bavarian capital was a garish stage set, with bad memories of Brown Shirts and braggadocio. There is a 1914 photo of a crowd on the Odeonsplatz celebrating the start of World War I. A wild-eyed young *fanatiker* turns out on closer inspection to be Adolf Hitler.

Klaus was no dummy. After a day or two of hurling pop-bottle gasoline bombs at American tanks in Nürnberg, he left the Hitler Jugend, hiked home to Flensburg, polished his English, became an exchange student to the United States, and enlisted in the 3rd Infantry Division as a translator, to get his citizenship. I could not explain to him the lure of Munich for a white-bread Midwesterner, whose previous idea of civic splendor had been the Johnson County, Indiana, courthouse. I'm not sure I can explain it now; all I know is that I spent the three most intense days of my life there, in the summer of 1958, walking every inch of the city (it seemed), visiting every beer hall (it seemed), and wandering for hours in the oddly named English Garden with the towers of the Frauenkirche floating in the distance like a dream.

How to explain something that was a pure explosion of the senses, a poem in gilt and stucco, a divine breath of the warm South? I will be quoting Keats about "the blushful Hippocrene" if I'm not careful. Beer and bratwurst played a part, but not all that big a one. So did the relief of a three-day pass from Army disci-pline. But mostly I was drunk with a city whose every paving stone seemed afire for me with youth and romance. I think I had a hotel room. Perhaps I slept during the 72 hours, but if so I don't remember when.

So what did I see, do, experience in those hours?

A vignette arises. I am eating roast meat and onions on a stick outside the Augustiner Keller, in a crowd. Surely no food has ever had this sharp, all-conquering smell before. Only saffron is exotic enough to explain it, though it may be merely garlic. A little later I am sitting (in my self-consciously GI civvies) in the quietest res-taurant of my life, with dim light filtering through stained glass, and ordering venison for the first time from a severely correct Herr Ober. (A lot of these memories have to do with food: its smell, savor, texture. Munich is one of the world's great cities just to eat one's way through.) When not eating or drinking, I am soaking up every building, statue, strasse, store, and vista with the avidity of someone who has only three days to live. It was some-thing, I imagine, of what a blind man feels when the operation has succeeded, the bandages come off, and the whole wild, disorient-ing world of sight and color bursts in upon him. Too much, too much, and never, never enough.

To get down to earthy cases, I have tried the famed Hofbräu-haus by daylight, found it pleasant, and am now back at midnight in the Schwemme—the swim, the horse pond, the blowsy base-ment beer hall where busty Bavarian *mädels* carry five foaming steins in each hand. I have drunk a <u>lot</u> of beer. A whore is work-ing on me at the table—a nice lady, older, a bit the worse for wear, but ready to take a lonely GI to her capacious bosom. And I am not exactly averse to the idea, despite inexperience in such matters, but why would I want to go home with her when all Mu-nich is out there to be ravished? So I temporize and evade. A man nearby—her friend, confederate, maybe just a knowing Münch-ner—observes to her that I'm clearly not the kind who likes pretty girls. (I know enough German to understand all this.) How to save my macho honor, or dishonor? I apologize to her, praise her beauty, but add that "jeder Mensch ist nicht so einfach"—"Every man is not so simple." What a goof I am! I half expect her to say, in my mother's old phrase, "I'm not mad, just disgusted," but she makes a wry face and goes off to greener pastures (or ones not so green).

As if to reassert my shaky manhood, I go the next afternoon to the Marienbad public pool where the girls wear next to nothing and are falling out of that. No interest in sex from them, just in getting every possible photon of sunshine onto every centimeter of bronzed Bavarian flesh.

It's a little later still in the English Garden. I've finally slowed down enough to sit on a bench near the Chinesischen Turm, an obvious GI on holiday, and contemplate the vistas of this incomparable park. A panhandler approaches with a story of needing train fare to see his dying mother in North Germany. I listen and say, "Leider nicht, Ich habe kein Geld." Nonplussed, he tells the whole story over again, and again I say no. He draws himself up in a fury and spits at me the worst thing he can think of: "You're not an American—you're a German!"

The days, the endless afternoons, are full of summer light. In the Nürnberger Bratwurst-Glockl, with its sign showing a bell made of sausages, kitchen fires burn brightly, awakening gleams in pewter plates on the walls. At the Rathaus around the corner, the figures of the Glockenspiel come out each hour to march and play their tunes. A block away, the Karl Valentin Museum holds quirky memorabilia of the great Munich folk comic. (Sometime during the three days I have seen a film with Valentin and his delicious foil, Liesl Karlstadt.) Valentin, the story goes, was dragged offstage by the Nazis after saying, "Guess what? I saw a black Mercedes today and there wasn't an S.S. man in it!" Returning after the war and prison to a tumultuous welcome, his first words on stage were, "Guess what? There *was* an S.S. man in that Mercedes!"

I have poked my head, it seems, into half the churches of Munich; the Bridgeses are a family of church crawlers. The golden baroque sunburst above the altar of St. Johann Nepomuk in the Assamkirche still dazzles me. I have been to the zoo—Hellabrun, "bright fountain"—where a woman has left her baby with me for an hour until I wonder if I've become an involuntary father. I have been past the German Museum, the Alte Pinakothek art museum, the Hofgarten. I have drunk coffee in the Café Annast on the Odeonsplatz. The Oktoberfest must wait for another visit, with Klaus this time, but I have argued with an unregenerate Nazi in the Pschorrbräu at midnight and pissed against the wall of the Maximilianeum at 2 a.m., hoping no policeman was watching.

I have also bought a little book, just published, by Wilhelm Hausenstein, titled *Liebe zu München*—"Love to Munich." The chapters are evocative: "The City and Its Panorama," "Meaning and Destiny of the City," "Of Art and Artists." Despite my limited German, I can see that these little essays are really love letters. The author's knowledge and his sensitivity to the city far exceed mine; I have adopted his title for this essay with humility and gratitude.

In the years since my three-day visit, I've returned to Munich several times, though never with the lover's first crazy passion. I spent a happy day once showing the city to a plump little New Yorker who had stopped off on her way to a kibbutz in Israel. I made an appointment long in advance with a friend to meet in the Bratwurst-Glockl at a date and time certain. I was there, he wasn't, the more loss to him.

I have worked in Munich as a reporter for an international news service, covering a horrible plane crash that also incinerated a streetcar full of Münchners. I have spent an afternoon listening to a brass quintet in an obscure suburb, and have drunk beer at dawn with farmers in the Viktualienmarkt, not an especially good idea.

I once spent most of a day going from shop to shop trying to buy an air-pressure gauge that would tell my spelunking brother how deep he was in a cave. I had to invent a vocabulary: "Tiefenmesser," depth gauge, and "Höhlewanderer," cave explorer. I may have told some startled clerks that my brother was wandering in Hell and needed to know how far down he was. But everyone listened, tried to help, walked me to the next block to point out a store that might have such a bizarre device. I never found one, but would not have missed for the world that day in Munich among wonderful Münchners.

Eventually I took my wife and children to Munich, and I believe they loved it nearly as much as they did Venice, Paris, or London. But how to tell them what it was like to be young, with all the world before me, in the city of my dreams? Can it ever be explained, by anybody? Only years later, when I read Baron Corvo's anthem of praise and hopeless passion for Venice, did I understand what had happened to me during those three days in Munich: that my soul had been jerked clean out of my mouth and made to encompass a city, a country, a world.

And what was the city, the country, the world of Munich? Yes, it was a stage set; when I saw the repeating sandstone façades along Ludwigstrasse near the Theatinerkirche (the Theater Church!), I knew what Klaus meant. Yes, it spawned the Nazis and is next door to Dachau. It is huge and beery and vulgar. It has also been Germany's center of art, music, film, journalism, science, debate. Yeats was right about how close the places are of creation and excrement.

After a highway altercation, a Berlin truckdriver sued a Münchner for saying, "You slob, we had culture in Bavaria when you Berliners were still eating acorns in the woods." A judge threw out the case on the ground that truth was a defense. Munich was the capital of a slightly mad kingdom, and it has never forgotten. In my three days there I experienced for the first time a coherent world—what a great human city really is, a true *Weltstadt*. Munich took me in her arms, and if the embrace at times was that of a whore in the Schwemme, I knew there was pure gold in her heart.

[2005]

CODA

THE FALL OF 2006 found Karen and me in travel mode again. The bank account was reasonably healthy and no major appliances had broken down lately. (That would happen the next year.) We decided to make a three-week Middle European trip that would include seeing the Lipizzaner horses in Vienna, drinking beer in Munich, and visiting Horst and Maria Piewak, friends since Army days, in Würzburg. While at Piewaks, we would celebrate Karen's 65th birthday.

Vienna went well (horses ditto), although Karen was taking medication for some lingering sciatica. Reaching Munich by train, we dragged our bags to the subway and then headed on foot for the Hotel am Victualienmarkt near the center of town. Or at least we thought it was near the center. But as we trekked down street after street, it seemed to recede. By the time we found it, Karen was in pain. And by the time she had trudged up three flights of stairs (no elevator) and fallen over the top step, it was more than a mild inconvenience. She took a slug of heavy painkiller, collapsed in bed, and was out like a *Bierleichnam,* a beer corpse, at the Oktoberfest.

I had a moment of panic and self-pity—no, several moments. What to do? Would this get worse? What about all the things we planned to see and do in Munich? Had we been crazy to make this solo trip at our advanced ages, rather than signing up for the Elderhostel bus? And, more importantly, could we get a room on a lower floor or move to another hotel?

Then common sense kicked in, and also the good advice of a book I was carrying on Buddhist breathing meditation. We needed to live within our conditions, which on reflection were not all that bad. We had money, and Munich has excellent medical services. We both speak German. I talked with the obliging hotel owner, who said we could move to the first floor if we didn't mind a narrower "French bed." We didn't. I walked a block to the Victualienmarkt, Munich's farm market, and loaded up on fruit, bread, and wurst for supper. By the next morning, Karen could move enough to get downstairs. Then, by easy stages, we made it to the biergarten of the Victualienmarkt, where we could sit all day if necessary, drinking coffee, reading newspapers, and people-watching. Live where you are, in the present moment, the book said.

That's what we did, essentially, for a couple of days, although Karen soon was improving enough for short excursions beyond the V-markt. I quit worrying about what we weren't seeing, and enjoyed being with her. We made it to lunch at the Nürnberger Bratwurst-Glockl, three blocks away, even though it took rest stops at a coffee shop, beside one of the plastic lions that were prowling the city, and on a pile of lumber in the Rathausplatz, the town center. After a day or two we got a little further, to the Augustiner Keller, for lunch. I took off on my own to revisit the English Garden and the Assamkirche with its amazing altar.

The Pope was in town (and involved in controversy over a lecture he had given on Islam). One night we had supper at the Deutsche Eiche, a gay restaurant down the street from our hotel. The bar was festooned with portraits of the Pope wearing a rainbow halo. Who knew?

On about the third day, I looked up from my *Süddeutsche-Zeitung* in the Victualienmarkt and remarked that the Pope had left town, and that the Oktoberfest was about to start. "Pope's gone, time to party!" Karen said. The crisis, if it had been one, was over.

We went on by train to Würzburg, where Horst and Maria moved into their travel trailer so we could have their apartment. They threw a birthday party for Karen, and we taught them to play euchre. Their kids (and a granddaughter) showed up to see us, and one of them, a tour-bus driver, ferried us around the Bavarian countryside in the glorious autumn weather, stopping frequently to drink *federweiss*, the new and potent "feather wine," in outdoor gardens.

I came home thoughtful. Age (and illness) forces change upon us. The culture (and advertising) tells us we don't have to change—we can have it all, forever. But we can't. All that we have, really, is the breath we're taking now, in whatever place we happen to be. We have to work with that.

Munich half a century before had been a fantastic carnival of experiences and sensations—and of freedom from the strictures of Army life. But I had never felt freer than sitting in the Victualienmarkt on a September morning, with my long-loved wife, and not a place to go nor a plan to follow.

Munich had taken me to her heart in youth, and now, in a different way, she had solaced me again.

[2007]

A ROAR AND A CLOUD OF DUST

BY THE SIDE OF THE EDD SHEPPARD Memorial Highway, a country road near Paragon, Indiana, cars are turning off the pavement in a brown haze of dust. We have reached our destination by luck, after scouting the back roads in vain for directions posted on telephone poles or fence posts.

That destination—for Jerry, our wives, and me—is dirt-track racing at the Paragon Speedway (founded by Edd Sheppard), and dust is one of the things it's about. Others are speed and smash-ups and sitting on plank bleachers from late afternoon until early the next morning, watching sprint cars, street stocks, and "bombers" roar and slide their way around three-eighths of a mile of former Indiana cornfield.

But dust is the first and lasting impression. Entering a grassy parking field downwind of the track, we pass a car so soiled that our fingers itch to scrawl something on it. "Wonder how long it's been parked here?" Jerry's wife, Sheron, wonders. "Probably half an hour," Karen, my wife, replies. That's dust, bigtime.

Dirt tracks are also about noise and competition, but at 6:30 on a Sunday evening in July, the Paragon Speedway is as relaxed as a church picnic. We buy our tickets at a neat white gatehouse and saunter up a hill, the other side of which slopes to an oval

27

track with short straightaways separating sprawls of banked earth at each end. A small infield with a pond is off-limits to spectators. Beyond the track is a pit area full of vans and trailers, then two metal grain silos followed by miles of corn, richly green after the past week's thunderstorms. Beyond that, distantly, the hills that everyone outside Indiana has trouble believing exist here.

The race crowd, already gathering, is relaxed and happy. People chat and settle themselves on hillside bleachers made of weathered planks or aluminum strips, laid across stumps of creosoted telephone poles. Some have brought lawn chairs to straddle the planks, and their clothing is as casual as the seating arrangements. I'm a first-time dirt tracker and am overdressed—the Levis are okay, but my shirt has a collar. The upper-body covering of choice here is a T-shirt, sometimes with a snappy motto: "Go fast or be last." Or more aggressively, "We bust ours so we can kick yours."

The track is muddy, and Jerry—a racing writer in his spare time—explains that it has been soaked on purpose, in what will prove a futile effort to hold down the dust from tonight's big racing field. This field includes 45 sprint cars and smaller numbers of street stock cars and bombers. The sprints are a step up in size from midgets. The stocks and the slightly longer bombers look like your family car after a moderately serious collision.

When the sprints take to the track, the noise is like a hundred circular saws ripping through pine planks. But amid the din are also moments of great beauty. Watching 20 brightly colored cars slide around a turn, spraying fans of dirt, is a child's dream of racing. These are the wind-up toys we played with as kids, dragging them out of a big toybox at a cousin's house—stubby and rounded at the back, sloped in front, a big number 22 in bright red against a lemon yellow body. As they charge out of a turn, they're a perfect poster for racing. "Saturday Night Thunder" shouts a T-shirt, and that could go across the bottom of the poster.

A ROAR AND A CLOUD OF DUST

The sprints go like demented dune buggies, but when they stop—spinning out, stalling, colliding with each other—they're helpless. They have no gears or clutches; a Jeep or tow truck has to drive onto the track and push, goosing their engines back to life. Then they're off again, like beetles on amphetamine, sliding, throwing dirt, busting a gasket to catch up with the tail of the pack, to which they are now exiled.

I know nothing about the technical side of all this, and Jerry wisely doesn't try to educate me. The Paragon track is more primitive than many, but its races are sanctioned by the United States Auto Club, or USAC. Since the track isn't high-banked, speeds are moderate. The sprints make a circuit in 15 to 16 seconds, at between 90 and 100 miles per hour. The track record is 14.9 seconds, set by Robbie Stanley in 1980.

Stanley died last summer in a crash at the Winchester, Indiana, track, pointing up the darker side of going fast, which all the skillful driving, padded helmets, and rollbars in the world can't conceal. Injury and death will not spoil this evening, but there will be plenty of spills as cars bump each other or slide too far up on the turns and careen into neighboring fields. There are no guard rails, which is just as well, since these would damage the car and driver more than simply rolling to a stop in clover. A screen protects the crowd from flying debris, and anyone who's still nervous can move a little higher up the hill.

Drivers can go high or low through the turns. Low seems to make sense, since that path is shorter, but Jerry says there are compensating advantages to riding the outside rim. And anyway, he adds, "real men go high on the turns." The shorter inside groove is referred to derisively as "the huggie pole."

Like all racing, the Paragon show is unabashedly macho, even for the handful of women drivers like Brenda Buster, whom the track announcer refers to all evening as "the young lady." Buster is evidently just learning; her times are slow and she finishes far back, even in the "last chance" qualifying races for drivers who have failed earlier.

This raises the question of how anyone learns to drive on dirt, in races Jerry describes as "about the closest you can get to being out of control without totally losing it." The turns at each end of the oval are so close together that the cars simply slide through them, their front wheels braced in the direction of the skid. They seem almost to stop for an instant, before the wide rear tires take hold, halt the sideways slide, and send the car charging forward again. "Squat and dart," my wife calls it. One Indiana school teaches the basics of sprint driving, but in the end, Jerry observes, "it's like ski-jumping. You just have to go out and do it." Dirt-track racing with its unique driving skills is giving way slowly to faster racing on paved tracks, "and someday you may not see any of this."

Tonight's crowd is mostly young, with a strong family flavor. Some couples have brought their children. Beards and ponytails abound. Coolers supplement sandwiches and soft drinks from a concession stand on the hilltop above the bleachers (hotdogs, $1.50, garnish them yourself at the end of the counter). But this is not a hard-edged, beer-swilling crowd, just central Indiana people out for a night in the open after a week of hard work on the farm, at the office, or doing the laundry. For seven hours of racing they've paid $15 each, and maybe another dollar for a souvenir program. The program contains the track rules, pictures of past winners, a program number for giveaways during the evening, ads for motor tune-ups and crushed stone, and a photo of contestants in the speedway's annual bikini contest.

The Paragon track is a lovely place to be on this cool evening with a few sunset clouds above the cornfields. Others besides race fans are enjoying it, too. Glancing up, we see what look like parachutes, but turn out, as they drift silently toward us, to be two ultralight aircraft, with skeletal bodies hanging insect-like beneath oblong canopies of blue and white sail.

A ROAR AND A CLOUD OF DUST

The track announcer comments good-naturedly on what fine seats the ultralight pilots have provided themselves. He also reports that one race driver is 44 today and will celebrate his ninth wedding anniversary tomorrow. Even the USAC officials, flinty-eyed about lining up the cars properly, are otherwise good-natured. In one stock race, a car loses its hood and a scrap partly blocks the driver's vision. He wants to keep running, but an official flags him off. The driver does another lap defiantly, then flips the flagman the bird before roaring off to the pits. He's back in a later race, with no penalty. "At this level, things are pretty loose," Jerry says.

The sprint qualifications are followed by those for street stocks and bombers, both resembling conventional cars that have been attacked by glass- and upholstery-eating army ants. Some are sprucely painted and look nice enough to drive to church tomorrow morning. Others look beyond the help of God or baling wire.

After the qualifications, heats, last-chance runs, and a final sprint race for all non-qualifiers, the evening grinds down after midnight to the 30-lap sprint feature. The non-qualifiers' race was interminable, a succession of spins, yellow lights, and restarts. But the feature racers have all the right stuff, handling their cars expertly for 20 laps before one or two minor mishaps bring out the yellow briefly.

The race is a dirt-track epiphany of screaming engines, billowing curtains of dust, and a dozen racers diving together into turns that seem too tight for half that number. The winner is the "birthday boy," and the announcer has more to tell us about him. Not only is he 44 today and married nine years tomorrow, but his wife's birthday is Monday!

The crowd applauds. Children, recruited earlier, hand the driver a trophy. His relatives hug him, and he's invited to "say a few words."

31

"That's all the words some of these guys know," Jerry says, with friendly cynicism.

Much of the crowd is heading home by now, but the night isn't over; the feature races for street stocks and bombers are still ahead. The bombers, wallowing like bathtubs after the nimble sprints, are still roaring behind us as we walk to our car.

It is 1 a.m. We have been sitting on planks for more than six hours. Our eyes sting with dust and we shout at each other, into eardrums numbed by noise. The once-tranquil night has become surreal. Are there drivers inside the bombers, or are they like the psycho truck in *Duel*, hurling themselves malevolently toward morning?

The moon, pale and high when we arrived, is setting as we drive away. In that far-off afternoon, one of the blue and white ultralights had sailed across it, a tiny, soundless galleon. Now, as the dust and noise recede, this is the image that returns, with the scrap of a childhood lullaby: "Wynken and Blynken and Nod one night, sailed off in a silver shoe . . . ."

The Indiana night gathers us into its quiet darkness, and we are on our way toward home and sleep and dreams.

[1995]

CAGES FOR ELEPHANTS

On our kitchen counter is a blue-and-white ashtray from the "Hōtel des Volcans, Goma, Congo Belge." It depicts a lake and three peaks trailing plumes of smoke, and is a souvenir of a trip my uncle, William Bridges, made to the Congo in 1946. And there is another memento—a sheaf of letters that told me more than I had known before about this passionate man who hid his emotions beneath a modest manner and self-deprecating humor.

NOTHING IN MY UNCLE BILL'S previous life—whether in rural Indiana, Paris, or New York City—had quite prepared him to build cages for elephants.

But in the fall of 1946, he was in the Belgian Congo, charged with doing just that. The Congo government had given three elephants to the Bronx Zoo—the result of a casual conversation months earlier between Laurence Rockefeller and the Belgian minister plenipotentiary. The zoo had sent Bill, its curator of publications, to arrange matters and see the elephants aboard ship. Bill spoke French, could be counted on not to embarrass the zoo or his country, and could write about the experience for the zoo's magazine, *Animal Kingdom*.

It was not an easy mission. While he didn't have to nail the cages together himself, he had to find someone who could. And there were other uncertainties. He was in Leopoldville, and the zoo's elephants were part of an arkload of animals, drifting in low water along the Congo River from Stanleyville, a thousand miles upstream. No one knew exactly when they would arrive in "Leo," or when the freighter *Tamerlane* would make port in Matadi to take them aboard. Or just how they would be gotten on the train from Leopoldville to Matadi. In fact no one knew exactly which

elephants the zoo would get or how big they were. The cages had to be high enough to hold the elephants but low enough to squeeze through rail- way tunnels. Bill later told the official story for readers of *Animal Kingdom*, but some more personal details went into the 20,000 words written to his wife, Lynn, during his two months in the Congo. Roughly half that time was devoted to the elephants, and it was often tedious, bureaucratic labor—filling out forms, attend- ing official lunches, making an obligatory call on the Congo's governor-general, for whom he had polished some compliments in French and a small joke. The elephants, he planned to say, were the biggest gift ever presented to the zoo.

He did it all efficiently, but it was *work*. He was not, as he complained several times, "seeing Africa."

"I must keep my mind on the job I have come over here to do," he told Lynn.

But he also had been a reporter for the *New York Sun* and the Paris edition of the *Chicago Tribune*, and he couldn't help observ- ing. He went walking at night in Leopoldville, recording young blacks huddled over tiny fires, or sitting silently in the dark. And he reported to Lynn on the busts of Belgian women—they all seemed to be either size 60 or 18, he wrote.

During the second half of his stay, he did not quite leave work behind, but it was writing work, gathering information for articles in *Animal Kingdom*. He was on home ground here, and he made an amazing journey, logging 1,200 miles by car and 2,500 miles by plane. Much of this was in the distant northeast of the Congo, near its borders with Uganda and the Anglo-Egyptian Sudan. But he also got to the vast Albert Park game preserve and walked across the border into Ruanda-Urundi—present-day Rwanda.

Before any of this could happen, though, he had to get those cages built and the zoo's three elephants headed toward New York. He lost no time in starting. Within a day of reaching Leopoldville, he was at the U.S. consulate, presenting his credentials. He found that a key player was already in Leo—Pierre Offermann, chief game commissioner for the Congo, who had chosen the elephants and had a rough idea of their dimensions.

Offermann was also important to Bill's plan to see other parts of the Congo and write about them. After their first meeting, he told Lynn that Offermann was

a man of about 45, I should suppose; tanned, rather unsmiling, dressed in khaki shorts and khaki jacket—the usual uniform of officialdom here. . . . He is quite a fellow, by all accounts—speaks good English although he prefers French, and we did most of our discussion in French. I could wish that he were a little more open, more jocose, more responsive to a smile, but we shall get along fine. I am hoping that he can make the tour of Albert and Garamba [national parks] with me. . . . I want to get him talking, for I have discovered that I have plenty of material on the dry bones of the National Parks, & need the anecdotal side to fill it out. He knows the stories.

He and Offermann debated whether to wait for the elephants to arrive before getting cages built, or to start construction immediately. Word came in the pages of the *Courier d'Afrique* about the progress of the "ark" on the upper reaches of the Congo River. Eleven elephants were aboard, along with two lions, a hippopotamus, and a serval. The elephants had been marched nearly 500 miles from an "elephant domestication station" in the far Northeast. Several of them, and the other animals, were bound for the Antwerp zoo.

Bill decided not to delay starting the cages. But by the end of the first week, his letters had taken on a tone of dismay laced with determination. "Everything is at sixes and sevens for the moment, with construction of the cages still not settled," he wrote. "But I have several other possibilities & will whip it if it is whippable."

He made the rounds of several companies that could not deliver cages promptly, before settling on the Synkin shipyard. Soon he was reporting rapid progress, with one cage almost done, another three-quarters finished, and the third cut out and nearly ready to assemble. "It is extraordinary how they have worked," he wrote.

Then he waited for the elephants, filling the time by testing his cameras, making a radio program, attending a consulate party, and stocking his bathtub at the ABC Hotel (left) with snails that he and a photographer had collected. Bill was staying at the rather seedy ABC rather than the posh Regina, because it overlooked the Congo River, a bit of the romantic he couldn't quite suppress. "It should be called the XYZ," a consular official warned him. Bill called it "a hurrah's nest," but never could bring himself to leave its river view. He also took a cruise in a pirogue, "trailing my fingers in the Congo and plucking a water lily now and then." In his bush jacket, he wrote Lynn, "I look tropical as all hell."

The barge with the elephants, the lions, the hippo, and the serval reached Leo on a Friday evening, 19 days after leaving Stanleyville. Early next morning, Bill and Offermann supervised the offloading and the march through town to the Leopoldville zoo:

> [The elephants] walked down a gangplank after about 15 minutes of urging & effort, each with a black boy on its back, and immediately waded into the river for a drink and a bath. The procession formed and they came up the slope from the river, with the boys chanting some wild, rhythmic song, & and a standard-bearer, carrying a pronged pole, leading the way, the sergeant-in-charge walking behind, & a score of blue-uniformed red-fezzed police bringing up the rear. It was picturesque & dramatic, & I hope I got a movie of it. . . . The elephants marched through town without trouble, & are now in the zoo. I have spent most of the day out there, making up my mind about which ones I want; what I get is another matter.The mahouts (they call them cornacs here) have learned who I am, and salute me. They are fine-looking boys, tall & lithe, in dark olive-drab shorts and singlets, and they speak only Lingala, no French.

Bill told more in *Animal Kingdom* about the "wild, rhythmic song." It was as old, he wrote,

> as elephant training. Now in the corrupt and almost unintelligible tamil (words brought into the language by traders long ago), now in the slurred and half-formed Lingala, the song meant this: "The journey is almost over. Your days of labor and fasting are done. Here there is plenty of food. Here are good people. They will not harm you. Continue, be good elephants."

In *Animal Kingdom*, Bill disclaimed any expertise at elephant selection, but added, "I *have* haunted the Leopoldville Zoo since the herd arrived, and I have seen them in the smoky dawn before the cornacs have brought their armloads of breakfast brush; I have seen them in mid-morning, at noon, in mid-afternoon, and in the quick dusk when they had been disturbed all day by photographers and curious members of the European community." Thus, he was happy when Congolese officials picked the three elephants he had already tabbed as the best tempered and most docile. These were a young male, Zangelima, and two females, Doruma and Bamangwa. And they fit their cages!

But getting them into the cages and onto the train for Matadi presented new problems. They had to be caged at the zoo, with the cages pushed up ramps onto trucks. They were then taken to a rail yard, where the yard's travelling crane could lift them aboard a flatcar. The cornacs actually rode each elephant into its cage and then lashed a front foot to the cage so the animal couldn't back out—a dangerous operation, Bill said.

The cornacs were rewarded a few days later. Bill wrote:

> I made a presentation of about $2.50 each to the cornacs who had brought the elephants down the river—a little more to the ones who had gone to Matadi with our three. . . .They marched up in formation and saluted. I saluted back & then made them a speech of thanks in English, and [they] filed by to receive their gift. They took it, not as we would with one hand—but in cupped, outstretched hands—a form of politeness among the Ngala people. I shook hands with each one, said, "Vote the straight Democratic ticket," saluted, and took the next boy in line. It went off extremely well and when the column broke ranks after marching down the road, the boys skipped and gamboled like so many high school kids. They were heading for the native city, and I expect the cafés and the girls had a big time last night.

Bill also teased Lynn a bit, writing: "I was amused to notice that three black girls that I had encountered kept a straight face until I was past, then burst into giggles. Just like country girls anywhere." (Lynn was a country girl herself, from a farm near Trafalgar, Indiana.)

Bill and Offermann followed the elephants to Matadi, where Bill turned them over to Bob Montana, a Bronx Zoo keeper who had been sent over to care for them during the voyage to New York. Then he wrote to Lynn, and some of his hitherto suppressed excitement came through:

> Exactly three hours ago, at 1:15 p.m., the *Tamerlane* and her three elephants in cages disappeared in a pearly haze around the bend in the Congo. I stood on the balcony of the hotel overlooking the whole harbor, with the Congo and the high, brown sloping hills spread out before me, and watched her slip downstream. Did I have a lump in my throat and a tear in my eye? I did not! I was damned glad to see her go . . . The zoo sent me here to make cages & ship the elephants, & that's done. Now I'm going to begin seeing Africa. . . .

Then his handwriting got very big and he wrote, "The elephants are gone. And the bastards are in cages, too! Whoopee!"

Earlier, some of this exuberance had overflowed into a telegram to Lee Crandall, his chief at the zoo:

> BONVOYAGING ARK TWENTYSIXISH THEN ABLE PHOTOGRAPH JOURNALIZE UPCOUNTRY NEED REMAIN OCTOBER ONEISH HOME POSSIBLEST WIRE WHETHER SPAREABLE.

"Poor fellow," Crandall remarked to his staff. "We should have told him to put ice in that stuff, and not drink it straight."

* * *

Bill never intended his Congo letters to be read by anyone other than his wife. But he didn't destroy them, and they lay in a folder for more than 20 years after his death in 1984. When I finally opened the folder, I found the record of an unexpected friendship, some emotional responses to Africa—and an idyll.

There were also glimpses of the love affair between Bill and Lynn. In a moment of homesickness, he wrote, "From the way I feel today, about two weeks is as long as I can bear to be away from you." Her presence in New York, he wrote "makes it more charming than the whole of Africa."

Occasionally there were echoes of their early years in Paris, where these two Hoosiers were married in 1924. He called her "Cherry" (from *cheri*) and at one point wrote, "Don't you love the way I throw in African expressions. It's just to *épater le bourgeois*" [shock the bourgeoisie].

The unexpected friend was Pierre Offermann, the game commissioner, who did fly with him to the northeastern Congo, as Bill had hoped he would. By this time, after their labors with the elephants, they were on a first-name basis—had even "bonded" (a term Bill would have despised). They flew first to Stanleyville, where Bill described a party with "mad Russians." Then it was on to Aba near the Sudanese border, where they rented a Mercury and travelled to the elephant domestication station at Gangala, from which the zoo's elephants had come. Finally, after 400 miles, they reached Buta, where Bill interviewed Brother Joseph, a missionary and expert on the okapi, a rare cousin of the giraffe.

It was an intense journey, during which the native chauffeur managed to drive the Mercury into rivers twice—villagers had to pull them out. He also ran over a Basenji dog and a goat, and sent natives diving for ditches. Bill later described one such incident, during a rainstorm:

Through the muddy windshield I saw one ancient shrivelled widow miss her footing and tumble into the ditch; a cascade from our wheels fell on the pitiful heap as we passed and obliterated her ritualistic streaks of white clay. It was senseless, dangerous driving, but there was no controlling our demon driver.

Bill omitted that story from his letters, but told it several years later in *Animal Kingdom*, where it jumps out shockingly from a placid narrative. One reads anger and shame, suppressed at the moment, but coming out forcefully later.

Bill's visit to Brother Joseph is passed over briefly in the letters, but was the subject of a later article in *Animal Kingdom*. Bill had read a florid account by an earlier visitor, and it played on his imagination—the imagination he liked to claim was prosaic and unremarkable. Quoting the earlier author, he wrote: "Cannibals! Tropical storms! The torrid sun and the graves of thousands of white men!" It was the perfect setting for rare animals, he wrote, including the okapis Brother Joseph was famous for rearing. Back in New York, he had proposed to Fairfield Osborn, the zoo's president, that he visit Brother Joseph. Osborn agreed, and Bill got out of the office quickly before he could ask any questions.

But instead of the scene Bill had imagined, Buta turned out to be quite civilized and "the prettiest town I've seen in the Congo." He had expected Brother Joseph to be "a sort of combination of St. Francis and Frank Buck," but he found a modest lay brother whose French he had trouble translating. He still got a good story.

From Buta, Offermann flew back to Leo, and Bill returned with the Mercury to Aba. Then he went to nearby Kurukwata for an idyllic several days of recuperation after 800 miles on the African road. This was at the home of a Russian agriculturist, Pierre de Schlippe, and his family. And Bill needed the rest. "I am so full of Africa, I could bust!" he wrote. "I can't take any more—I simply can't!"

"Africa is just too damned tremendous and overwhelming—at least, I think it is, for I let myself go, storing up impressions. Result—my mind wears out."

The De Schlippes took him in and let him sleep. He told Lynn:

> How I wish you were out here on the verandah with me this morning. I am at the De Schlippe's house—the agricultural substation manager—and the sun is just climbing into the tops of the trees in the forest reserve that begins immediately beyond his lawn. There was a hard rain before dawn; the sky is clearing now, and water is dripping from the trees. A file of black men just now came silently out of the forest and cut across a corner of the yard, on their way to the little plant where De Schlippe extracts oil of citronella. There are white-maned colobus monkeys calling back in the forest, and some bird keeps up a continuous e-e-e-e cry. A cricket. And not another sound. It is mighty peaceful and pleasant to me. . . .
>
> I've had no time to get laundry done, but one of the boys here is doing it. This house swarms with servants. This morning, about 6:45, I was—I thought—awake; certainly I was conscious of the bird and animal noises in the forest. But I was lying with my face to the wall, and happened to see a shadow pass. I turned—and a black boy had come in, barefooted and silent, had cleaned everything off the night table, and had put down a tray of coffee. The boys slip around the house, never saying a word, doing everything. I'd hate to make an enemy of one—he could surround you before you knew it.

Bill pursued a farming/soil conservation story in Kurukwata by interviewing Chief Yona and residents of a nearby village. He also attended part of a village dance that began on a Saturday night and continued until late Sunday. The chief's son, Dramile, was dealing with a domestic problem—his new wife, already pregnant, had gone home to her family because Dramile hadn't been able to come up with her dowry of 10 goats and 20 hoes. "I am happy to have contributed two hoes toward making Yona's daughter-in-law an honest woman," Bill wrote.

There were other touches that made it clear how much he enjoyed his two or three days with the De Schlippes. The house had running hot water—"actually the first hot water I have had since I left Brussels," Bill wrote. "Mme. De Schlippe says it is 'just like New York!'"

The respite at Kurukwata also allowed him to get his notes in order and his film repacked in rice, which the servants heated to dry it. "The process puzzled them," Bill wrote. "They knew I was a foreigner, taking notes about things. They asked Mrs. De Schlippe if I had never seen rice before!"

The De Schlippes drove him to Aba to catch a plane to Albert Park. But before that, there was a happy moment on the lawn where the De Schlippe daughters, Bess, 4, and Caty, 7, were playing. One of the family's working elephants trumpeted, "and Bess looked startled," Bill wrote. "I heard Caty say, in French—'Don't be frightened; it's only an elephant!'"

"I liked them greatly," Bill said of the De Schlippes, "and De S. and I talked and argued and talked again, and had a wonderful time."

Time, however, was running out on the Congo trip. There were several fretful days in Aba, waiting for a plane and enduring the hotel manager, a classic colonial bore "who has been out here 20 years & now is afraid to go home."

Bill eventually cancelled his Albert Park visit to return to Leo and battle Pan-Am over his plane reservation home. The flight to Leo took him again through Stanleyville, where one of the "mad Russians" offered to throw a party for him "and consume all the vodka in the province." But there wasn't time for that.

In Leo, he had a last meeting with Pierre Offermann, and reported to Lynn:

> We had dinner together last night and talked elephants until 11 p.m.—an unheard of hour here, where everyone goes to bed around 9. We also wrecked a bottle of scotch. You know how it is.

But then he got a sudden chance after all to grab a plane for Albert Park. He flew once more over the vast Congo rain forest ("purple in every direction until it is lost in the distant clouds") and wrote his last letter from the Hōtel des Volcans in Goma, near the entrance to Albert Park on the Congo's eastern border:

> If I choose to look out of my window, I can watch the plume of white steam and smoke blowing toward the Southwest from the flat summit of the Nyiragongo Volcano, and if I turn my head just a little I can see the clouds perched on the slopes of Mikeno and Visoke—the great extinct volcanoes where the gorillas live. [Evidently, the *three* smoking cones on the hotel ashtray were a bit of artistic license.] And then I can look a little farther to the right, and see the green and brown mountains of Ruanda-Urundi, with terraced fields of bananas and fresh green vegetables. Unfortunately, I have to get up and walk to the front door of my two-room pavilion to see the blue-green waters [of Lake Albert] on one side and rosy-pink (sunset-lighted) mountains on the other. One can't have everything.

Earlier in the day, he had walked 2½ miles across the Ruanda-Urundi border to Kisenyi, with

> a black boy to carry my knapsack full of cameras. For a long time, to let him rest, I sat on a stone wall under a giant euca-lyptus, and watched a family of blacks bathing and washing clothes in a little cove. The sky was bright blue, the air pleasantly cool—I was having myself a vacation. An enforced one, for I am keen to get into the park and see game.

Although there is no letter about it, he did get into the park at least long enough to be photographed (next page), wearing a pith helmet, on a volcanic slope inhabited by mountain gorillas.

Such tranquil moments were to be fewer in the years ahead, both for Bill and for the Congo. A comment in his 1946 letters is poignant in retrospect: after exulting over the departure of the elephants, he adds, "You can see the state I'm in. Oh, well, something awful will happen that will bring me back to earth." Bill returned to the Congo in 1948, but this time it was to accompany an animal collector into the jungle in search of the rare Congo peacock. The trip nearly became a disaster when the collector broke his ankle in a swamp and Bill had to organize a rescue party. And within a year after that, his beloved Lynn was dead of cancer.

The Congo won its independence in 1960, but the years since have been ones of turmoil and bloodshed. Goma was overwhelmed by refugees from the genocide in Rwanda, many of them doubtless fleeing along the same peaceful road that Bill had walked to Kisenyi.

One wonders what became of Pierre Offermann and the gracious De Schlippe family. There is an Internet reference or two to a 1951 article by Offermann on "The Elephants of the Belgian Congo." Pierre de Schlippe published an elegant book in 1956 on *Shifting Cultivation in Africa: The Zande System in Agriculture*. He dedicated it to his father, who had been an agricultural adviser to the czar.

Beyond that, only silence.

The zoo's elephants arrived safely in New York. The male, Zangelima, quickly became Barney, but had to be destroyed in 1952 when he became unmanageable and dangerous. Bamangwa (Minnie) succumbed to a paratyphoid infection in 1950. Doruma (Pinky) died on March 1, 1970.

[2007]

45

WINE TREE

At first,
only something
flickering at eyecorner,
the molle tree. (Jose says "moll-yuh,"
as the double L makes "yama.")
Andean willow, "tree of many vertues
casting forth small boughs
whereof the Indians make wine."
Of many names also:
Peruvian pepper,
mastick,
lentisk,
Schinus molle,
featherhead
among the serious trees.

The Incas, those Romans,
planted it beside their roads,
a green relief from sun
and all that stone.
Jose spots it
from the train,
leaps off,
brings back a branch
leaking its white liquor.
Tonight the whole room reeks of it.

[1997]

THE PHOTOGRAPHS OF MARTIN CHAMBI

I am lying in bed, in the dark,
thinking of the light
of Martin Chambi, who photographed
all Cuzco in the '20s and '30s,
leaving behind in the Casa Cabrera
the silver and cyan images
of Senorita Torero and the 1926
Cuzco football team,
of sloe-eyed Estelle Iberico,
belle of 1935, my birth year,
and the Fabrica de Tejidos
de Benjamin de la Torres,
motorcar emporium with statues
of Hermes and Vulcan over the door.

And I am thinking, in bed, in the dark,
of Chambi's light in the Hospital
de la Almudena as it rains down
on an invalid in her chair
through the vines of an arbor,
the name for which I have forgotten;
and also, just before sleep
overwhelms me, of the fat man
with moustaches in the photo
of the Cuzco Equestrian Club,
whose imperishable top hat
lies on the hedge before him
now and forever, as I lie in bed
in the dark, thinking of the light.

[1997]

47

"The mountains are all around us like a crowd."
—*William Bronk*

A STONE CITY

TWO WRITERS, Richard Halliburton and William Bronk, led me to Machu Picchu.

Halliburton was an adventurer who, in the 1930s, visited fabled spots around the globe and wrote *The Book of Marvels*. Once we kids of the '40s figured out that it was "marvels," not "marbles," we ate up Halliburton's accounts of climbing the Great Pyramid, of attempting to visit Mecca as a pilgrim, and of going to Machu Picchu, the "lost city of the Incas" hidden in the fastnesses of the Peruvian Andes. It was all "superficiality and shallow romance," one journalist wrote, and we loved it.

I came to Bronk much later, in the 1970s, while reviewing a book titled *Little Lives*. This was a collection of gossipy tales, from a fictional town in upstate New York, written by "John Howland Spyker." Spyker concluded his book with a portrait of the town's principal literary light, William Bronk. There was considerable internal evidence that Spyker *was* Bronk, although pains had been taken (including a post-office box in Spyker's name) to blur the identification.

While puzzling this out and enjoying the fun, I discovered that Bronk was a respected though somewhat reclusive poet, who had spent much of his life running his family's lumber business in Hudson Falls, New York. He wrote precise and mysterious verse—with a metaphysical cast—and he had been to Machu Picchu.

Both Halliburton and Bronk were still in my mind 20 years later when I had a chance to lead a student trip to Peru. By then, I had read a lot of Bronk, listened to him on tape, and discovered an essay, "An Algebra Among Cats," which described his visit to the Andes. (This was in an oddly titled book, *Vectors and Smoothable Curves*.) His trip had taken place in the indeterminate but seemingly remote past, when only a few tourists—and those with some difficulty—got to the Inca city. It's only 50 miles from modern Cuzco, but is in a nearly impenetrable maze of mountains, on the saddle between two peaks. Not really impenetrable, of course, but it seems that way as one creeps up a steep valley on a little yellow train that clings to the edge of a whitewater river.

Bronk was no Halliburton, but he may have succumbed to a bit of romance himself by citing a theory that Machu Picchu was built by a pre-Inca people, the Aumatas, in the abyss of time. Scholars now believe it was begun about 1438 A.D. by the first great Inca emperor, Pachacuti, and lasted only a little over a century, before the Spanish conquistadors overthrew the Incas. It most probably was a retreat for Inca royalty, well-staffed with priestesses, farmers, and mechanics. It was abandoned within a few years of the arrival of the Spanish, who never found it, leaving that to the bumptious American explorer, Hiram Bingham, in 1911. Natives, of course, knew it was there and led Bingham to the vine-covered ruins.

But if Bronk was uncertain about its origins, he was dead on in his evocation of Machu Picchu as a place where every other consideration has been sacrificed to verticality, to rising. The city was built among the mountains the Incas worshipped as gods; as Bronk notes, it still feels like a holy place. One senses this most at nightfall, when mist rises from the Urubamba river 2,000 feet below, and the mountains seem to grow, move closer, and lean over the empty city.

I find myself writing "city" in preference to "ruins," because Macchu Picchu does not seem wrecked and desolate in the manner of Pompeii. It is entire, a carefully planned and executed cityscape that delights architects and artists—and stonemasons, who are quickly lost in adoration of the large and small granite ashlars that form Machu Picchu's houses, temples, walls, and walkways. One famous stone was cut with 32 angles to fit a particular spot. One thinks of diamond cutters in Amsterdam. One also gets tired of being told that the unmortared stones fit so perfectly that even the thinnest knife blade can't be thrust between them. This is true, but I can't slip a knife between the stones of the George Rogers Clark Memorial either. What fired Bronk's imagination wasn't this surface fit, but rather that the fit extended all the way through these sometimes highly irregular blocks of stone. He caught better than anyone I know the sublimity of such precision:

> who had to spend such easing care on stone
> found grace inherent more as idea than in
> the world, loved simple soundness in a just joint,
> and the pieces together once though elsewhere apart.

When I went to Machu Picchu in January, 1997, the trip was fast-paced and full of events and momentary crises. (A pregnant student worried us by jumping off Inca walls; another fell in love with a Peruvian soldier and had to be rescued.) But there were moments when both Bronk's and Halliburton's vision of Machu Picchu seemed very close.

We began our three-day excursion by bus from the old Inca capital of Cuzco, climbing to the 12,000-foot height of Tambo-machay and then descending into the valley of the Urubamba River. On the way, we stopped for views of Andean landscapes— a river, a little town, polders of light and dark green, with a man plowing far below.

We boarded our train at Urubamba, rather than Cuzco, where Bronk described his own departure:

> The railroad yard was deserted. Presently, the stationmaster came and unlocked his office. Alberto spied our car at the end of the yard and went to get it as one might go to get a

horse from a pasture. He came back with the driver and a kind of station wagon mounted on railroad wheels. We got in and immediately started; no one else was going to Machu Picchu that day.

At the end of the train ride—the Station of the Ruins—a bus took us up the switchback road to Machu Picchu. Tourism has arrived since Bronk's day, and we found the hotel outside the gate bustling and the site itself dotted with daytrippers. But we were to be there overnight, so didn't need to hurry.

Cliff Cain, the other leader, and I walked through the site to the Intihuatana—the "hitching post of the sun"—where pilgrims were laying their hands on the small obelisk, in search of psychic energy. We looked at Inca walls and found the 32-faceted stone. We walked to the "watchman's hut" above the city and then for a quarter-mile along the Inca Trail by which backpackers can approach Machu Picchu. We chatted with two American nurses, Dawn and Barbara, and later passed two of our own group, dawdling and eating wild strawberries. When we got back to Machu Picchu, the daytrippers had gone and the city was almost deserted in the evening light. Streamers of mist drifted across the stones—gray but softened by lichens to brown with hints of green. We walked back to the Intihuatana and this time had it to ourselves.

We had dodged showers all day, but at dusk the sky cleared, and I went out of the hotel and looked across the city to Huayna Picchu, the "sugarloaf" peak visible in so many photos. The sunset glowed behind it, and a phrase, "the presence of mountains" came into my mind. Bronk wrote: "The mountains are all around us like a crowd. They are so massive it seems impossible that so many could be so close. We are *in* them. It is like lower Manhattan seen from a position halfway up from the ground, from a setback on one of the buildings."

The next morning, some of our group climbed Huayna Picchu. Bronk had warned that "the path up and the view down are terrifying to anyone not inured to heights." We didn't find them so, perhaps because the trail is better than in Bronk's time and vegetation screens the precipices. The view from the summit, a thousand feet down to the Inca city, is worth some trepidation.

There were other adventures. One student fell sick and was treated by Dawn, the nurse from the Inca Trail. I evidently had talked about how Inca roads were shaded by molle ("moll-yuh") trees, because on the ride back to Cuzco our guide jumped off the train and brought me a branch. In the higher elevation of Cuzco, some of our group came down with altitude sickness, or *soroche*. Visiting a well-known potter, Pablo Seminario, I stepped backward and ruined a tray of tiles ready for firing. (Seminario was gracious about it and perhaps could afford to be—one student had just paid $547 for a huge ceramic piece!)

Bronk, during his visit, was blessedly free of such dramas and diversions. His way of thinking, in poems and elsewhere, resembles music and mathematics, and he compared Machu Picchu's location to standing "in the very middle of a trumpet voluntary, exultant and assertive and serenely composed." How satisfying it is, he wrote, that Amazonian Indians were moved and delighted when an ethnologist played Mozart's music for them. Both the ancient city and the music suggested to Bronk something essentially human, which we can recognize even at a great distance.

"Machu Picchu is entirely outside our tradition," he wrote, "so remote from us in time and space as to be untouched by it. It confirms and corroborates us. We find here our own image reflected, and it is as though we were to find an algebra among cats, or a Christianity among the people of Mars."

One may argue that Bronk exaggerates the remoteness in time of Machu Picchu. But I cannot argue with his feeling that it is a perfect abstract of a city—the heart of what "cityness" means for humans. In the modest scale of its buildings, its gentle flights of steps hewn in the stone, and its incorporation of the mountain's contours in its design, it resembles the scale and playfulness of Venice. Both are as intricate as the treehouse in *Swiss Family*

53

Robinson. To borrow a Bronk metaphor, they are habitations children might create and want to live in forever.

To anyone who has read Bronk extensively, it's easy to see the correlation between this abstract city and his poems, and to understand why Machu Picchu appealed to him so much. "What is behind this world?" he always seemed to be asking. His mind and spirit yearned to see things whole, in their essential nature, and could not. He wanted, like the stonemasons of Machu Picchu,

> *. . . to give shape to a world*
> *and oh, it is always a world and not the world.*

As I learned more about Bronk, who died in 1999 at the age of 81, I was glad to know that he had lived a seemingly happy life in his small town, whatever existential angst he may have had. He had been romantically involved for many years with a Hudson Falls woman ("a comely girl friend for whom I once lusted," Spyker wrote), but they kept to their separate houses. A friend with a Hudson Falls connection once brought me a snapshot of Bronk's house—large, frame, well shaded. Its calmness brings me back to Halliburton, who never had a real home and who died, at half Bronk's age, while frantically trying to sail a Chinese junk across the Pacific. For him the world was, in William James's famous phrase, "a buzzing, blooming confusion," and every place was new and different. The gap between Halliburton and Bronk is that between a tour guide and a Zen master.

I have been to Machu Picchu with both of them, but in retrospect my thoughts turn to nightfall, with the mountains crowding near, a looming moon, and a silent city of stone. Halliburton is the enthusiasm of youth, Bronk the consolation of age. But get Bronk's book yourself and read "An Algebra Among Cats." It would be hard to find a more perfect evocation of a place.

[1997]

54

IN JAPAN WITH LAFCADIO HEARN

PATRICIO LAFCADIO Tessima Carlos Hearn . . . .

Born 1850, in the Ionian islands, from one of which, Levkos or Leucadia, he took his name. Son of a British Army surgeon and a beautiful but somewhat unbalanced Greek mother. Abandoned by his parents at the age of seven. Raised in Dublin by a fanatically Catholic aunt. At 12, packed off to school in France and a year later brought back to attend an Irish college-prep school, where he lost the sight of his left eye in a playground accident.

Down and out for a year in London. Then at age 18 given a one-way ticket to New York and Cincinnati, where a cousin refused to take him in. On the streets in Cincinnati until he met two unusual men. One was Henry Watkins, an English printer and disciple of the utopian socialist Charles Fourier, the other John Cockerill, a legendary Pulitzer editor recently arrived to run the *Cincinnati Enquirer* after having killed a man in the newsroom of the St. Louis *Post-Dispatch*. Watkins virtually adopted Hearn. Cockerill gave him a reporting job.

Lafcadio Hearn: A skinny, short (5'3"), lank-haired, half-blind young man—an exotic, a sensualist, infatuated with language and the supernatural. Editor Cockerill has left a description of his new reporter:

> One day there came to the office a quaint, dark-skinned little
> fellow, strangely diffident, wearing glasses of great magni-
> fying power and bearing with him evidence that Fortune and
> he were scarce on nodding terms. When admitted, in a soft
> shrinking voice he asked if I ever paid for outside contribu-

tions. I informed him that I was somewhat restricted in the matter of expenditures, but that I would give consideration to what he had to offer. He drew from under his coat a manuscript, and tremblingly laid it upon my table. Then he stole away like a distorted brownie, leaving behind him an impression that was uncanny and indescribable. . . . Later in the day I looked over the contribution which he had left. I was astonished to find it charmingly written.

On the *Enquirer*, Hearn proceeded to set the good burghers of Cincinnati on their ears with stories—like the Tanyard Murder Case—so sensational they would scandalize the *New York Post* or the *National Enquirer* today. A very short excerpt, describing the finding of the tanyard victim's body in a furnace:

> The brain had all boiled away save a small wasted lump at the base of the skull about the size of a lemon. It was crisped and still warm to the touch. On pushing the finger through the crisp, the interior felt about the consistency of banana fruit . . . . The eyes were cooked to bubbled crisps in the blackened sockets, and the bones of the nose were gone, leaving a hideous hole.

Something of Hearn's approach to journalism at the time can be gathered from his contribution to a short-lived comic weekly in Cincinnati:

> The Ghoul [Hearn's name for himself] resolved to spring French sensation upon the public. . . . The French school of sensation, embodying the extremes of horror and the agony of aesthetics, was the highest order of sensation, and might therefore be improvised into a medium of education.

Hearn was hounded out of Cincinnati because of his liaison with a mulatto woman. For a time he was down and out in Memphis. Next he became an essayist for New Orleans newspapers, then a freelance writer in Martinique, where—to my mind anyway—he first began to make himself into a writer by getting control of his material. Listen to this description of the *porteuses*, the carrying women of Martinique:

> Let me tell you something about that highest type of professional female carrier . . . . the type of *porteuse* selected for swiftness and endurance to distribute goods in the interior parishes, or to sell on commission at long distances . . . . At 16 or 17 she is a tall, robust girl—lithe, vigorous, tough—all tendon and hard flesh;—she carries [on her head] a tray or basket of the largest size and a burden of one hundred and twenty to one hundred and fifty pounds weight;—she can now earn about 30 francs (about six dollars) a month, by walking fifty miles a day, as an itinerant seller. . . . There are no corpulent *porteuses* for the long interior routes; all are built lightly and firmly as racers. There are no old *porteuses*;—to do the work even at 40 signifies a constitution of astounding solidity.

By this time, Hearn had written his first books: *Some Chinese Ghosts, Stray Leaves from Strange Literature, Two Years in the French West Indies.* On April 12, 1890, he arrived in Yokohama on assignment to do a travel book for Harper & Brothers. He never left Japan.

Hearn went from Yokohama to Matsue, an isolated city on the Sea of Japan, beneath a brooding medieval fortress. There he found a purity of Japanese life that enchanted him. And there he began becoming Japanese himself. A friend realized that this strange, gifted Englishman could not survive on his own and arranged a marriage with Setsu Koizumi, a samurai daughter who was something of an outcast herself, because her first husband had deserted her. Actually, Hearn married a whole family, taking the responsibility not only for Setsu but for eight or nine of her relatives. In the following years, he and Setsu became parents of three sons and a daughter. In 1895, after leaving Matsue, Hearn became a Japanese citizen and took Setsu's family name, becoming Koizumi Yakumo—"Little Spring, Eight Clouds." In the remaining few years of his life, he wrote, taught in Japanese colleges, and with his last major book, *Japan: Toward an Interpretation*, became the foremost interpreter of Japan to the West. Hearn died in 1904, and is a venerated figure in Japan, although virtually forgotten in the West.

A few years ago, my wife and I traveled to Matsue, not because of Hearn's significance, but because we (or at least I)  wanted to see the places he had written about, and discover whether any echos remained of his beloved city. When I told a Japanese student that we were going to Matsue, he said, "Oh, that's remote," and I'm happy to report that it still was, at least a little.

Hearn did some of his best writing in Matsue, in the study at left, and some of the things he wrote about are still there. It's a lovely city, modernized but with many blue-roofed temples as well as canals and gardens. Magnificent cinnamon camphor trees flank the city's wooden castle, which is as solid as when Hearn described it:

> A vast and sinister shape, all iron-gray, rising against the sky from a cyclopean foundation of stone. . . . looking somewhat like a huge pagoda, of which the second, third, and fourth stories have been squeezed down and telescoped into one another by their own weight. Crested at its summit, like a feudal helmet, with two colossal fishes of bronze lifting their curved bodies skyward from either angle of the roof, and bristling with horned gables and gargoyled eaves and tilted puzzles of tile roofing at every story.

There is an old samurai residence at the foot of the castle hill. The Hearn museum, very small, is next door, with such things as Hearn's writing desk, his famous white suit, the cages in which he kept pet insects, and—most poignant to me—the sheets of news-print on which he wrote English words to teach his oldest son. "The cat eats the rat," said one, in broad brush strokes.

Hearn also wrote about the gardens outside his house, which are still there and well-tended:

> In order to comprehend the beauty of a Japanese garden, it is necessary to understand—or at least to learn to understand—the beauty of stones. Not of stones quarried by the hand of man, but of stones shaped by nature only. Until you can feel, and keenly feel, that stones have character, that stones have tones and values, the whole artistic meaning of a Japanese garden cannot be revealed to you.

In *Glimpses of Unfamiliar Japan*, Hearn describes awakening in Matsue:

> The first of the noises of a Matsue day comes to the sleeper like the throbbing of a slow, enormous pulse exactly under his ear. It is simply the pounding of the ponderous pestle of the *kometsuki*, the cleaner of rice. The measured, muffled echoing of its fall seems to me the most pathetic of all sounds of Japanese life; it is the beating, indeed, of the pulse of the Land.
>
> And now from the river-front touching my garden there rises to me a sound of clapping of hands. . . . From the long high white bridge come other clappings, like echoes, and others again from far light graceful craft, curved like new moons—extraordinary boats, in which I see bare-limbed fishermen standing with foreheads bowed to the golden East. . . For all the population are saluting the rising sun—O-Hi-San, the Lady of Fire, the Lady of the Great Light.

My wife and I stayed in a *ryokan*, or traditional inn, in Matsue; morning came to us much as it had to Hearn, though without the beat of the *kometsuki*. We also visited Lake Shingi, the small inland sea that borders Matsue, and sailed by Yomegashima, "the Island of the Young Wife." Hearn had told that story, too.

It is said that it arose in one night, noiselessly as a dream, bearing up from the depths of the lake the body of a drowned woman who had been very lovely, very pious, and very unhappy. The people, deeming this a sign from Heaven, consecrated the islet to Benten [the Goddess of Eloquence and Beauty], and thereon built a shrine unto her, planted trees about it, set a *torii* before it, and made a rampart about it with great curiously-shaped stones and there they buried the drowned woman.

But despite seeing such things in Hearn's city, I felt only the most tenuous connection with him there. We eventually gave up our literary pilgrimage and simply enjoyed Matsue—which was, of course, what Hearn had done a hundred years before us. We bought flowers for Mrs. Sunimatso, keeper of the Horaiso ryokan. We bathed together in its conjugal hot tub, and watched old gray Grandfather Carp in the pool beyond our window. We took our dirty clothes by cab to the "coin rawndry," which is the actual term in spoken Japanese. And behind Matsue Castle we drank excellent coffee in a café called the Hide Out, which also featured an ancient Rex motorcycle and some classic music—Chet Atkins on guitar and Hank Williams singing "Wabash Cannonball."

One day, we left Matsue and went by bus to the village of Bessho, to see a museum with work by the famous paper maker Eishiro Abe. There was an entire white suit made from *washi*—paper twisted into strands and woven—and a *washi* cat. On the return ride, I saw something that took me back for an instant to the time of Hearn. A wasp had settled on one of the bus windows, and a Japanese man reached out and very gently *petted* it.

It was good to have visited Matsue, although ultimately my interest in Hearn is as a writer—or, more accurately, as someone who created himself both as writer and human being out of the most unpromising materials. He once described himself thus (please remember that this was an Englishman writing in the Francophobic age of Victoria):

Your ancestors were not religious people. You lack constitutional morality. That's why you are poor and unsuccessful and void of mental balance and an exile in Japan. You know you cannot be happy in an English moral community. You are a fraud—a vile Latin—a vicious French-hearted scalawag.

A few years before his death, Hearn wrote to his old friend and almost-father in Cincinnati, Henry Watkins:

I often wonder now at your infinite patience with the extraordinary, superhuman foolishness and wickedness of the worst pet you ever had in your life. When I think of all the naughty, mean, absurd, detestable things I did to vex you and to scandalize you, I can't for the life of me understand why you didn't want to kill me. . . . What an idiot I was!—And how could you be so good?—And why do men change so?

Hearn also wrote to Watkins the testimony of a hard-working, professional writer: "I have been obliged to learn the fact that I am not a genius, and that I must be content with the crumbs from the table of Dives."

His wife, Setsu, once talked about the likes and dislikes of this odd husband, whom she married first and later came to love:

I may name again some things that Hearn liked extremely—sunsets, summer, the sea, swimming, banana trees, cryptomerias [Japanese cedars], lonely cemeteries, insects, *kwaidan* [ghostly tales], Urashima, and *Horai* [songs]. . . . He was fond of beefsteak and plum pudding, and enjoyed smoking. He disliked liars, abuse of the weak, white shirts, Prince Albert coats, the city of New York, and many other things.

[1992]

The Wabash River at Vincennes Indiana, during a winter in the early 1960s that froze it almost bank to bank near the Lincoln Memorial Bridge. At right, Earl Howell stands near driftwood piled against one of the bridge piers.

River Days

"The Wabash has been designated as Indiana's official state river."—News item.

"OH, NOTHING MUCH. The river goes up and the river goes down."

That was my father's reply in the 1950s when anyone asked what was happening in Vincennes, Indiana, where we lived. And indeed the rise and fall of the Wabash gave a rhythm to our lives, peaceful usually but now and then rising to a furious crescendo.

Day after day, in the bitter February of 1950, the river pressed toward the top of the floodwall that ran from the George Rogers Clark Memorial, along First Street, and north to Ebner's ice plant and Kimmell Park. Workmen heightened the wall with mudboxes and shored up weak spots with sandbags. Delivering newspapers, I rode my bike through axle-deep back-up water at Fifth and Perry streets. Students who volunteered to fill sandbags were let out of school, and I spent a day or two on a work brigade, stopping as often as I dared for coffee and doughnuts at the Salvation Army van. The floodwall and sandbags held, and we felt we had triumphed over the worst that nature could throw at us.

My wife, who grew up in unprotected country north of town, remembers the river lapping almost at her back door: "The chickens flew up in the trees, and we had to take my horse to a neighbor's on higher ground."

Years later, when I worked for the Vincennes paper, a dweller near the river taught me something about fairness and objectivity in reporting. Steele Polk, president of the Niblack Levee Association at Oaktown, asked, "Why is it that when we do something good, like building a new levee, your paper says 'north of Vincennes,' but when the levee breaks it's always 'near Oaktown'?"

Most of the time, the river murmured almost unnoticed alongside our lives. Summer evening picnics stretched into velvet nights, with stars shining over the Illinois shore and now and then a lantern-lit johnboat drifting down on the current. The boat may have belonged to a mussel fisher, survivor of an industry that once shipped tons of mussel shells each year to Muscatine, Iowa, "the Pearl Button Capital of the World." Vincennes had a riverside community of mussel fishers then, but construction of the Clark Memorial in the 1930s wiped out most of this "Pearl City." By my reporting days in the 1960s, only a few shanties remained on the bank. (One, I remember, was occupied by Mrs. John Kennedy, a robust riverwoman who bore little resemblance to the Mrs. JFK in the White House.)

There were some memorable times on the river, including the day Red Skelton, the comedian and Vincennes native, came home to dedicate the bridge named for him. "I learned to swim in the Wabash," he said, "and it sure was dark in the sack with those kittens." Some winters the river froze nearly across. In a photo, my colleague on the paper, Earl Howell, is halfway out on the ice, planting a long staff like a conquistador claiming the river for the king.

Some of us went bird-watching in the woods below Westport, practiced cross-country running on the Allison Prairie levee, and camped out in Robison Hills on the Illinois side. And when I returned at 25 from being a soldier and wire-service reporter in Europe, I spent a long evening gazing downstream toward the St. Francisville ferry, wondering if I was home for good and what life might still have in store for me.

It never occurred to me to think the Wabash should be Indiana's official state river. I guess I thought it always was.

[1998]

The Pearl Fishers

That summer night we saw
a single lantern burn
just where the current turned
out of the Embarraw.

A johnboat going down
to troll the mussel bar
bore that slow-moving star
athwart our little town.

Pearl fishers passed on
with voices indistinct
until their lantern winked
and vanished. I sit alone,

remembering long after
how we had talked at ease,
a star among the trees
and voices over the water.

The Soufriére Hills volcano on Montserrat in 2003. The three-bladed white object is an abandoned wind turbine.

Two Islands

THE MESOZOIC MONSTER

IN MONTSERRAT, you wake up with volcanic ash between your teeth. It's a reminder of what someone has called "the Mesozoic monster" at one end of this lushly green Caribbean island—the Soufriére Hills volcano.

The world became aware for a few months in the 1990s that Montserrat, a British dependency exactly the size of the Dallas-Ft. Worth airport, was in trouble. During 1997, the *New York Times* ran a dozen stories, telling how 19 islanders had died in one eruption, how the capital of Plymouth had vanished under ash and been abandoned, and how a British warship was standing offshore in case the whole island had to be evacuated. Then the journalists went elsewhere, and the world went back to sleep as far as Montserrat was concerned. The volcano didn't.

There is a Montserratian proverb: "Eat a toad for breakfast and nothing worse can happen to you the rest of the day." The Soufriére volcano is a spectacularly large and ugly toad.

* * *

Living next to a volcano is like having a nasty neighbor who drinks too much and gets violent with explosives. Rather than deal with him, some people move away. Others are too stubborn, or have too much invested. So they stay and become part of the tight family of those who live daily with the problem.

Montserrat's population was about 11,000 before the eruption and now is less than half that. Among those who stayed are Shirley and Lou Spycalla, who operate the Erindell Villa Guesthouse on Gros Michel Drive in Woodlands, about halfway up the island. My wife, Karen, and I had arranged to stay there during our two-day visit and were the only guests for one of those days, in a pleasant room next to a pool turned to pea soup by ash. "Erindell" is a fanciful reminder of an early Irish connection to Montserrat—something the tourist industry played on, when there were still tourists. "Drink from the burn, you'll be sure to return," says a sign, edged in Kelly green, next to a wayside brook.

Everybody on Montserrat knows Shirley and Lou, and Shirley spends much time with the phone and e-mail, keeping up with news and gossip. She has little use for the island's British population, especially the contract workers brought in after the disaster. "What? Are you people still here?" she says, mimicking a worker's supercilious wife. And one woman told her, "I'll be glad when the Montserratians leave, so we can get their nice houses."

British workers and their families get "stress-buster weekends" on neighboring Antigua, as well as holidays to Miami and London, she says. They were told to come in suits, with briefcases, and some contracts called for them to be given whole houses, while locals were living in shelters.

The locals watch the Brits closely. It was observed that several days before an evacuation order was announced for the Belham Valley, British residents were already moving out, and into better replacement housing in the north.

The more one listens to such stories, the more Montserrat seems like a small town of an earlier day, a contained world whose residents do not feel this as a lack. In one sense, the island is more part of the world than ever, because of the post-eruption immigration to Great Britain, the United States, and the rest of the Caribbean. People stay in touch by e-mail, but the chat is still all about the island. Listening to it is a little like eavesdropping on tourists from the same midwestern town who have run into each other in Paris.

Everyone is on a first-name basis, and they say things to each other that would result in pistols at dawn in some parts of the world. If Shirley spouts off on the Internet, a half-dozen respondents will tell her, in different and colorful ways, "Shirley, put a cork in it."

And sometimes the edge is sharper. "Thank you for that kick in the face," says one e-mailer who has been feuding with another. Somehow, this large, close-knit, and dysfunctional family manages to stay together, partly because there's no place to go and partly because to go would be to admit defeat.

Shirley tells stories about local characters and businesses, including Ram's Emdee Supermarket, where, she says, customers "are a nuisance" because they interfere with restocking the shelves. And Lou has a delightful story about Rose Willock, the manager of Radio Montserrat ZJB. Willock was on the air, interviewing the British overseas development secretary, Clare Short, who at one point exclaimed, "Rose, you don't listen! I just answered that question!" So Rose started listening, Lou says, and nailed Short for saying, "They'll be wanting golden elephants next," a comment about Montserratian claims for compensation. It was a quote that haunted Short for a long time.

There is a charm to all this, but also something a little claustrophobic. A good friend of Shirley and Lou's is Joe Phillip, who drives a taxi around Montserrat and also runs the island's "Evergreen" listserv, named for a famous tree that was a gathering place in Plymouth. Joe picked us up at the dock when we arrived on the Opale Express ferry from Antigua and dropped us off there when we left.

After he drove away, I realized that I'd forgotten to return our room key, so I went into "Moose's Place" near the dock to find a telephone. This was a typical Caribbean cantina with a noisy domino game and Moose himself behind the counter. "Why do you need to telephone?" he said. "Just give me the key and I'll give it to Shirley." Which in retrospect I should have done. But I asked again to use the phone, and Moose announced loudly to the bar that I was a damn tourist who didn't trust him, and what was I doing in Montserrat anyway? (He did let me call, finally, and Joe Phillip drove back and got the key.)

* * *

There was a time when cruise ships stopped at Plymouth, and an entertainment industry featured musicians like the pop music star Alphonsus "Arrow" Cassell. But all that began ending on July 18, 1995, with rumblings and a "phreatic" or steam eruption in English's Crater on Castle Peak in the Soufriére Hills. Things quickly got worse. August 21, 1995, was "Ash Monday" with 20 minutes of near-total darkness over Plymouth (followed in the next few days by Hurricanes Luis and Marilyn). Plymouth was evacuated for a few days, as were communities south and east of the volcano.

Early 1996 was relatively quiet, but in April lava began moving down the Tar River valley and more residents had to leave. Ashfalls made life gritty over most of the island. In September, a lateral explosion struck the town of Long Ground, and all residents south of the Belham River (roughly the southern half of the island) were asked to leave.

On June 25, 1997, the volcano's dome collapsed and sent white-hot flows of superheated lava down its sides, devastating eight settlements and killing 19 people, some of them farmers who had ignored evacuation orders and gone back to care for their cattle. Not long after that, the island's population dropped to 4,000, and it appeared there might have to be a complete evacuation.

Bennette Roach, publisher of the *Montserrat Reporter*, remembers those days with a journalist's relish for disaster. "I was into this thing," he says. "Anything that happened, I was there." During one of the early eruptions, while other residents were fleeing north, Bennette was driving south, to get closer to the volcano.

Karen and I are talking with Bennette and his daughter Camille over lunch at the Attic, an airy roadside café. The conversation continues later at his home in Olveston, where the *Reporter* occupies three small rooms on the ground floor, with a pressroom in the garage. Bennette took over the business in 1994, just a year before the eruption, from a political party that had gotten in legal trouble. The paper, actually a sideline to his printing business, kept publishing in Plymouth until June, 1997. He got one press out but had to leave a bigger one behind. When he last saw it, he says, "it looked like something from the 12th century, covered in ash."

Bennette is 58, but looks younger, even though his neat beard is tinged with gray. "I'm getting older. I'm very tired," he says. He studied journalism many years ago by correspondence course and also explored law and criminal investigation. In his paper, he campaigns relentlessly for redevelopment, for a new airport, and against misuse of reconstruction funds from Britain. The paper also runs a feature called "Jus Wonderin,'" which pokes sly fun at everything from the volcano observatory to colonial officials. "Jus wonderin' if we can invite the U.S. in Puerto Rico to target practice on our volcano. Jus wonderin' if we can put Montserrat up for auction on eBay."

The *Reporter* prints 500 copies a week, which Bennette says is saturation for the 4,000-plus residents who remain on the 37-square-mile island. He would like to expand the paper's web site if, like any other publisher, he could figure out a way to make it pay. Before the volcano, he had 20 employees, 16 in printing and four on the paper. Now he has eight in all, including one reporter, Catherine Rodriguez, who likes her job but hopes someday to be a travel writer for Condé Nast. One or two other people write for the paper occasionally, including an "expat" American editor who provides volcano limericks.

Bennette calls himself a Montserratian "all the way," even though his home town of St. Patrick, like Plymouth, no longer exists. He says contemptuously of a politician: "He's afraid of the volcano." And he adds, "If you accept the words of the vulcanologists, that it won't go further, you take that lead and decide that you're going to rebuild Montserrat. That's what you do."

When his journalist's hat is on, Bennette dislikes unnamed sources, bureaucrats, and press releases that substitute for face-to-face interviews. "I want to know what it is that you don't want to tell me," he says. But he also has a sense of the job's responsibility. "The bad names journalists get, they usually bring upon themselves," he says.

"I make it possible for people to say what they want to say, as long as it's not libelous. In this place, in this little place, there's a lot of vindictiveness around."

His own days of non-stop volcano coverage, when the government gave him helicopter rides to news scenes, are long gone. Today, the volcano continues to belch ash, lava, and hot rocks, but after destroying or menacing half the island, there's not much more it's likely to do. In a sense, it's old news, and something else has to fill the newspaper. Bennette tells Catherine Rodriguez, "When you go home tonight, lie on your bed and think about electricity. There's a lot of stuff you can find out about electricity."

* * *

Shirley has lined us up for an on-air interview with Rose Willock, after interviewing us herself to make sure we pass muster. A cab takes us to Radio Montserrat's studio in Sweeney's, where Rose is waiting to put us on the station's Family Radio service. She took over the Radio Montserrat job in 1990 after 10 years as program manager at the Antilles Radio Corp. and is a veteran of hurricane coverage, having done her first emergency broadcasting in 1979, when Hurricane David hit the island of Dominica.

"We were the lifeline for Dominica and the world," she says.

"But the volcanic crisis has been more sustained. You never really know what to expect." In a disaster, she says, "radio is a centerpiece that can hold it together for you while you sort yourself out. It's absolutely integral.

"You get calypso coming out of other islands. We've matured past that."

Radio Montserrat moved six times during the crisis. "The little sprinkle of ash we're getting today is nothing," Rose says. When her station's service was interrupted, she used phone lines to broadcast through a station on Antigua. The Caribbean is prone to natural disasters, she observes, "and we have to have agreements with other islands for hurricanes—and now for volcanoes, we know for sure."

Both Bennette and Rose know well that much of their audience is now scattered from England to Canada and the United States, as well as to other Caribbean islands. The Internet is the link for this Montserratian diaspora, Rose says. The emigrés listen to radio on the Internet "as if they were home." Bennette says that every time someone finds the *Reporter* web site, "he sends a letter in."

It's an easy, relaxed interview, and Rose is an excellent listener, letting Karen and me tell why we happen to be here, all the way from Indiana. She even lets us get in a plug for our local college, in case any aspiring Montserratian youths might want to apply.

Then suddenly we have company, Karney Osborne, who has dropped by to see Rose. Karney is 80, retired, and a legend in Montserrat broadcasting, although his career actually goes back to early days in Newfoundland. On Montserrat, he rebuilt Radio Antilles at O'Garra's after Hurricane Hugo in 1989, only to have the

200,000-watt station wiped out for good by the volcano. O'Garra's, Erindell, St. Patrick's—do those names tell you anything? Karney explains that many Irish emigrated to Montserrat during the potato famine of the 1840s. Now history has come full circle, he says, and Montserratians are going out into the world again.

Karney corrects me in kindly fashion on my pronunciation of St. Kitts and Nevis ("It's Nee-vus"), and chats for a few minutes about broadcasting—how you "have to read as though you're not reading" and also "learn to leave the white space" in your radio commentary.

Lou tells us later that Karney is Rose's boyfriend, and despite the considerable disparity in ages, I can believe it. He's a charmer.

* * *

Some myths about Montserrat need to be dispelled. It is open to visitors, although they must arrive by ferry or helicopter, since the volcano has gobbled up the airport. There are places to stay, like the Erindell Villa, where Lou will cook you an excellent chicken dinner, served in the family kitchen. Taxis will take you wherever you want that isn't in the volcano "exclusion zone." The northern half of the island is still beautiful, green, and on many days free of ash. The devastated southern half is impressive in its own way, and a helicopter service will give you a tour within a few hundred feet of the smoking cone. But it's heart-breaking to read guide books that still describe Plymouth and the Great Alps Waterfall, and the Galway soufriére, or hot spring. "Gone, gone, gone, gone," Bennette says.

Volcanic danger is not a myth—think Mount St. Helen's or *Dante's Peak*. Caribbean volcanoes do not put forth photogenic streams of lava like Hawaiian ones. Their sticky magma piles up, then collapses, and sends deadly flows of lava, ash, and super-heated gases down the mountain faster than anyone can run or drive. The Soufriére dome is higher than it has ever been since the volcano awoke from a sleep of centuries. It is ripe for a big collapse. During this first week of January, 2003, the volcano observatory is reporting 843 rockfalls and 120 long-period earthquakes. On our second night in Montserrat, Shirley drives us up to the Volcano Observatory, where we have a good view of the cone and can see an occasional trickle of lava, or a glowing rock bouncing down the slope.

Ash is not a myth, either. On the morning of January 8, a curtain of brown rain appears to be falling out of a cloud over Plymouth. It isn't rain, it's pulverized rock. In the early days, Bennette says, "we had inches of ash the way you have inches of snow."

If you owned a carwash on Montserrat, you might get rich.

* * *

On the verandah of the Gourmet Gardens Restaurant, 25 evacuated residents of the Belham Valley are talking to a lawyer about suing the government to get their homes back. We've trailed along with Bennette, who is covering the meeting for the *Reporter*. The lawyer talks about civil rights, but the residents, mostly expatriates, want to talk about the government's unfairness. "They're making new rules every time they turn around—it's unconscionable," a woman says.

The residents are among 300 evacuated several months ago from the Belham River Valley, which could fill up with lava if the dome collapses to the northwest. Their homes are untouched so far, but they can visit them only at stated times, which they say change arbitrarily. How does the government decide, they wonder, that 2 to 6 p.m. on Monday is safe, but 10 a.m. to 2 p.m. on Tuesday isn't?

There's a system of alarms for volcanic activity, and "last night the alarms were going off like crazy," a resident says. "But alarms can be set any way you want."

These are ordinary citizens, not militant but aggrieved, who just want to go home. Most are middle-aged, the men in sports shirts and the women in blouses, with skirts or pants. One man sports a long beard and a cane.

"When I returned to my temporary quarters . . . ," a speaker begins, then breaks off. "I almost said 'home.'" The government has "ungodly powers," another says. The colonial governor comes in for much criticism. "There are lots of things you can't talk to him about," a speaker complains.

This meeting, Karen whispers to me, sounds for all the world like a property-owners association grousing about a zoning board—except that these people have lost their homes to a volcano.

Among those present is the limerick-writing editor, Don Brandt, formerly of the Wilmington, Delaware, *News Journal,* and one of the founding editors of *USA Today.* He and his wife, Alberta, retired to Montserrat a year before the eruption. Today the line of the exclusion zone runs through his yard and across his driveway—a difference of 50 feet and he would still have a house.

The lawyer keeps trying to bring the discussion back to the practicalities. This case will be won, not by emotion, but by research and by putting pressure on the government—"the embarrassment factor," he calls it. And now, he continues, we need about 15 people willing to put in money, to defray the likely costs . . . . He will probably get the money. These are people who are not leaving. Some have cut their ties with their old homes. Everything they have is here, and they don't want to move again.

Lou Spycalla is not leaving, either. In fact, he has just bought a second car, a 1990 Mazda 626, for a dollar from a friend who couldn't stick out living with the ash. Inside he found an unused Bose radio. "Dammit, keep everything," his friend told him. Now all Lou needs is a carwash.

TWO ISLANDS

Since this was written, the Soufriére volcano has continued to belch ash, with some major "events" but without another catastrophic eruption. A new airport has opened at Gerald's in the north, but ferry service has been suspended. Don Brandt, the editor, died in the summer of 2007, of lung complications after a dozen years of breathing volcanic ash, still barred from his home. (On a trip back to Delaware, he was asked why he stayed on an island that at times has been knee-deep in ash. "Because I have a shovel," he said, "and people need help.") The Montserrat Reporter *is still "jus wonderin, who is in charge since no one seems to know of any plans if volcano really blow."*

GOING TO SABA

FOR SOME TIME, I had wanted to go to the Caribbean island of Saba. I knew only a little about it—that it was five square miles of volcanic mountain, that it was pronounced Say-ba, and that a Dutch princess had climbed to its summit and declared it "the highest and smallest place in my kingdom."

It was famous for being difficult to reach. A guidebook described the harrowing descent to an airstrip on the island's one flat point of land: "Just close your eyes and remember that the pilot wants to live as much as you do." Like so much in tourist literature, this was a lie. The 16-seat Winair plane from St. Maarten made a routine landing at Yuancho Yrausquin Airport, beside a minute green-and-white terminal. Ed Peterson of Eddie's Taxi Service agreed to drop me at several points around the island, and by 8 a.m. on the last day of the year I found myself alone in the sunshine outside the locked Church of the Holy Rosary, in Hellgate.

I had hoped to look at handmade lace in a building behind the church, but it also was locked. So for a few minutes I sat on some stone steps across from the church door and looked at the sunlit space in front of it, a piazzetta. The Italian term was apt; this corner of Saba is almost Mediterranean. Hellgate, despite its menacing name, is a hillside of white, red-roofed houses with names on their gates like Susanna's Cottage and Sunrise House.

Below them is the island's one road, called simply The Road, built with pickaxes and dynamite in the mid-1900s. Along the road are Saba's four communities—Hellgate, the commercial center of Windwardside, St. John (site of the high school), and The Bottom, so called because it occupies the crater of an extinct volcano. The Bottom is Saba's capital and despite its name is still 900 steps above Fort Bay, where the first settlers landed. If a Dutch *huisvrouw* wanted a piano, it had to be lugged up those 900 steps.

There was an air of patience about the day. I watched for the next plane to land, but the sky remained empty. Wait, an interior voice said. Something will come.

Ed Peterson had told me I could walk the road to Windwardside in half an hour. We would meet there at 1 p.m. and drive to The Bottom. I began walking. The Road was a deep pleasure this bright morning, with Mt. Scenery rising to a cloudy summit on the right and the island dropping swiftly to the Caribbean on the left. The distant land between the airport and Old Booby Hill lay in deep green folds, modeled by the eastern light. No one else was on the road. The rhythm of walking came easily—lean into the hills, let your legs carry themselves on the downward slope. Lichen spread its slow bloom over a low stone wall beside the road, beyond which were vines with yellow trumpet-shaped flowers.

Windwardside was a bustle of cafés, art galleries, and boutiques selling the island's famous lace and Saba "spice," a home-distilled liqueur based on 151-proof rum. Dive shops abounded; Saba has virtually no beaches, but its sunken littoral is a celebrated marine park. After a quick lunch in Scout's Place, I met Ed and we drove on to The Bottom. He dropped me near Queen Wilhelmina Park, a small square overgrown with knee-high grass.

TWO ISLANDS

Two workers were applying red paint to the white shingles of a gazebo. Pointing to a church a block away, Ed said, "You might want to look at the mural," and drove off.

The church seemed like a good place to start. The mural over the apse was modern, by a local artist; the Virgin and cherubim floated above a stone house with Saba's characteristic gingerbread gables. But back outside, I began to feel a strangeness about The Bottom. What had looked from the road above like a colorful, perhaps lively, Caribbean town, took an odd turn when one was in it. It had no commercial center, and where were the government buildings? There was a fire department and, some distance away, a police station, as well as a handsome two-story house covered with flowering vines, which I later learned was the lieutenant-governor's home. But there were no offices or shops, only an occasional cantina and "My Grocery," a hole in the wall that expanded inside to a labyrinth of aisles and levels packed with everything from milk to suitcases. But it carried no hats, and in the intense sun I was starting to need one. Few people were about, and those few spoke little English. No, they said, no hats in The Bottom. Try Windwardside.

Hatless, I wandered in the heat. Half a dozen young Sabans lounged outside the grocery. One hacked at a coconut with a machete. The gazebo workers had disappeared. I walked away into a deserted quarter where goats grazed in a vacant lot. What kind of a capital city was overrun with goats? Street signs bore the names of dead generals and colonial politicians. From a bar, under a tent in a field, angry voices rose. "Fuck it!" seems to mean the same thing in several languages.

It was hotter now, and my head was burning. The afternoon was taking on a sinister edge. What was I doing here, with an hour and a half to kill before Eddie's Taxi returned? If it returned. Wait, the interior voice said again. Sit and wait. Everything will come to you.

In the shady yard next to the church, I sat on a wall and ate the candy bar and nuts I had brought with me. A taxi came by ferrying tourists, who looked out at the church like actors peering from a TV screen, before being carried onward. A motor whined around a corner of the church. After a while, a wiry man carrying a weed-eater emerged from behind the church and greeted me in English. We talked while he fastened a new plastic cutting cord to his machine. His name was Richard Hassell, he said. I asked if he was related to Josephus Lambert Hassell, a self-taught engineer who pushed through The Road, against all expert advice. "No," he replied, "there are a lot of Hassells—brown, white, black."

He said he had been a sailor and knew one-quarter of the job of steering "The Edge" ferry from St. Maarten 12 miles away. He knew half the job of being a martial artist, and now, with his weed-eater replenished, he was about to tackle with his full abilities the overgrown lot behind us. "You have to approach these things in the right spirit, with energy," he said, flourishing the weed-eater with the hint of a Samurai swordsman.

When he had gone, I walked down the street and sat on another shaded wall next to a small stadium where boys were hitting a tennis ball with sticks. Now and then a ball flew over the stadium wall and rolled across the space in front of me. Sometimes the boy who ran out to retrieve it was quick and lithe, hurling it back over the wall with grace and elasticity. Sometimes the boy was slow and awkward, and the ball hit the wall and had to be scooped up again.

Up the street, dreamy calypso poured out of a café. A burro grazing in a field ambled over to look at me. If I went to sleep now, I thought, would I have the experience of a photographer friend who dozed on his campstool in the desert and woke surrounded by watching animals? The aura that had bothered me earlier, of restrained menace, had dissipated.

TWO ISLANDS

At that moment, two little girls, one holding a tan puppy, came scrambling over the wall next to me. "You have a camera— take our picture!" one cried. Holding the puppy, they struck the

pose, I took the picture, and they climbed, laughing, back over the wall. "Happy New Year!" we called to each other, and they were gone.

Ed was due in a few minutes. I walked back to the little park. The loungers were still there, but they were just loungers now, killing time on the year's last afternoon.

On the drive back to the airport, I asked Ed about the goats. "They're a terrible nuisance," he said, "always eating the gardens." In the airport's tiny waiting room, I came face to face, inexplicably, with one of the little girls from the photo. "Come and take my mother's picture," she said. But I hesitated, thinking of explanations, and she wandered away. I didn't see her again.

[2003]

The architecture of the Jewish Museum Berlin, with canted windows and sloping walls, can be unsettling to visitors.

RETURN TO BERLIN

CRUSADING WITH BILLY

THIS SPRING, while my local church was following the preparations for a new Billy Graham Crusade, I was revisiting the site of an earlier Graham appearance—the Berlin segment of his German "Crusade for Christ" in the fall of 1960.

This time my wife, Karen, was along, and I was leading a group of 20 journalism students, from four U.S. colleges and universities. In that earlier day, I was a reporter for United Press International in Berlin, where the arrival of Billy Graham—if not quite as big news as the airlift a few years earlier—was certainly the biggest event of a quiet summer and fall.

I remember that UPI's German manager, Wellington Long, had been intrigued by some of Graham's public comments and ordered full coverage of his stay in the beleaguered city, just in case he said anything politically provocative. The Berlin staff obliged with daily stories about Graham's appearances "close to the Iron Curtain." In fact, most of the Crusade took place in a tent several blocks from the boundary with East Berlin. But for the final afternoon, Graham spoke in the open, from a platform raised on vacant ground next to the burned-out Reichstag building and within sight of the Brandenburg Gate and the East Berlin "vopos"—the people's police. The final rally drew 90,000 Berliners, by a police estimate.

"Be sure and be there," we were urged earlier by Graham's press officer, who had been reading our stories and knew an easy sale when he saw one. "We're going to be even *closer* to the Iron Curtain."

My story called Graham's final sermon "a thundering jeremiad," and that seems accurate enough. Throughout his three-week crusade—in Essen, Hamburg, and now Berlin—he had exclaimed repeatedly, "There is a day of judgment coming!" and had urged his listeners to repent. It was solid, fundamentalist preaching. "Are we living in Noah's times?" he asked the Berliners. "What do you think?"

Graham painted a world far gone in sin, materialism, and obsession with sex, accentuating this with a visit to Hamburg's Reeperbahn vice district, where he preached to 10,000 outside a saloon called "Kitty in the Milk Bath." In Berlin he also said German youth were looking for a leader, a flag, and a slogan, and that Christianity must supply all three. It was a remark that made some commentators nervous.

I remember that the final rally featured spirited singing—could George Beverly Shea have been the leader?—and Graham's by now familiar exhortations. Loudspeakers carried his warnings to the far edge of the crowded field and brought them echoing from the fire-blackened recesses of the Reichstag building, where German leaders had once addressed Parliament (and where they would again after reconstruction a few years later).

As they had for the earlier tent meetings, many people had slipped over from East Berlin, where the crusade was officially frowned on. But this was before the Wall, so no serious effort was made to stop them, although the vopos were assiduous in checking papers as they returned to the East.

Graham's press people estimated the total crowd in the three German cities at three-quarters of a million, and there seems no reason to doubt that figure. They also counted more than 16,000 "decisions for Christ."

When Karen and I visited Berlin this spring, there was still a vacant lot next to the Reichstag, but it was full of construction equipment and materials—a sign of the huge building boom that began in Berlin when the Wall came down in 1989. And the Reichstag was no longer a blackened hulk—it was the restored and gleaming home of a unified German parliament. There were only a few reminders of the war and immediate postwar years— Martin Niemoeller's cell in Sachsenhausen concentration camp, which we visited, and the evangelical church erected in the Ploetzensee suburb of Berlin as a memorial to the prisoners murdered nearby by the Nazis. The arena-style sanctuary is bordered with grim paintings of prisoners in death cells. We also visited Berlin's dramatic new Jewish Museum, with its windows and walls at odd angles to keep visitors from feeling too comfortable. The tactic works.

I found the building where UPI had had its second-floor office in 1960, and took pictures of it, turning my back on a rousing political demonstration along the Kürfurstendamm by Kurds, who were protesting the death sentence in Turkey against rebel leader Abdullah Ocalan. If I had had time, and could have found my way to it, I would have visited the suburban village of Steinstücken. In 1960 it was a tiny exclave of West Berlin, totally surrounded by East Germany. On rare occasions, a western military team drove a Jeep down the road to it, just to show they could. I hope the residents are leading happy, quiet, unpolitical lives these days.

It would also have been fun to see if I could find again the Rialto bar, which in 1960 had the furtive reputation of being the only nightclub in East Berlin. It was up a dark side street in suburban Pankow. A sign on the door said, "Closed due to overcrowding," but a kindly doorman let me in, and a husky platinum blonde took my order. "A scotch and water," I said. "Your passport, please," she replied.

And there were other memories, like Wellington Long's story of CBS correspondent Howard K. Smith's famous book, *Last Train from Berlin*, at the start of World War II. Long said that Pat

85

Conger, the United Press bureau chief in Berlin, liked to tell people, "Yes, I put him on that train. Then I went back to work."

But by this spring, Berlin had long since moved on from such scenes. Most impressions were of a free, vigorous, and lively city. The sense of being under siege was gone. Sidewalk cafes were filled with patrons enjoying, among other things, the jelly-filled pastry known as "Berliners." President Kennedy is still revered for his ringing support of the city during his visit there, but it hasn't been forgotten that he should have said just, "Ich bin Berliner." His actual words, "Ich bin ein Berliner," mean literally, "I am a jelly doughnut."

A PERSONAL HISTORY OF A PLATZ

WHEN I REVISITED BERLIN, there were two parts I especially wanted to see. One—easy to locate and dispose of psychically— was the block on the Kürfurstendamm where I had worked in 1960 as a young UPI reporter. The other was Potsdamer Platz and its adjoining Leipziger Platz, which I had not even visited in 1960, but to which I felt attached by the thinnest of personal threads.

The thread was a story told by a German friend about her childhood, and I had used it long afterward in a poem:

> . . . . *In Berlin, Frau Grötsch*
> *pointed to postcards of the Kaufhaus Wertheim*
> *before the war. Her sisters carried her*
> *to see the Christmas lights, then ran*
> *through snow to catch the tram under a clock.*
> *She closed the book. "Das war die schone Zeit,*
> *aber der Krieg hat alles weggerissen."*

Indeed, the war "had torn it all away." The area, once the center of Berlin, had been blasted out of existence and the ruins

86

razed. Its desolation was as complete as Carthage's, and it stayed that way for 45 years—a grassed-over wasteland in the city's former heart. The clock, on the Verkehrsturm or traffic tower in Potsdamer Platz, had stopped both actually and symbolically, while the wall that divided Berlin ran almost exactly through its former location. Potsdamer Platz became a "ghost station" on the subway, through which trains could pass but never stop.

Now, in 1999, all this was changing. A huge construction project was under way on Potsdamer Platz. I wanted to visit it and see if any trace remained of my friend's childhood city. At the same time, I knew that her city had been only the latest on that spot, and that there was more history and memory behind it.

The shape of the future Potsdamer Platz was already clear on a Berlin map of 1685, where a ganglion of country roads fanned out through farms and woodlands from the city gate at the Potsdam Bridge. There were no street names on the map, but one could imagine in the tangle the future paths of Potsdamerstrasse, Linkstrasse, Bellevue, and Stresemannstrasse. And one could see the possibility of an influx that would make Potsdamer Platz the heart of Berlin and necessitate Germany's first traffic light, on the same tower as Frau Grötsch's clock.

It was never "a proper platz," a guidebook said, describing it rather as a five-cornered traffic knot on the old high road between Königsburg and Aachen. When King Friedrich Wilhelm I built his palace at Potsdam, Berlin expanded in that direction, and by 1795 Prussia's first all-weather road ran through the old rural intersection. In 1823-24, the renowned Berlin architect Karl Friedrich Schinkel rebuilt the Potsdam Gate, adding the small colonnaded structures—the "Torhäuschen"— on each side that remained as reminders of the old city wall until their destruction during World War II.

The region beyond Potsdamer Platz had developed in the early 1800s as a district of quiet villas, but its peace ended with the building of a railway station near the platz in 1838. From then on, growth was rapid, with the swelling of traffic, the opening of Berlin's first subway under the platz in 1907, and the building of hotels, restaurants, and cabarets. The guidebook described the

glitter of prewar Potsdamer Platz, where at night as many as 3,000 guests might be found in a dozen different "salons of entertainment and diversion," including one where international cuisine was served in rooms named the Greek Taverna, the Bistro Francaise, and the Wild West Bar. Around the corner were the studios of Germany's first radio station. And just up the street, in the 1930s, was the Reichskanzlerei of Adolf Hitler.

Nearby also, on Leipziger Platz, was the fairy-tale department store of Frau Grötsch's recollection—the Kaufhaus Wertheim, more correctly the Warenhaus Wertheim, stretching along Leipzigerstrasse for 330 meters, its floor space double that of the Reichstag, with 83 elevators, three escalators, five kilometers of pneumatic tubing, and a thousand telephones. It was arguably the most gorgeous department store ever built. Walther Kiaulehn described its decor in his 1958 book, *Berlin: Destiny of a World City*:

> How they trembled, those great garlands of incandescent lights, glittering still in memory, throughout the Great Hall. How the light glanced and sparkled from those chandeliers of crystal and Bohemian glass. The atriums were brilliant, some of them 25 meters high with walls of semi-precious stone, as in the unforgettable Onyx Saal. The fountain court

was of Istrian limestone with mosaics and gilded terra cotta. And where but there could one find a Carpet Room of Italian walnut, with its lanterns of gaily colored stone, or an East Asian Room, where one sat on huge rolls of raw silk and glimpsed the smiling lips of the gilded gods?

Kiaulehn reproduced pictures of the Warenhaus Wertheim's handsome exterior, designed by Alfred Messel, with ground-floor arches and tall mullioned windows artfully concealing the number of floors, all of it surmounted by a graceful double mansard roof.

Today, a temporary three-story structure, the Infobox, overlooks what is left of Leipziger Platz. The Infobox is bright red and resembles a construction trailer on stilts, which is appropriate in view of the enormous construction projects going on all around it. (I counted nearly 60 cranes at work in different parts of the city. The construction crane, goes the joke, is the city bird of Berlin.) In front of the Infobox, somewhat removed from the original site of the Verkehrsturm, is a replica, with a clock and a row of horizontal (now purely ornamental) traffic lights on each of its six sides. It is the only thing Frau Grötsch would recognize.

On the roof of the Infobox, I asked a guide to point out the site of the Warenhaus Wertheim, and he gestured toward a still desolate vacant lot stretching up Leipzigerstrasse. Although redevelopment of the Potsdamer and Leipziger platzes was planned together, the developer of the latter was unable to carry the project through. Sony and Daimler-Chrysler, the developers of Potsdamer Platz, have done better, and a nearly finished assemblage of glistening glass and steel towers now rises on the former site of the Palast Hotel and the Weinhaus Rheingold.

The public relations director for Daimler-Chrysler's part of the project explained that a decision was made in the spring of 1989 to build the company's headquarters on the spot, as an expression of confidence in Berlin. When the Wall came down that November, "we suddenly had a new challenge," she said. What Daimler-Chrysler and Sony decided to do was to build "a new city" on the wasteland that belonged emotionally to neither the East nor the West—or perhaps belonged to both. The project has been carried out brilliantly, and one assumes profitably. Daimler-Chrysler's part of it contains 18 buildings, only two of them used by the company. The rest are rented out by its real-estate arm, and occupancy is full, the spokeswoman said.

I asked if any archeological work had been done on the site before construction, and she seemed momentarily puzzled, although later she said that some artifacts found during excavation—bottles, etc.—would be put on display eventually. But she clearly was not concerned with history, and why should she be? Even the street plan of Potsdamer Platz has been changed, eliminating finally the centuries-old "five-cornered traffic knot." A huge new railway depot is being built under the intersection. There is an "Alte Potsdamerstrasse" within the complex, but it is a brand-new street, with bright sidewalk cafes, trees, and a Marlene-Dietrich Platz.

I sat for an hour in one of the cafés, nursing a "Berliner Weisse"—beer with a shot of raspberry—and watching passersby. At an adjoining table, a young man sat reading a newspaper for most of the hour. But as I was about to leave, a lovely girl appeared, embraced him, and sat down to share his table. Was she an hour late? Had he come early to catch up on the news? It didn't matter. They were radiantly happy, and oblivious of any history but their own.

Perhaps all the history of places—my own, Frau Grötsch's memory of running through snow to catch a streetcar—is as personal, and as mutable, as that.

[2000]

Lost Villages and a Train Wreck

IF A COURT EVER SUBPOENAS my notes for news stories published half a century ago in the *Franklin Evening Star*, I'm ready—at least if the notes involve the ancient history of Johnson County, Indiana.

In the summer of 1953, I was a cub reporter writing stories about the county's "lost villages and ghost towns"—settlements laid out during the 19th century and sometimes actually built, but which had long since disappeared into farmland or beneath urban sprawl. I had saved the stories, and went back recently to re-read them. Then I got out my notes and re-read *them* to see if I had missed anything. By now my wife was rolling her eyes. My paper fetish is well known—if it has writing on it, I save it.

Once in a while this pays off, and it did this time. The research showed that my handwriting was as bad 50 years ago as it is today. But I also found a note that in pioneer days the Johnson Trading Station in the Union Village community (now Providence) sold "rotgut" near the present site of the Christian Church, a fact I had neglected to tell readers in 1953.

But mostly it was thought-provoking to look at the printed accounts from 1953, and see how many recollections I had gathered from residents in their 70s and 80s, who still remembered clearly what families had lived where in, say, 1880. There is still a Pushville crossing on Highway 31 north of Franklin, but even in 1953 I hadn't been able to find the story behind the name. When I confessed ignorance in the newspaper, however, a letter came immediately from Elmer E. Henderson of Greenwood, enlightening me:

Most of those who lived in the vicinity of that crossroads back 60 years ago were spending the time one rainy day in the blacksmith shop then owned by Jim Vest. At that time a blacksmith helper by the name of Dick Glass, and a good blacksmith, too, was working for Vest. Someone suggested that the place be named and the name of Pushville was suggested by Mr. Glass. The crowd then wanted to know why he would name it "Pushville." He replied that [it was] because he thought it would "push it like the devil to ever make a town."

Henderson's words have the ring of authority, and I see no reason to deny Dick Glass the title, "Father of Pushville."

Other, better-known stories also re-surfaced. The most famous "lost village" was Far West, so called because it was at the county's western extremity, on the bluffs of White River. The story, recorded by earlier historians than I, is that the commission voting on a site for the state capital came down to a choice between Far West and a village a bit farther north called Indianapolis. Jacob Sutton, a tanner in Far West, reportedly cast the deciding vote against his hometown because he foresaw that his smelly business would not be welcome in the heart of the future metropolis. Far West managed to hang on for a few years, with one or two general stores, a "hotel," a church, and a tollgate. In 1953, an elderly gentleman named Ed Surface told me he remembered the tollgate, and that it was run by a Stotten Fletcher, who owned land in the vicinity. But by 1900, the community had gone. When I set out 50 years later to find its remains, there was only a bit of grassed-over roadbed, a barn lettered with "Far West Farm," and a pig sty where I took shelter from a rain shower.

Besides finding the barn, I spent a pleasant afternoon in nearby Bluff Creek, talking with a bright and spirited old lady, Mrs. Otis Shufflebarger. She remembered Far West and showed me two letters to her grandfather, Christian Kegley, dated exactly a century earlier, with "fare west p.o." as the postmark.

LOST VILLAGES AND A TRAIN WRECK

In 1953, I also drove to Urmeyville, northeast of Franklin, where I found practically a civic renaissance. The old No. 5 county school building was still there, used as a workshop and storage place. But about 10 small houses were occupied, mainly by workers and their families brought in by industrial expansion in the neighborhood. Urmeyville, once a ghost town, was alive and well.

A little north of the Pushville crossing on Highway 31 is the Worthville Road, which enshrines the name of a railroad switch that had only one house—but one with a history. Charlie Henry, 85, told me in 1953 that the family who lived there ran a store in the house and sold groceries and boots. Railroad section gangs stopped there to drink from the well and eat their lunches in the yard, he said. And a later occupant, Jim Coons, was famous as a coon hunter, but met his death on a rainy evening in 1883 when he was hit by a train while walking home along the tracks from Whiteland.

Some villages, like Plattsburgh, seem never to have progressed beyond a developer's dream and a plat map filed in the county recorder's office. But the town of Turpey, west of Providence, had a founder of note. This was Sam Montgomery, described to me by William Day, his son-in-law, as a "red" Irishman with a temper to match. Montgomery built a store and a sawmill about 1870 and named his "town" for an Indiana senator. With the steam engine that ran the sawmill, he also threshed wheat and ran a clover huller and fodder shredder.

"But it would have taken a preacher to work alongside him without making him angry," Day said.

Turpey eventually had several houses, a gunsmith, a post office, and a blacksmith. In 1953, the county's school superintendent, Custer Baker, told me he remembered boys gathering at Montgomery's sawmill to throw their hats into the sawdust pile and then wrestle with the owners of the hats they drew out.

Just over the hill from Turpey, there was reputed to have been an Indian village and a silver mine. Day recalled that an old man named Sam Demaree came to Turpey several times to search for silver but never found enough to make a mine practicable. "He didn't have a family or anything, and he just wanted to get out in the bush," Day said.

When, years afterward, I needed a two-syllable town name for a poem titled "American Archaeology," I exercised my poetic license and used Turpey. But the community described was really Cottletown (or Cottleville), a long-gone village south of Trafalgar in the southwest corner of the county. On a rainy day in 1953, I found the site and a "tunnel of light through trees," which once had been a road. Then I had to ask a neighboring farmer to get his tractor and pull the *Evening Star*'s car out of the mud.

There had once been a sawmill at Cottletown, but by the time I arrived, only a trace remained of a road through the woods, and one or two pear trees that may have been planted by settlers. I did manage, though, to talk with Grand Cottle, 80, of Edinburgh whose grandfather, James, ran the sawmill. James ("Uncle Jim" to his neighbors) was a great woodsman, and helped to clear much of the land in southwest Johnson County, his grandson told me. He remembered the old man well—powerfully built with a full beard, he said.

The summer of 1953 ended, my college classes resumed, and I never got around to researching other lost villages and ghost towns. Lancaster was a canal town that failed because its canal was too shallow, my fading notes say. Anita, a vanished rail stop, still enjoys a slight vogue because of some determined local boosting. But what became of Rowe, Bud, Kinder, Frances, and Banta? Until a few years ago, Banta had a general store, and the first issue of the *Trafalgar Times* on July 7, 1916, told of a tragedy there at a baseball game between two churches. Miss Margaret Hill, 17, snagged her little finger while jumping out of a truck, and tore it off. The news story ended laconically by reporting that "the ballgame was won by the Banta team, which piled up a 22 to 0 score."

Some of these places are still on maps, but they await another summertime reporter with time on his hands. My interest in finding them has faded along with my notes.

That interest was rekindled briefly in the 1980s when a student, Gwen Rodenberger, and I hiked some stretches of the abandoned Big Four railroad, which once ran diagonally across the county. Gwen was writing a history paper, and we fought our way through brambles along the old roadbed (and ate blackberries), but after that my interest declined again.

At some level, though, it has continued. How much history, how many poignant stories, are lost irretrievably—and almost necessarily, for what archive could hold them all? As a journalist, I watch with interest as the absorbing local news of the day slips off the front pages, becomes folklore, or disappears forever into the oubliette of the unrecorded (or at least unvisited) past. Even great disasters pass from the knowledge of all but historians.

Memory is fallible. When I wrote a memoir a few years ago, I found newspaper accounts confirming some famous family stories—but the storytellers were often shaky on details or wrong on the dates, sometimes by years. I am no better. While writing this, I set out to verify a story I've known most of my life, about a terrible train accident long ago in Johnson County. What I found is worth telling in some detail, as a cautionary tale for amateur historians.

What I heard, perhaps 60 years ago, was that a locomotive had struck a wagon or buggy filled with people, killing seven or eight of them. The accident was said to have happened at Branch's Station, a flag stop on the Big Four railroad between Franklin and Trafalgar. I may have heard about it during the summer of 1947 when I was living on my Aunt Laura Vandivier's farm. Branch's Station was just beyond our fields, and I walked

95

over its now vacant site on my way down the tracks to buy candy or a Nehi cream soda in Trafalgar.

There were no details attached to the story, though, and no date.

Years later, a friend, Harvey Jacobs, wrote an unpublished novel which began with such an accident—the only survivor (the story's eventual hero) was a baby swept up on the cowcatcher of the locomotive. Jacobs was a Trafalgar native, and when I read the manuscript after his death I thought, "Oh, that's the Branch's Station tragedy."

So I went to the county museum the other day, expecting to find the story without much trouble. But there was nothing. I then e-mailed a cousin, Ivan Lancaster, who knows everything worth knowing in that part of the county. He hadn't heard of a wreck at Branch's Station, but he called Marie Pitcher, 95. Another blank.

There followed a round of phone calls to octo- and nonage-narians, none of whom knew of the terrible accident. They knew of others, like the wreck of a northbound Pennsylvania train that went through a bridge over Blue River at Edinburgh on Sept. 17, 1922. But there were no casualties in that one. A fatal car-train accident at Christmas, 1960, on the Illinois Central line, was clearly not my tragedy. Neither was the mishap reported around 1900 by the *Pea Ridge News*, involving "Mr. Hunt's old gray cat," which was hit by the Big Four locomotive while "snoozing away on the track." The cat "was a genuine mouse grinder, and the end of its brilliant career will be mourned throughout the county," the story said.

I called Harvey Jacobs's widow, who wasn't sure whether the episode in his novel was based on fact or not. Eventually, I reached Max McCaslin, 94, who knew Branch's Station inti-mately—in fact had once eaten his lunch in a house there, while it was being moved on rollers across the railroad track. (It took two tries to reach McCaslin at the Morning Pointe retirement home—when I phoned the first time, he was calling a Bingo game.)

Alas, McCaslin also knew nothing about any fatal train accident, although he did recall a derailment on the Day farm between Branch's Station and Trafalgar—"my wild guess is that it was about 1924 or 1925." McCaslin said someone had placed a piece of metal on the track, perhaps to straighten it; the locomotive's guide wheels jumped the track, and a work train had to come from Martinsville to get things squared away.

He had some other unrelated, but fascinating, information. The farmer on whose land the train derailed had later killed himself, he said. (When I got back to Cousin Ivan with this, he knew all about it. In fact he and his brothers now owned that farm, he said. The barn where the farmer died was gone, but the next barn up the road, the site of another farmer's suicide, was still standing.)

McCaslin knew a lot about the Big Four ("Old Jerk") and its fabulous slowness—so slow, I once was told, that hogs ate the grease from the journal boxes as the cars dawdled by. My grandmother, as a young woman, had ridden Old Jerk to her job in a Franklin dry-goods store, and the crew sometimes stopped along the way to pick flowers for her. McCaslin said the crew members also liked to hunt. They would stop the train in the country, shoot live steam into the ditch alongside, and then pot away at fleeing rabbits.

I could have told McCaslin some stories of my own. Old Jerk was once owned by Ambrose Burnside, the Civil War general of whom it was said that "he had a modest opinion of his own abilities, and that opinion was amply justified." And a little beyond the Day farm was the farm of my great-great-grandfather, George Bridges, whose son John ruined his lungs at 14 while fighting a field fire started by sparks from a locomotive. That would have been in 1852, and John died relatively young, in 1879.

But what about McCaslin's lunch in the middle of the railroad track? Old Jerk was halted for an hour, he said, so that his family's house could be moved on rollers across the rails. He and some teenage friends thought it would be fun to eat lunch while in transit. But as they ate, one of the rollers shifted, dropping a corner of the house. McCaslin said one boy (he named him) "took out of there like he was shot, but it didn't even crack the plaster."

Cousin Ivan made one more try to reach another of the Oldest Inhabitants who, he thought, might know something about the Branch's Station wreck. When she didn't, I gave up. My terrible accident was mythical.

But the accounts in my *Franklin Star* articles were not, and recently I decided to take another look at Far West, Urmeyville, and Cottletown. After all, I knew where they were or could easily find their plat maps again—my notes also recorded their locations on the county map.

On a hot July night, my wife and I set out for the short drive to Urmeyville. The "tarvy" road ran past a golf course, non-existent 50 years ago. Approaching Urmeyville, we passed spacious brick homes—the suburbs, we joked. Urmeyville crossing was where it had always been, but the casual houses and meandering paths of 1953 were now neat cottages with paved drives, and even a new log home. There was a street sign at one corner! Surprisingly, Schoolhouse No. 5 was still there, though sadly dilapidated, with one brick wall knocked out to accommodate a truck.

A day or two later, we drove south of Trafalgar, on the other side of the county, to the center of Section 23, Township 11, Range 3. This was the putative site of Cottletown, but the "tunnel of light through trees" was gone, or obscured by a field of corn. A road that might have been one mentioned in my story ran back into it, but you don't drive into an Indiana cornfield these days without the risk of being taken for a meth dealer. We left Cottletown to oblivion.

On the way home, we drove through downtown Trafalgar, which George Bridges helped lay out in the early 1800s. It was looking poorly. Where a brick building had housed a hardware store was now a vacant lot—I had phoned there once looking for sash weights and been told by a clerk, "I think we've got some of them critters." But the store's stock was so jumbled that the "critters" were never found. Another grassy plot was the site of Ma Butler's café, where I ate a prodigious chicken supper in the 1950s with the Big Four train crew. Business was booming along a nearby highway, but the center of Trafalgar was fulfilling the estimate of an earlier traveler: "a small punkin that withered on the vine a long time ago."

Far West, when we reached it, was even more gone than Cottletown. The barn, the fragment of road, the pig sty—all had disappeared under a highway interchange and the outlots of fast-food franchises. A mile away, we stopped at Mrs. Shufflebarger's old home in Bluff Creek, to see who lived there now. The house was badly decayed and overgrown, with a morose yard goose on the front porch. I knocked three times, but there was something sinister about the house and its dank, shadowy yard. I began to imagine people with guns, and meth cooking in a rat-infested kitchen. After the third knock, I waited a few seconds and then fled—to the car, the highway, and the sunlit present.

After an except from this essay appeared in a historical newsletter, I got a phone call from Betty Legan Smith of Parma, Ohio, who had read the newsletter. She still had her grandmother's scrapbook with a clipping about a fatal accident at what the newspaper called the "deadly" and "notorious" Branch's Station Crossing. A train had indeed struck a buggy, killing Guy Martin Dragoo and injuring several others. The date? Aug. 24, 1908. The clipping said the buggy passengers had been discussing an earlier accident at the crossing "just before the train was upon them." Of course I had to find the earlier accident, and with the 1908 date it wasn't difficult. A farmer, Charles McDonald, had been killed when the Big Four struck his wagon, on July 27, 1907. None of my nonagenarians had known any of this; 1907 and 1908 were just over the horizon of living memory—and no one had told them the stories.

[2007]

THE GRAIN ELEVATOR AT NEEDHAM

After the mill closed, they began
dismantling the lower beams and stanchions,
ladders and walls,
but one day found
they could no longer reach the machinery
in the tower and would have to knock
the whole thing down.

Our biggest man in those days
had been ambassador to the Sublime Porte,
but when his house was knocked down
at auction, it was found
that the silver samovars had rusted
and the Izmir carpets
were moths and dust.

Difficult to salvage anything
of a past so transient, when all night
trucks roar at each other
on the interstate,
and in the cemeteries
car lights of lovers circle
the passionate dust of the pioneers.

THREE WRITERS

'THE OBSCUREST OF MORTALS'

ONE CHRISTMAS IN THE LATE 1940s, a church youth group to which I belonged visited the Knox County Home (or Farm or Infirmary) in the country outside Vincennes, Indiana.

In a grimmer age, the Home would have been called simply the county poorhouse. And it was Dickensian in appearance—a gaunt brick structure, two or three stories, set alone in a field. Its rooms were high-ceilinged and dingy, though not unclean. We were greeted by the matron, who introduced us to the home's residents, a company of the crippled, sick, and mentally deficient consigned to the county's care, in a time before health plans and nursing homes. Perhaps we sang Christmas carols to them—my memory is vague on exactly why we were there.

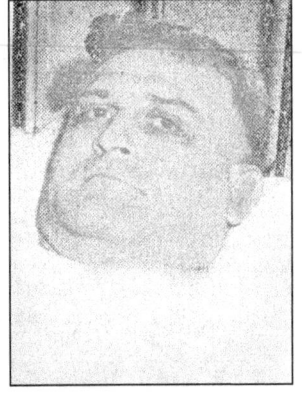

Then she took us into a bedroom, where we met Henry N. Dick.

Dick was in bed, surrounded by a farrago of books and papers, his leonine head propped on a pillow as in the 1944 newspaper picture at right. The matron explained that he was a scholar and author, and he talked with us for a few minutes—about what, I no longer remember. But something about the visit remained with me. Maybe it was just the impression of this large-headed man, bedfast, but clearly hard at work. Though he seemed happy enough to see us, there was a sense of our being a diversion from a bigger undertaking of some sort.

Years later, when I was a newspaper reporter in Vincennes, I looked Dick up in the local library and found that he had written a 2,300-line epic poem on George Rogers Clark's capture of Vincennes during the Revolutionary War. This had been published by the Hobson Book Press in Cynthiana, Kentucky, in 1944, as a slim paperbound volume that also included "The Hymn of Deborah," Dick's versification of the Book of Judges.

The poem didn't strike me as very good. I probably had some idea of interviewing Dick for a feature story, but never got around to it. I was a young reporter, and the Home was a rather dismal and disquieting place.

But Dick stayed in my mind over the next 50 years, during which I became a poet myself and more aware of what was involved in writing 2,300 lines of anything. Dick got into one of my own poems, written with much literary license and a comment of which I now am slightly ashamed. Addressed to a writer friend, it read:

> Susanna, I can't tell you why
> the magic happens one night
> and not another, so instead
> I'll tell you about my friend Henry,
> who wrote ten thousand lines extolling
> George Rogers Clark in heroic couplets,
> unread, uncelebrated, and in sober fact
> pretty punk,
> but just as _there_, by God, as Xenophon.
> And Rafinesque inventing the Walum Olum,
> with pictographs to prove the Lenni Lenape
> came from Siberia to Crawfordsville.
> And my brother-in-law's
> delirious buddies who fell
> for inspired fakery in a Hoosier cave
> and wrote a book to tell the delighted world
> how Egyptians discovered Indiana.
> We just keep hitting that old piñata,

hoping a blue eyeball will fall at our feet
and we'll pocket it,
and walk off whistling, right past
the guards and into the green fields
of the Holy Ghost.

Dick's epic wasn't 10,000 lines, of course, and he wasn't actually a friend. When I recently found a copy of *Clark's Anabasis* and *The Hymn of Deborah* (on an Internet old-books site), it didn't deserve the "pretty punk" comment either. Dick's work is competent and not embarrassing at all. His poem leans a bit on the antique diction of older epics, and is perhaps too step-by-step a description of Clark's campaign across southern Illinois and Indiana during the winter of 1779—a campaign that helped secure the Northwest Territory for the new United States. But the poem is a serious work that is indeed *there*, whatever its faults.

I went back to the library a few days ago, to see what else I had missed on my earlier visit. There was a 1944 newspaper story about the publication of Dick's book. It explained that arthritic paralysis of his legs had left him bedfast for 22 years, since his freshman year in high school. After a failed operation, he had lived with an elderly couple before moving to the county Home in 1935. He began writing his poem in 1927, when interest was high in the forthcoming 150th anniversary of Clark's capture of Vincennes, and continued working on it through the Depression and World War II until friends finally arranged its publication in 1944. A typical couplet expresses Dick's feelings about the great frontier general, who died ill, poor, and unregarded:

How slow are men to recognize the worth
of heroes and great captains of the earth.

When Dick died in 1960, the *Vincennes Sun-Commercial* ran a front-page obituary, calling him a self-taught "poet and scholar." Mrs. Cardinal, the matron, called him "just an awfully good, good man." According to the story, he could read and speak Latin and Greek, and knew mathematics thoroughly. He also played the guitar and was expert at checkers. Before leaving for the hospital where he died, he had given his television set and his dog to another Home resident. The obituary added that he had finished 1,100 pages of a new work about Epaminondas, the early Greek statesman and general.

There was a copy of something else in the library archives—a letter Dick wrote on the Fourth of July, 1951, to an acquaintance in Vincennes. "Maybe you'll be surprised to get this letter from the obscurest of mortals," he began. Then he told in a few lines how he had lived his life:

> *Long ago, when I was young, I developed an interest in a few subjects and my studies throughout the long passing years have kept my head above the waters of despair which so often seemed so eager to swallow me up. I have kept myself busy. Too occupied to pay much attention to my misfortunes, I haven't shed many tears. Despite the bleakness of prospect, I have thus been able to find a remarkable lot in life to amuse me. Hence I can say that, while I've not been happy, [through] all the griefs, sorrows, and disappointments that have crowded my way, I have seen and felt some of the glamour of life. This is a truly wonderful old world. None would tell better than one like me who has lost so much of it.*

THE LAST ADVENTURER

YVES-GUY BERGÈS WAS A WRITER with whom I once spent a strange two days during a tour of Taiwan for VIP journalists. The arrangements for the tour were a little strange themselves, since Bergès and I were the only ones on it and we travelled in separate cars, meeting only when our drivers stopped to show us the next tourist attraction.

But in those brief meetings I got a certain amount of information about Bergès. He was a large man, who looked to be in his

70s and limped badly from a broken ankle—the result of "dodging bullets in Dubrovnik" several months before, he said. He had been a *Paris Soir* correspondent in the 1960s, and had gone with Arnaud de Borchgrave, the celebrated international journalist, to the Congo, where he had been captured by insurgents. At the time of the moon landing, he reported the reactions of a Stone Age tribe in Colombia, after which he wrote a book, *The Moon Is in Amazonia.*

I began to have the feeling that I had encountered a legend, although in truth I had never heard of him before. Also in truth, he seemed a bit of a bore—the aging journalist who can't give it up, or give up talking about it. He was in Taiwan writing a story for *Geo*, globe-trotting on his own now—his wife hadn't been able to take the life, he said—and filing stories by fax.

We trouped together through the Hsingchu Science-Based Industrial Park, where our names were posted on the park's VIP welcome board. (I was a VIP only because a Chinese friend had told the government I was one—but, like Bergès, I was trying to justify my celebrity by sending news stories home.) It was 1992, and we saw a replica of the satellite dish Peter Arnett had used to report from Baghdad, and a ship's antenna used for a Bush I meeting with Gorbachev on Malta. Then we were whisked away to the Encore Gardens, an almost unbelievable triumph of oriental kitsch, where we walked up and down fake mountains, with Bergès dragging his shattered ankle. We went to a water-organ concert and watched fountains leap in time to booming music. "We'll get 'Carmen' next," Bergès said. "I won't get my story written tonight. This is costing me a thousand dollars!"

The show was mercifully short, but then we did a night walk through the Gardens, a sort of Chinese Disneyland, gaudily lit, with steps outlined in green neon. We walked past an illuminated seven-story pagoda, flowerbeds planted in the shape of hideous masks, a carousel with giant plastic cartoon figures as riders. "Everytime I think it can't get worse, it does," my diary entry says. "Rows of red parasols, a lighted column with a dragon twined around it, a revolving statue of Confucius. Good God!"

The next day, Bergès and I visited an "aboriginal park"—this time a well-planned exhibit featuring the cultures of native Taiwanese peoples. But as we headed back toward our cars, Beethoven's "Hymn to Joy" began blaring from a loudspeaker, followed by the "Anvil Chorus" and "Carmen."

"See, I told you," Bergès said. "I haven't kicked around the world for nothing. There'll be another water show."

And there was, with the music blasting through "Brittania, Rule the Waves" to (so help me) the "Hallelujah Chorus," a crescendo of water, and a plastic cherub peeing into the audience. "Nunc dimittis," the diary says. "I've now seen (and heard) everything."

There was no Google in 1992, but when it eventually arrived I tried to find out more about Bergès. There was not a lot, at least in English. There were some references in French, but his book on the Colombian tribe had never been translated. He had "collaborated" with a Rolf Steiner on *The Last Adventurer*, a book about Steiner's exploits with the Foreign Legion in Vietnam and Africa. (I read it—it was competent ghostwriting—but Bergès's name on the title page was the only reference to him.) Bergès apparently was the only western journalist on the spot in Teheran on Sept. 8, 1978, the Iranian Revolution's "Black Friday," when troops of the Shah massacred hundreds of protesters. He describes diving for cover as soldiers fired into the crowd.

But of his life, his resumé, and by now probably his date of death, there was nothing. My parting view of him was of a tall figure, limping away toward his own last adventure, not boring anymore, and strangely brave.

ONE HUNDRED YEARS WITH SAM PUGH

I'VE NEVER MET SAMUEL F. PUGH, but I do him reverence. Who would not praise a man who has survived for a century and who acknowledges with gracious words the family and friends who have published the little book of his "poetry and prayers" that I am holding. Only 38 pages, but it sparkles with Sam Pugh's vitality, as does his photograph on the cover—an alert centenarian, with big glasses and a nattily dotted tie beneath his sweater. He is smiling, happily and a bit toothily, at someone off camera.

Beyond this, I know almost nothing about Sam Pugh. His book was given to me by my daughter-in-law's aunt, who I believe knows him personally. She thought I would enjoy the work of another poet, and I do. She also said he had been in business many years in Indianapolis.

Revise that comment about believing she knows Sam Pugh—of course she does. A birthday napkin bearing a red, orange, and green "100" is tucked into the booklet, along with an invitation to a party on June 5, 2004, at the Robin Run Village Community Room, 5354 West 62nd St., Indianapolis. "No gifts, please."

As a fellow writer, I appreciate that comma after "gifts," and also the 30 poems that make up Sam Pugh's *parvum opus*. They are arranged as "celebrations with" (not "of") Nature, Children, Life, and Prayer. They are not (and now I have to say it) poems that are likely to appear in college literature texts. Most are simple meditations—now and then sing-songy—on birds, autumn, "Little Boat," and "As I Grow Old."

But there are surprises. The longest poem, a two-pager titled "Violets," is a tribute to his wife and his memory of her as a young woman, choosing violets above all other blooms in a San Francisco flower market (as, I am thinking, she also chose this modest, kind man). Sam Pugh has read widely in good poets, and he drops some names easily and appropriately—Amy Lowell, Langston Hughes, Robert Pinsky. The verse in which they appear is titled "Where Are the Poets?" and it ends:

Could it be one of us?
We will need to dig deeper

107

than we've dug before.
Can we do it?
We can and will.

Samuel Franklin Pugh has done it, and my eyes are moist as I read his "Epilogue," subtitled "Come Walk With Me":

Years ago, when I was a boy in Missouri,
I used to gather black walnuts in the autumn
woods. When I crushed the green walnut hulls
with half a brick, then dug the hard nut out to dry,
my hands were black with stain. But the winter
flavor of those delicious kernels made it all
worthwhile. Now, decades later, I realize that
everything I've touched, every place I've been
and every person I've met has left some imprint
on my life. Some experiences were so strong
that they changed my viewpoint, my attitude,
my convictions, and my way of living—like
walnut stains.

Sam

[2007]

THE ENGINEER OF CONSENT

ON AUG. 6, 1992, my wife and I were in Montreal at a convention of journalism teachers. We were looking through the voluminous program for an interesting speaker, when my eye fell on "Edward L. Bernays."

"That's impossible," I said. "He'd have to be 100 years old." Bernays—the famed creator, with Ivy Lee, of professional public relations. Nephew of Sigmund Freud. Coiner of the term "engineering of consent." The man who told the world that Ivory Soap floats.

He was listed as the luncheon speaker at a professional division meeting, and we sneaked in after the lunch to hear him. He was, in fact, 100 years old, a dapper little man whose eyes barely peeped above the podium. "When Woodrow Wilson appointed me to the Creel Committee," he began—and he was certainly the last man alive who could make that statement. Wilson had formed the Creel Committee, or the Committee on Public Information, in 1917 to manage wartime propaganda, and Bernays was already famous.

"I served on the first committee that used ideas as weapons of war," he continued. "It occurred to me that if ideas could be used as weapons of war, they could certainly be used as weapons of peace."

But in modern public relations, he said, "anyone—nitwit, dope, or brilliant individual—can use the term . . . . Public relations today suffers from an unfortunate number of incompetents." There are no standards as there are for other professions, "and I believe there should be. . . . I believe that licensing and registration are mandatory if we are to transform public relations into a respected profession."

The idea that this would lead to government control is "rubbish," he added. "A public-relations practitioner is an applied social scientist who advises on social attitudes and actions." The term must be defined to save it, he concluded.

Bernays told of being approached by a woman seeking advice. He asked what she did, and she said she was in public relations. "That's not what I asked you," he responded. "I asked what you do." Her reply? "I pass out circulars in Harvard Square."

He described public relations as "a generalist vocation" that students majoring in many subjects could practice, although he did allow for formal courses, "probably on the graduate level." He also told the assembled teachers that codes of conduct like those for PR practitioners are useless. "None of those codes are enforceable and none are ever enforced."

Bernays spoke vigorously for 20 minutes, hardly sounding like someone a century old (he lived on for another two and a half years). When he finished lambasting current PR practice, there was a standing ovation, and I thought, "When you're 100 years old and the founder of the field, you can say anything you want."

I had watched him during the preceding (dull) program, and he paid more alert attention than much of the audience. His secretary, a woman about twice his size, occasionally leaned over and called something to his notice.

He stayed around afterward, talking to people and, I think, signing programs. He was still around the next day, greeting people in the hotel lobby. Finally, the secretary said, "Come on, Edward, time to go." He put on a little brown hat, and off they went down the escalator.

[1992]

THE SINGERS OF ST. KILDA

AFTER THREE STORMY NIGHTS in an open boat, an intrepid scribbler named Martin Martin reached the Scottish island of St. Kilda on June 1, 1697, and began a literary tradition that continues today.

Martin's little book, *A Late Voyage to St. Kilda*, is a travel classic that addresses compactly the people, geography, and customs of this most westerly of the Outer Hebrides (except for the Rockall seamount). He even adds some spice with an account of "the Imposter," a lunatic who had gone to the island proclaiming himself to be John the Baptist with a new revelation for humanity.

It sometimes seems as if every visitor since Martin has felt compelled to write about the experience, and I am no exception. I went to St. Kilda in the summer of 2000 for an archaeological dig, sponsored by the National Trust for Scotland, and described it later in poems and a memoir. The tiny archipelago has only one accessible island, Hirta (sometimes spelled Hirte), and is uninhabited most of the year except for sheep, thousands of seabirds, and the crew of a radar station. It is a treeless and starkly beautiful place, as well as a very steep one. Cliffs drop straight down more than 1,000 feet to the Atlantic. It's no wonder visitors are stirred to write.

But St. Kilda had its own population until 1930, and its own literary tradition, scanty and fragmented now but still of interest. The islanders lived by catching seabirds and crofting—farming on very small plots. Not surprisingly, much of their literature consists of elegies for friends and relatives who went "over the rocks." This is still happening; the year before my visit one work-party

111

member wandered off and fell to his death. But not all the island's literature is tragic; there is at least one fine love song, usually titled "St. Kilda Lilt" ("Iorram Hirteach"), which is worth printing.

He:
Away bent spade, away straight spade,
Away each goat and sheep and lamb;
Up my rope, up my snare,
I have heard the gannet upon the sea!

Thanks to the Being, the gannets are come,
Yes, and the big birds along with them;
Dark dusky maid, a cow in the fold;
A brown cow, a brown cow, a brown cow, beloved,
A brown cow, my dear one, that would milk the milk for thee,
Ho ro ru ra ree, playful maid,
Dark dusky maid, a cow in the fold!
The birds are a-coming, I hear their tune!

She:
Truly my sweetheart is the herdsman
Who would threaten the staff and would not strike!
Dark dusky maid, etc.

He:
Mary, my dear love, is the maid,
Though dark her locks her body is fragrant!
Dark dusky maid, etc.

She:
Thou art my handsome joy, thou art my sweetheart,
Thou gavest me first the honied fulmar!
Dark dusky maid, etc.

THE SINGERS OF ST. KILDA

He:

Thou art my turtle dove, thou art my mavis,
Thou art my melodious harp in the sweet morning.
Dark, dusky maid, etc.

She:

Thou art my treasure, my lovely one, my huntsman,
Yesterday thou gavest me the gannet and the auk.
Dark, dusky maid, etc.

He:

I gave thee love when thou wast but a child,
Love that shall not wane till I go beneath the earth.
Dark dusky maid, etc.

She:

Thou art my hero, thou art my basking sunfish,
Thou gavest me the puffin and the black-headed guillemot.
Dark dusky maid, etc.

He:

The mirth of my eyes and the essence of my joy thou art,
And my sweet-sounding lyre in the mountain of mist.
Dark dusky maid, etc.

She:

May the Being keep thee, the Creator aid thee,
The Holy Spirit be behind thy rope!
Dark dusky maid, etc.

I once recited this is the presence of a distinguished poet, who sniffed and said, "The Song of Solomon." It is, of course, but is still remarkable for an isolated island where nearly all energies were expended on survival. There were singers even here.

We have the photograph of one, Oighrig Nic Cruimein, or Euphemia MacCrimmon, who looks like a wild druidess of the North Atlantic, and who passed on the poem above, which she described as a "conversation" between her parents before their marriage. It is one of a handful of poems she managed to communicate to a folklorist, Alexander Carmichael, on May 22, 1865, while Carmichael was visiting St. Kilda. The poems were gotten down under difficulties, Carmichael said, amid a crowd of residents and naval officers, the shouts of children, and the barking of dogs. And also the disapproval of many, who thought these old songs were "part of the foolish past."

The main modern chronicler of St. Kildan songs is Mary Harman, who catalogued nearly all the known ones in her book, *An Isle Called Hirte.* There will be no more; the last 35 islanders were evacuated more than 75 years ago by the mainland government, which—with bureaucratic logic—gave some of them jobs as foresters.

Harman reports that "in the seventeenth century the St. Kildans were fond of music, song, and dancing. The only instrument they had was the jew's harp, though visitors sometimes brought pipes or a violin. Some had a talent for composition, their subjects being mainly love songs and laments for relatives, extolling their courage, abilities, and affection for their family. The women sang while harvesting, working at the quern, spinning or waulking cloth; the men sang while rowing." She notes that the person most responsible for preserving their songs was Neil Mackenzie, a pastor on St. Kilda in the 1830s, who encouraged residents to tell their stories and sing, during the long winter evenings. (A few years later, the Rev. John MacDonald, the dour "Apostle of the North," put an end to such frivolity.)

Harman divides the songs into elegies, love songs, religious songs, and a small miscellaneous group. Her list of 50 songs includes 36 different titles, 20 of them from Mackenzie's collection. The other 14 are variations. I found texts for 48 in the National Library of Scotland; the two missing ones do not seem significant. I also located a fragment or two not catalogued by Harman.

Aside from "St. Kilda Lilt," the most commonly cited St. Kilda song is an elegy on the death of a youth while gathering eggs on Hirta's neighboring island of Soay. This is a lugubrious affair, described either as a lament by a young wife for her husband or by a widow for her son: "Cursed be the cliff where thy feet lost their hold . . . . I lost my sweet Iver. Ah, me, he'll never return." Nine of Harman's 50 titles are variations on this melancholy theme. There are also six versions of a song about a St. Kilda maiden, sometimes identified as Marion Gillies, and her unrequited love for "Campbell of Islay."

But scattered among these sentimental poems are a few that repay closer study. A "St. Kilda Waulking Song" is pleasant in English and might be worth retranslating (waulking = thumping woolen cloth vigorously on a board to thicken or felt it):

> *I would make the fair cloth for thee,*
> *thread as the thatch-rope stout.*
>
> *I would make the feathered buskin for thee,*
> *thou beloved and importunate of men.*
>
> *I would give thee the precious anchor,*
> *and the family gear which my grandfather had.*
>
> *My love is the hunter of the bird,*
> *who earliest comes over foreign sea.*
>
> *My love the sailor of the waves,*
> *great the cheer his brow will show.*

Another song, identified by Harman as "It was no crew of landsmen," tells of a boat crew either lost or marooned during a voyage from the island. The first two verses in the Gaelic read:

Cha b'e sgioba na faiche
Ghabh Di-Ciadaoin an t-aiseag:
Gura sgeula nan creach mura beò sibh.

Gur h-e chum sibh cho fad uam
Am muir ard 's a' ghaoth chas oirth,
Chor 's nach d'fhaod sibh a' cheartair seò dhi.

An early English translation, hopelessly wooden, reads:

It was no crew of landsmen
Crossed the ferry on Wednesday:
'Tis tidings of disaster if you live not.

What has kept you so long from me
Is the high sea and the sudden wind catching you
So that you could not at once give her sail.

A few months ago, I began working through the Gaelic with the help of a dictionary and a Scottish friend, Ann Wakeling, from the work party in 2000. The word "faiche" (fai-shuh) proved interesting, because it can mean a sand crab's hole, but might also be the name of the boat involved. There was the suggestion of a woman waiting at home, engaged in household chores, and also—Ann said—of a Gaelic idiom she herself uses when she drops a bowl and breaks it: "Oh, my doom has come!" Eventually I wrote the following, which is perhaps less a translation from the Gaelic than a new poem:

Good sailors all, the crew
of the little Faiche,

small as a sand crab's hole,
who crossed over on Wednesday.
Good sailors, but they slipped
from my hand, broken

like a dish. Oh, what keeps you
so far from me?
Are you still even living?
On the steep sea, a shearing wind
caught at your sail,
spilling the air.

There is also a longer poem, in Gaelic, about the Well of Virtue in St. Kilda's northern valley. I have drunk water from this well but may need more before attempting a translation. (I once asked an expert on Chinese poetry how long one should study a language before starting to translate. "Oh, about 10 minutes," he replied, with a laugh.)

The history of St. Kilda is an ancient one, which I researched in some detail before going there in 2000. The Norse had been there in 800-900 A.D.; there is no saint named Kilda, and the island's name may be a corruption of the Norse *skildar*, for shield.

In the months before the trip, I did my usual overpreparation; among other things, I pulled Martin Martin's 1697 classic off the Internet and bound the pages into my own copy, which I carried to the island. My final packing list included 120 items, somehow crammed into two duffels and a small bag. A pair of Wellington boots never got used—the dig was too slippery. A can of high-powered insect repellant held off Scottish midges, and a camera tripod, carried upside down with one leg in the air, discouraged dive-bombing by bonxies—great skuas.

Our work party (13 people, including two actual archaeologists) met in Oban on the west coast of Scotland and traveled overnight by motorship to reach St. Kilda, 40 miles out in the Atlantic. For two weeks we excavated a dwelling site above the former village, where we ate and slept in houses restored by the National Trust. The Trust owns the islands and preserves them as a wildlife refuge.

When not excavating, we hiked the two-mile length of Hirta, did "bonxie dances" on the beach (running in circles while waving our arms), and pursued individual missions, from bird-watching to gathering wool shed by the island's Soay sheep. We also became friends—when I wrote a brief memoir of the dig, what struck me most was the lack of a single hard word in two weeks. As our cook, a veteran of several digs, put it, "This is the hardest-working, happiest, just absolutely bloody luckiest bunch of dirt monkeys I've ever seen."

Our excavations found pottery and bone that pushed the date for human habitation of the archipelago back a thousand years earlier than the Norse, to the Middle Iron Age or 300 B.C. (plus/minus 300 years). I wrote my own poem about that, called "Limited Knowledge":

After 2,000 years, you dig
deeper to find less
of the shepherd and his wife—
a handstone he may have used,
some fragments
of the pot she made,
pressing triangles
into its braided band.
Perhaps she broke the pot,
or it sat here
until the roof fell.
Perhaps it held grain.
Perhaps they ran and hid
in the scree hole, where pirates

killed them.
Perhaps the pot was what
they couldn't carry
when they left
a relentless country
where nothing but stone
could stay.

[2000]

**View between cleits on St. Kilda toward
Mulloch Sgar and the archaeological dig.**

LEAVING ST. KILDA

There is no saint,
there is no island.

Hesperides, Hebrides.
Behind us,
the doors of the sea
are closing over Skildar,

which has
no saint at all, only
a name the Norse left
for barrier, shield,

which is not
one island even,
only a cloaking name
for many islands.

The boat moves
in the sun's power.
Skildar's old poets
sleep under Oiseval.

The ocean quiets
and weaves
with little winds
a winding of black linen.

Dead men fall down
into the sleep-nets
of the woven sea.
. . . .
The boat bears us
from dream to dream,
turning us
to the world.

There is no saint,
there is no island.

THE ABSENT

You know how sometimes a crowd's
photograph is keyed
to silhouettes? (This hat is John,
that shoulder Cousin Kate.)

On the Street this morning I see them,
black shapes cut from the day,
bent over knitting or headed
with fowling rods toward the cliffs.

They refuse to emigrate or be given
over wholly to history. One raises
a hand with a rock to gesture
against time and violation.

They make a space in the air
one has to step sideways
to get around. The birds see them and rise
crying into the desolate sky.

121

Venice's Scuola San Marco (also called the Ospedale Civila or City Hospital) and its elaborate *trompe l'oeil* façade.

BY VENICE OBSESSED

WHEN I WENT TO VENICE, my Uncle Stephen gave me two tasks. He asked me to go to "the bookshop (last on the right) in the Calle di Canonica beside the Clergy House just north of San Marco," and buy a copy of *La Chiesa di S. Maria Formosa* by G. Bortolan and A. Niero. I found the church history for him, but the timing was wrong to fulfill his second request, which was:

> Go to the Campo of SS Giovanni e Paolo at sunset some evening – stand on the bridge opposite the entrance of the church – and report whether the hospital (Ospedale Civila) casts a shadow on the façade of the church. Canaletto and other painters have painted it that way. J.G. Links, who is editing a revised edition of W.G. Constable's two vol. work on Canaletto, and I have been exchanging ideas on the possibility of this. Our best engineer working with facts on hour of sunset at that latitude on June 21 says it is possible on June 21st. Links is going to Venice at the end of June to see for himself. I'd love to scoop him.

Oh, Stephen, how much fun it would have been to answer your question and show Links, author of the best modern walking guide to Venice, a thing or two! But my family and I were there in May, not June, and the research would have been inconclusive.

That was 1974, and Stephen's letter—dated April 18—has just fallen out of a small trip notebook I kept. Also tucked in the notebook was a clipping he sent of a column from the *Long Island Press* by William A. Rusher, who had just toured Venice with a copy of Links's *Venice for Pleasure* in hand. Stephen called the column "a fresh bit of writing on the almost hopeless subject of Venice."

Why hopeless? Because it sometimes seems that half the people in the world have been to Venice, and that every one of them has written about it. Stephen's brother Bill, fresh from his first trip, decided to convey his enthusiasm to an old farmer in Nebraska with whom he corresponded. The farmer wrote back that Venice didn't seem to have changed much since his own visit in 1911!

As you can tell, I am circling the question of why I should add to the glut of words on Venice. It's because of Stephen, I think. He saw Venice, on his many visits, with an artist's eye, and shared that vision with my family and me, giving us tips on what to see, what to avoid, and what would delight or bore our boys (three of them at the time). He recommended his hotel, Paganelli's, on the Riva degli Schiavone just down from the Royal Danieli Hotel, and suggested that we have a project for the trip— in view of our family name, he said, we might take pictures of all 400 bridges over the canals.

Shortly after our return, he wrote a note saying that my wife, Karen, had just telephoned him "in a fine state of rapture," and had so fired his own imagination that he and a friend had already gone down to the Pan-Am office and booked passage, once again, for Venice.

Venice has so much for everyone that the only sensible way to approach it is to find your own enthusiasm and pursue it, whether this is the paintings of Canaletto or the cats that cross your path and peek out at you from windows everywhere in the city. Visitors to Venice should park their world-weariness at the train station, board a *vaporetto* on the Grand Canal, and sail off to a different world. It's like entering a miraculous, life-size toy that repays whatever you bring to it. If you bring a typical tourist's mentality, you may enjoy it for a day and then be put off by its summer smells, scaling paint, and the sight of orange peels in the canal. Stay longer and you may never leave.

That's what happened to a most peculiar writer, Frederick Rolfe, who styled himself Baron Corvo and wrote a novel about Venice titled *The Desire and Pursuit of the Whole*. Another writer, Sean O'Faolain, recommends Corvo's book to anyone visiting Venice, but this is partly a warning: "Corvo was taken to Venice for a brief holiday; refused to leave it; piled up debts; was reduced to pauperdom; thrown out of his hotel; rejected by his friends; tramped around his beloved city in the winter night like a homeless cat; got pneumonia; recovered; died and left this, his last, wonderful tribute to the Circe who had killed him." It is also "a very bad novel," he adds, which it is.

Stephen was able to tear himself away from Venice, repeatedly, but he also wrote a book about it. His obsession was churches, and with two friends—Richard Zimmerman and John McLaughlin—he wrote a guide to church-crawling in Venice. It's never been published and probably never will be now; its title, *A Venetian Keepsake*, is Stephen's admission that it was a personal memento. "This is not a guide book nor is it intended for those who boast that they do not know an apse from an atrium," he wrote in the introduction. "It is a labor of love."

And what a delightful one. I am looking through my copy as I write, and enjoying again Stephen's description (in full) of the Oratorio dell' Annunciata: "More evidence of restoration than age, but with signs of being loved as the ex-votos give witness. A nice one for those who collect small churches."

Reporting on Sant' Antonino, "a simple neighborhood church," he notes an old guidebook's report that "in 1819 a church-crawling elephant escaped from a menagerie, entered this church (what consternation and excitement!), refused to leave and was finally dispatched with a shot from a piece of ordnance."

Stephen himself dispatches San Simeone Piccolo, which arrivals see from the train station, in three sentences: "The elegance of the porch makes up for the clumsiness of the dome. The absence of a drum gives the effect of a man wearing a hat three sizes too large. Forlorn interior."

There is much more, including a list of churches "still standing but put to secular use" and another list of those "known to Flaminio Cornaro but now destroyed."

But this speaks mostly to Stephen's obsession, and every visitor to Venice should have his own. I see that I have two Venetian notebooks, both small. The first I filled before our 1974 visit—filled it with every scrap of information I thought might be useful in the city, including lists of landmarks, a map of the islands of the lagoon, what to look for in various art galleries, and a handwritten catalogue of 80 paintings by Giambattista Tiepolo, scattered among 34 museums, churches, and palaces.

The notebook has similar lists for Titian, Tintoretto, Carpaccio, Georgione, Bellini, Donatello, Cima, Lorenzo Lotto, Piazetta, and Veronese. After all, we were going to be in Venice for a week and didn't want to run out of things to do. In among the lists, I sketched floor plans of churches (I Frari and San Zanipolo) and the Doge's Palace (or Doggy's Palace, as Stephen sometimes called it after a scotch or two).

I wrote down the location in San Zanipolo (the Church of SS Giovanni e Paolo) of a monument to Alvise Trevisan, a young man "who died from his exertions in the gymnasium." My uncles had made a practice of leaving a red rose on the stone, and of course I planned to do the same thing.

The notebook also contains an account of the collapse of the Campanile in St. Mark's Square, at 9:47 a.m. on July 14, 1902, along with a comment on it recorded in the Venetian patois by Horatio Brown in 1905: *"Lu xè sempre stà galantomo, lu ga parlà; lu ga avisà, 'fe largo che casco'"*—"He's always been a gentleman; he spoke, he warned us: 'Away with you, for I'm coming down!'" The only casualty was a cat buried in the ruins. (The Campanile was rebuilt, and few tourists realize they are seeing a tower only a century old.) Near the Campanile are the city's two famous columns, dedicated to St. Mark and St. Theodore. The notebook reminds me that these were repaired in 1891 by Signor Vendrasco, and that the eyes of St. Mark's lion atop one column are not diamonds, as widely supposed, but faceted white agates.

At the back of the notebook I pasted a timeline showing, in minute handwriting, the entire history of Venice, from its founding in a swamp in 421 A.D. to May 16, 1797, when Napoleon invaded and put an end to La Serenissima—Her Most Serene Highness—at least as far as worldly power was concerned.

I was also collecting literary references to Venice, from O'Faolain to Corvo himself, who, when he was cold and starving, still saw only the stars above the canals, fluttering "like little pale daffodils in a night mist colored like the bloom on the fruit of the vine." I find bits of Ruskin in the notebook and of the scented prose of Gabriel D'Annunzio: "A sound of applause burst from the passage of San Gregorio, re-echoing in the precious discs of porphyry and serpentine adorning the house of the Darios, that stooped under their weight like a decrepit courtesan under the pomp of her jewels."

Finally, I had overprepared for the trip to the point of covering one kitchen wall with a map of the city drawn in chalk.

I was nearly as crazy as Corvo.

In retrospect, such drudgery was not the best way to get ready for Venice. Did I really need the names of all the islands in the lagoon, as well as the five "mythic" islands of Murano—Tremodià, Trencòre, Galbaia, Mortesina, and La Foléga? Did I need to know that William Dean Howells had referred to "the evanescent islands of the East?" (While writing this, I complimented my wife on trouping loyally through countless museums and obscure churches in windswept corners of the city. "I hadn't learned yet to say no," she replied.)

A much saner approach is described by Links in *Venice for Pleasure*, first published in 1966. It offers four simple walking tours, and is mostly, he says, "about the outsides of buildings, seldom about their contents. It is about Venice, the city, not about its possessions, and very little about its people." This last may sound cavalier but is realistic. Venetians have their own lives, jobs, a city government, and a police force. But unless you plan to go native like Corvo, you'll see very little of all this, which is as it should be. (My family and I did get swept up in a Communist parade at one point and marched happily along with the Venetians for a few blocks under the red banner.) Venice is a great world city—it expects you to be a tourist and indulge your obsessions, as long as you also contribute to the economy. The days when Venice held "the gorgeous east in fee" (Wordsworth) are long gone.

Links is the best antidote I know for tourist guilt. Stop often, rest, and look around, he writes. Enjoy yourself. Don't look at paintings unless you feel like it. You can see St. Mark's next time. His book has a few carefully chosen illustrations and some helpful simplified maps. Even so, getting around Venice on foot is an adventure. My son David and I started out one day to see the Carpaccios at the Scuola del Greci, and soon found outselves in a warren of streets. Consulting Links, I said, "We can go left and be at the museum in five minutes. Or we can go right and be hopelessly lost." "Let's go right," David said.

My obsession with Venice had an unexpected sequel. When I got home, I found that it had stirred me to poetry, and I began to study that art seriously. My first Venice poems were amateur work and are safely buried, but eventually I wrote one that could be submitted to a respectable poetry journal. It described a Sunday morning visit to the Church of the Gesuati on the Zattere, bordering the harbor:

An old woman kisses God's toe and goes out,
bees drip from the mouth of a priest.
Tiepolo's angels are flying somewhere

above the scaffolding, but spring
has come in from the Zattere.
A freighter is moving up the channel.
Coffee is being served at Nico's.

Three girls lean over the organ case to flirt
with the young organist. God hears
antiphonal laughter. He is here
in the person of an old priest
who has been walking under the trees
by San Agnese and has come in
to rest his feet. The girls please him.

They rise up the side aisle afterward,
momentary angels, graceful and smiling,
stooping to hug a solemn, dressed-up child.
Their love this morning is enough to cover
organists, little boys, even God.
They bob to Him, lord of the year,
who blesses and sends their blitheness into spring.

The editor of the journal rejected the poem and suggested gently that I learn to spell—it's the Church of the Gesuiti, not Gesuati, she wrote. Well! I knew my Venetian churches by now—the Gesuiti (with its chilly green marble) was on the desolate northern shore and had been described by Howells as "incredibly tableclothy" despite its painting of St. Lawrence "toasting so comfortably on his gridiron amid all that frigidity." The Gesuati is on the other side of town. I reported this to the editor, who was embarrassed into printing the poem.

Curiously, my second notebook, from Venice itself, is much shorter than the "prep" notebook, and quits entirely after a day or two. There is a sketch called "A Morning in

Dorsoduro," which is mainly a street-by-street account of a ramble with Links's guidebook at the ready. I'm happy to see that we stopped for coffee—something Links (and Stephen) favored doing often. We saw cats, and children playing. We saw a beautiful girl step onto a balcony for a moment and then disappear back inside. We were almost swept away by a flock of pigeons in a nameless *campo* near the Campiello Barbaro.

After that, though, the notes get sketchy. I had sunk into the city and wanted to see more and more, without the distraction of note-taking. There would always be time for that on another visit (and there was, several years later, although the first enthusiasm of travel was spent).

Stephen had foreseen all this and had the wit to give us excellent but fairly minimal instructions on getting around the city of his dreams, with children. Have one boy keep a diary, he said. Teach the older ones how to read a street map. "Set the task of looking for horses in sculpture." Make sure they see glass blowers at work, and "photograph your youngest on the back of the marble lion on the terrace beside San Marco," a lion polished by the backsides of countless children over the centuries.

But in the end, our children found their own memories of Venice. On the Grand Canal one morning, we saw a Venetian angler with two poles. When we looked again, David was holding one of them. He didn't catch anything, but I can imagine him responding to some new raver of Venice: "Yes, I remember fishing in the Grand Canal, in 1974. Doesn't sound like much has changed."

[2006]

130

TIME OUT AT THE 'TIME OUT'

BEHIND THE BAR, a clock inside a green halo of neon shows fives all the way around its dial.

It's always quitting time at the Time Out Bar in Van Buren, Indiana.

It was 11 a.m. in the outside world, just before I entered the Time Out, where I'm now eating the Hoosier version of fish and chips—a fish sandwich on a bun and a bag of Lay's barbecue chips. I'm here as a result of mentoring an intern, at a nearby newspaper, who a few days ago wrote a story about the Time Out. The intern called it the last place left to eat a sit-down meal in Van Buren, a hamlet of 800 souls just off Interstate 69 on the way to Ft. Wayne.

I'm headed to Ft. Wayne to visit another intern, but Van Buren lies nearly on my path, and I'm running early, and it's almost lunch time. And the Time Out is easy to find. It's just around the corner from one failed eatery, the M'eating Place, and down the street from P.J.'s defunct pizza parlor. And just across from the post office and a yard sale.

Yard sales are big in Van Buren this Friday morning—I have counted at least six while driving into town, past a red barn, the Lions Club Park, and the water tower. Other than the D & J Lubritory and the Weaver Popcorn Co., they're almost the only businesses. Except, of course, for the Time Out, which is doing a brisk trade among its regulars this morning.

"I left my cigarettes in the car, Daisy," a woman tells the bartender. "I'll be right back."

131

I've been in many bars in a long and sometimes misspent life, but the Time Out is classic, from its hand-painted name on paper pasted onto the front windows, to the fluorescent juke box, to a schedule of NASCAR races on the wall, to a green neon frog hanging from the ceiling in the back, next to the men's room, which has no doorknob, no lock, and a sheet-metal urinal. (Leaving it later, I nearly bump into a waitress, who says, "Boo!" and then "It's all right, honey.")

We can barely see each other anyway, because the Time Out is *dark*. Dark paneling on the walls, dark, grained formica tables, ancient dark flooring. Most of the light comes from neon signs for beer and Jack Daniels whisky—"Jack Lives Here, Old No. 7" says one. A stack of blue Bud Lite boxes occupies a corner next to the bar, and the front wall beside the door is draped with silver tinsel and black stars, like a leftover prom decoration. The Time Out seems caught in a time warp, an impression reinforced by an elderly Bob Barker still emceeing "The Price Is Right" on the TV over the bar. The bar is like a lighted ocean liner breasting the tide of darkness. An illuminated menu board gives the day's specials. Daisy and her helper draw beer from a spigot on the wall under the clock, which is next to somebody's wedding picture and a sign for "Free Metal Hauling."

Daisy brings my fish sandwich, bag of chips, and coffee. (I have long since, after a dismal experience in Germany, given up drinking beer before noon.)

"Is this the place the paper wrote about the other day?" I ask her.

"Sure is," she says.

"Well, I read that story down where I live, in Franklin, south of Indianapolis, and I just had to stop by."

"Our advertising worked, didn't it?" says Daisy, who apparently is not at all surprised that someone a hundred and fifty miles away has read about her bar and made a trip to see it. Others overhear us, and after a while Daisy's helper, not quite so laconic, is reminiscing about the day the press showed up.

"I hate having my picture taken," she says. "I won't even have it taken with my grandchild. But they just took it anyway."

The fish sandwich is good, the coffee plentiful, the chips . . . . packaged. Time passes, or does it? Thinking about it later, I can't remember seeing anybody (except the woman with the cigarettes) enter or leave. They were all there when I came in and they're all still there as I leave. When I arrived, the clock said five. As I leave, it says either a quarter of five or 5:45, take your pick. (Other bars have different novelty clocks—on one, the numbers run backward and a sign below says, "If this looks okay to you, you've had too much.")

Later, back home, Karen and I are sitting on the front porch in the warm dark, eating strawberries and ice cream, and talking about old bars in Vincennes, Indiana, our hometown—the Palm Café, the Manhattan, Alice & Woody's, Jiggers, the Little Owl. As a child, she sat in the car outside most of them while Fritz, her father, was socializing inside (except for the Little Owl, a shabeen up the C.& E.I. tracks, which not even Fritz would go into).

I tell her about the Time Out, and watching Bob Barker, and she tells me something that surpasses anything I could have contrived as an ending for my story. What I was watching on this Friday, she says, was Barker's very last live, on-screen performance after 50 years in television.

O tempora! O mores! and also *Tempus fugit.* Time, alas, does pass, even in the Time Out Bar.

These charred pilings beside the Yukon River in Whitehorse, photographed in 1986, marked where a steamboat burned.

'Word Lobster Has Been Spoken'

ONE DAY IN THE MID-1960s, a man walked into my office at the Hornell, N.Y., *Evening Tribune* and threw down a sheaf of brown and crumbling newspapers. He had found them in his attic, in a trunk containing effects of his mother's cousin, Ben Trenneman, a noted wrestler in the Klondike during the Gold Rush of the late 1890s. Was I interested in seeing them?

Well, of course. At that time, people appeared in my office with many things. Potatoes resembling famous people. A Christmas tree bulb that had burned every season for 30 years. One man brought me a Stradivarius violin he had found in *his* attic (at least the label pasted on the inside said, in Latin, "Antonio Stradivari made me, 1697"). Ben Trenneman's cousin left the newpapers with me and never returned.

Over the years, I've seen much mouldering newsprint, and most of these papers were ordinary: several copies of the *Dawson Daily News* (dull), one copy of the *Vancouver Daily Province* (duller), and—oddly—the "turned-rule" (black-bordered) edition of the *New York Herald* reporting the assassination of President Lincoln. There were also two copies of the *Yukon Morning Journal*, printed in Dawson in 1901. One reported the wedding of Chief Silas of the Moosehide Indians. It was one of the funniest (and most politically incorrect) newspaper stories I had ever read.

I suppose I wrote something about the Yukon newspapers—a column, maybe, on a dull news day—and then I put them away. Since I seldom throw out papers, they went along with me from Hornell to Louisville, Ky., and to Franklin College, where I began teaching journalism in 1979. In the mid-1980s, I had an academic need to publish something and also the means—an academic award—to finance the research. I dug out the Yukon newspapers. Why not go to the Klondike and find out more about the interesting and funny *Yukon Morning Journal*? I'd learned that it was on microfilm, but had never been studied. And the Yukon Archives in Whitehorse had additional information. Leaving my family at the Vancouver World's Fair, I flew off to Whitehorse on my academic boondoggle.

To Whitehorse, but not to Dawson itself, near the Alaskan border, 268 miles northwest of Whitehorse, as measured on my 3-by 4-foot topographic map of the Yukon Territory (Canada Department of Energy, Mines, and Resources, 1972). I could have visited Dawson, but the place I wanted to see did not exist there anymore. I would have found a modern Canadian town, with some tourist museums and probably a Klondike revue, played for laughs, with an equity actress as Diamond-Tooth Gertie. The city I wanted was in the microfilm and the drawers of barely catalogued materials in the Yukon Archives. So I spent a week in Whitehorse, reading the *Yukon Morning Journal*, and taking time off to visit a museum in a beached steamboat on the bank of the Yukon River. (Not long before, another steamboat had burned while moored nearby.) A museum guide took us into the purser's office and pointed out a 1922 Remington 16 typewriter, a duplicate of one I had inherited from my Uncle Bill. "You don't see that kind anymore," the guide said. "Oh, I have one in my office, right next to the computer," I responded. "Use it almost every day." The guide's look said, "You meet every kind of smart-ass in this business."

Whitehorse was a pleasant small town that might have been teleported from Indiana: a wide main street of mostly one-story shops, and a good steakhouse in the cellar of the Edgewood Hotel, with French onion soup, the cheese crust of which required a knife to hack through. There was another deluxe hotel with its inevitable revue, the "Frantic Follies," and my own adequate but cheaper hotel, the Regina, next to the deep green and fast-flowing Yukon River. On the other side of the Regina was a bar, a barn-like shed where Indians wandered in and out, day and night. On the way back to the airport, my cab driver confirmed, reluctantly, that, yes, there was a considerable problem with alcoholism. One day I walked out into the country, passing the Yukon College and a river with a fish ladder. In half an hour, I was in the the Yukon bush.

It was the Fourth of July, and signs in store windows welcomed "Our American Friends." Despite this, I was told, the tourist business was down. It had been hoped that the Yukon exhibit at the World's Fair would bring visitors. "But if it doesn't, it'll be a hard winter," my hotel manager said. "Back to moose meat, I guess." Daylight lasted until almost midnight, and this, with the relentlessness of the Yukon River, began to work on me, until I eventually wrote about it:

Only once I went as far north as I could
and saw the Yukon stampeding north all night
like a green freight train. Too long.
No sunsets came, and every time
I looked out, that damn river was still there.

I don't want many things to last forever,
or to live without sunsets going up
like shouts of gold. I think I know
why prospectors went dumb or crazy. Those days
were as near eternity as I want to come.

In the end I was grateful for the cozy Yukon Archives, and its adjoining hall, built around a central stone fireplace. The Archives staff was small but with a helpful director, Eileen Edmunds. There were not that many researchers digging through the records. (A

137

few months later I called Eileen to ask about getting one of my students a January internship there. "You were here in July, Bill," she said. "Do you know how cold it gets in January?")

The *Morning Journal* didn't disappoint. It was just as funny, quirky, and opinionated as I had hoped. Chief Silas had been just a start. The *Journal* brought the Dawson of the Gold Rush vividly to life for me, and eventually led me to the daughter of Eugene Allen, the real pioneer of Yukon journalism and founder of the storied *Klondike Nugget.*

But that came later. First I read all the copies of the *Morning Journal*, which began life on March 4, 1901, and expired a scant three months later, a victim of competition, lack of a news service from the "outside," and the fading of Dawson's free-and-easy Gold Rush mentality. Its owners were G.E. Daniel (a butcher turned business manager), editor Alfred L. Smith, and George E. Storey, a Seattle printing foreman who had been Eugene Allen's "chief of staff" on the original *Nugget*.

The *Journal* tried to be a Gold Rush newspaper after the Gold Rush had passed, and it was doomed from the start. But what a lot of fun it had during its brief life! Chief Silas was a fairly typical piece of flamboyance. The chief's wedding dance, it reported

> was greatly enjoyed by all, many new and original steps being presented. Chief Silas was a striking figure, wearing a dress coat cut on the bias and trimmed with gunny sack edging, giving him a picturesque effect that excited the envy of the younger bloods. His blushing bride was most becomingly clad in a waist of prismatic bunting, with a skirt of Army blanket overlaid with pale lavendar mosquito netting. Her delicate and shapely feet were encased in a pair of new moccasins and on her head she wore with modest grace a large-sized clam shell imported especially for the occasion. She was the cynosure of all eyes.

The account wasn't too much different in outline from what I had written during a brief stint as a small-town Indiana society editor in the 1950s, with peau de soie and veils of pink illusion substituting for the mosquito netting and Army blanket.

Since there was little real news in Dawson, the *Journal* had to make do with drama where it found it, including an account of a "pasty war" between bill plasterers for rival theaters. This apparently involved the trading of insults. "Word lobster has been spoken," the headline declared ominously. It also ran stories about the demise of Tim Sullivan in an "opium den," about a man who ate 247 oysters at a sitting before the police stepped in to stop "the bivalve fiend," and about the embarrassment of a man called out in his bathrobe to fight a fire. It told the latest on "Swiftwater Bill" Gates, that most outrageous of Klondikers (no relation, so far as I know, to Microsoft Bill), and reported how rival factions had taken turns demolishing and rebuilding a log cabin on a disputed townsite.

The tiny four-page *Journal* was the smallest of Dawson's four papers, but it made plenty of noise. It outdid its rivals in reporting mad-dog scares; one case of hydrophobia was enough to bring out the "Second Coming" type: "Hundreds May Die of Rabies."

The *Journal* also had a fascination with the poor, peripatetic Dawson prostitutes, who were forever being told to move on. It described them in terms that probably concealed a sense of civic guilt: the demimonde, daughters of Aphrodite, nymphs of the pave. It reported a suggestion to the Yukon Council that "a board fence six feet high be constructed around the demimonde," adding that the councilors had rejected the suggestion "with dignified scorn." (The *Yukon Sun* took a more ironic view, reporting after a vice crackdown that "Dawson has put on her pure white garment of virtue, and the half-world is in evidence within our city limits forever no more. We are the holiest people on earth, and don't you forget it.")

The *Journal* was ambivalent about gambling and moral reform at a time when the *Sun* was generally supporting the new virtue. It wrote:

> Since time was a callow youth, attired only in the scanty garb of inexperience, there have been drunkards and there have been gamblers. When the scythe of time, grown old and decrepit, shall have rusted and fallen from its haft, and Gabriel blows his last call, there will be those who are drunk and cannot respond, and those who will stop to see the next card.

The *Journal* drew a sneer from its rivals with a report that a watch chain—"evidence of prehistoric man"—had been found under 45 feet of gravel on Hunker Creek. That was too much even for the usually friendly *Nugget*. In a story headed "Prehistoric Nothing," it gave the "true history" of how the watch chain had been torn from its owner during a brawl at a St. Patrick's Day dance.

But if the *Journal* didn't mind a yarn now and then, it took mining seriously and showed a vigorous regard for truth when one of its reporters wrote about a gold strike of $20 to $150 a pan. That would have been an excellent yield indeed, but the *Journal* reported next day that the figures were the totals taken from two diggings. In a correction titled "The Wine Was Red," it explained that its reporter had "looked upon it and his report became somewhat colored. . . . Hootch hath no superior as a ready multiplier." The same issue reported that H.J. Baron, "late of Boston," would join the paper's reporting staff as its "bright young man," replacing James Boyd Nesbitt, "whose connection with the *Journal* has been severed."

Some of the *Journal's* most characteristic stories, however, were whimsies and tall tales to which no one could seriously object. It reported the "arrest" of Master McDonald for sailing his toy steamboat around the courthouse. There were several "Tales Told by Cranks"—sourdough yarns like the one about a prospector who assured himself of both bread and supple shoe leather by setting dough to rise overnight in his boots. Another told of a prospector who walked for three days "against the whirl of the earth" and found himself 4,000 miles from his destination.

The *Journal* also covered mining news extensively as well as all major local stories of the spring of 1901: the suppression of gambling, discussions of the miner's lien law and the gold royalty, the dedication of the Ogilvie Bridge, and a long legal battle between the Yukon Council and Mrs. Luella Day McConnell, during which Mrs. McConnell took to her bed and refused to answer court summonses.

During most of its brief life, the *Journal* treated its competitors good-naturedly. It observed on May 17, 1901, that "another day has passed and yet no scoop has been published. Florence [Florence Marvin, editor of the *Sun*] must be seriously ill." Soon after that, however, the *Journal* entered into a serious argument with the *Sun* over the proposed formation of a miners union. The *Journal* favored the union, and the *Sun* attacked its morning rival as "that quaint publication" and "the wildly struggling dodger that is attempting to create in others the belief that it is a newspaper." The *Journal* fired back at the *Sun* as "the silurian of the sloughs."

The use of "quaint" as an epithet for the *Journal* was telling. Dawson was changing—it was already a long way from the uproarious Gold Rush days of 1898, when Eugene Allen, a printing salesman from Seattle, stole a march on his rivals by typing the first issue of the *Klondike Nugget* and pinning it to a bulletin board in the center of Dawson.

For about a year, Dawson—a former moose pasture at the confluence of the Yukon and Klondike rivers—became truly "the San Francisco of the North," a boomtown of 30,000 constantly shifting residents, which ran 24 hours a day as the miners tore the gold from the creeks and were "mined" in turn by gamblers, dance-hall girls, prostitutes, and confidence men of all kinds. Gold itself meant almost nothing, and the miners disposed of it in a frenzy.

"The poor ginks have just gotta spend it," Diamond-Tooth Gertie, one of the dance-hall queens, observed. "They're that scared they'll die before they have it all out of the ground."

There was continuing tension between Americans and Canadians, and some abortive conspiring to establish a Klondike Free State that would seek union with the United States.

Journalists were also part of the frenzy. Gene Allen later described the long days of the *Nugget* staff: one reporter habitually worked, sang, and drank until he dropped, then crept off to sleep a few hours in "Little Willie's Cradle," the coal box in the kitchen of the Portland Restaurant. The party went on six days and nights a week, then stopped short for a sabbath enforced by the Northwest Mounted Police. It ended for good in the summer of 1899 when gold was discovered on the sands of Nome, Alaska, at the mouth of the Yukon River. In a week, 8,000 people left Dawson in the stampede to Nome.

Behind they left a nostalgia among journalists for the Gold Rush days, the time of youth, yarns, nicknames, and easy camaraderie, when all the social bars were down. Elmer "Stroller" White, the *Nugget's* popular columnist, lamented the days when police court was reported under the heading "Fun at the Forks," and included such fanciful offenses as "disturbing the dove of peace" and "making Rome howl." White cited with some admiration the work of a fellow reporter, Casey Moran, who "could dig up more news, and make a bigger mess of writing it" than anyone else in the Klondike. (Moran once reported the discovery of Noah's Ark on a mountain in Alaska.)

The Klondike went on mining gold, but it was never the same again, and little by little respectability reached Dawson. The Canadian author Pierre Berton, who grew up there, has written that it was much like "the small towns I used to read about in Booth

Tarkington novels, complete with dusty roads and shady walks, neat, flower-decked cottages and pretty steepled churches, with horses clip-clopping down the main street and the river running past our front door." My 1911 *Encyclopaedia Britannica* reported that Dawson had "all the resources of a civilized city in spite of being founded on a frozen peat bog." My 1972 topo map lists Grand Forks as "abandoned." No more "fun at the Forks."

The *Journal* couldn't revive the era its writers clearly loved. In May, 1901, it reported a civic festival in which Ben Trenneman, the relative of my newspaper visitor, had helped the Athletic Club team to a hard-won victory in the tug-of-war. Trenneman has been described elsewhere as "a star grappler on the coast before [the] Klondike dragged Seattle out of antediluvian sleep." But he collapsed in exhaustion after the tug-of-war, the *Journal* wrote, and had to be carried off "thoroughly gone." Not long afterward, in early June, the newspaper ceased daily publication, and by summer's end it, too, was "thoroughly gone."

I had a good time ransacking the records, although the "academic" paper I wrote never found a publisher. (It is on file in the Yukon Archives, however.) I did not care all that much. I had spent a week in the Dawson of the Klondike Gold Rush and lugged home a briefcase full of photocopied newspaper clippings and odd bits from the file drawers of the Yukon Archives. I have never thrown any of this away, naturally, and I got it all out a few nights ago. There were some things I had forgotten, and some discoveries.

Before going to Whitehorse, I had researched the Gold Rush in detail, as I do any place I visit with more than a casual purpose. "Tourism is sin," the filmmaker Werner Herzog said, and I expiate in advance by overpreparing. I knew the names of all the "creeks"—Gold Run, Dominion, Hunker, and Bonanza, with its fabulously rich tributary, the Eldorado. (The gold-bearing part of the Eldorado was only two or three miles long, my *EB* said, but "for its length probably surpassed any other known placer de-

143

posit.") All the creeks radiated from the Dome, 4,250 feet high. Gold was discovered on Aug. 16, 1896, and the first claim was staked the following day. By the next April, 1,500 people were in Dawson. Then there was the "starving winter" of 1897-98 before the boom really got under way the ensuing summer. At its height, in 1900, $22 million in gold was extracted from the frozen ground by thawing it with fires or steam, the *EB* said. Prospectors arrived from around the world, many of them greenhorns, but some already veterans of gold fever in Australia and South Africa.

In my files, I found a photocopy of a "newspaper," the *Klondike News*, that predated Allen's *Nugget* by ten months—Aug. 25, 1997. But it was not a real newspaper—more likely it was something "gotten up" to appeal to potential stampeders. An article, "How to Get to the Klondike," accurately described two paths—the all-water route from Seattle to the mouth of the Yukon and up the Yukon to Dawson, and the "backdoor route" by way of St. Paul and Edmonton on the Canadian Pacific, followed by a 50- to 60-day trek to Fort McPherson. "It is mostly downgrade all the distance," the story added. The writer seems not to have known of the water/land route via Skagway and White Pass, but substituted his own whimsical travel prospectus—a syndicate, he wrote, was planning a direct trolley line from Chicago's City Hall to Dawson.

The *News* also said Dawson's population was estimated at from 3,000 to 15,000, "mostly human beings."

There were other discoveries. Out of a drawer in the Archives I had copied three pages, written by D.E. "Dave" Griffith, about "Dawson's First Extra." The typed manuscript recalled the often-told story of a "Cheechako youth" who brought in a Seattle paper with the first detailed news of the Spanish-American War. The paper was sold, resold, and eventually read aloud at the Pioneer Hall to a crowd that had paid $1 each to hear it. In his manuscript, Griffith identifies himself as the "Cheechako youth" and points readers to Page 3 of the first *Klondike Nugget*, where, he says, his identity is established. And indeed it is.

As I looked through my stack of photocopied newspaper pages, I realized what a Klondike they were themselves of the era's social history. Earlier, I had looked at news stories. Now I lingered over ads, for J.A. Flynn's Big Burlesque with Jennie Gulchard and the Savoy Gaiety Girls, for the Mechanics Emporium and the White Pass & Yukon Railroad, for steam hoses from the Dawson Hardware Co. and "Swell Clothing" from Hershberg's, "opposite White Pass Dock."

But few libraries welcome old photocopies or for that matter the original, deteriorating newsprint. In the end all my research materials will probably go into the discard, as worthless as the "Stradivarius" violin I carried in the trunk of my car for a month before finally taking it to an expert. "It's just an old fiddle," he told me. "Con men made up the labels and sold them by the hundreds." (Real Stradivarius labels have the last two digits of the date written in ink, he said, "but the good con artists have learned to fake that, too.")

Before leaving the Pacific Northwest, I tracked down Gene Allen's daughter, Lucena Allen Swain, and passed a happy afternoon with her at her home in Belleview, Washington. Her father had talked and written about his love of the Klondike's social equality: "I've always figured that if we could just get rid of the veneer and the social bunk and just use common sense and live natural, we'd get a lot farther ahead." But his daughter had a slightly different take on it. After the Gold Rush, she said, "I think he had lost something. There was no more glamour for him. He never wanted to work for anybody—he wanted to be the boss."

He was also "quite a colorful person," she said. She recalled a family gathering on Allen's 35th birthday at which his father asked sententiously, "Gene, how old are you today?" Gene replied, "I'm 35 years old, and if I'd saved a dollar a year, I'd have $35." The story has survived in the family as an example of Allen's irreverence and devil-may-care attitude. He was pretty clearly a bit of a rolling stone, not quite a good fit in conventional society.

"He liked to get things started, but then he would lose interest," Mrs. Swain said.

Her mother, she said, "was a very gentle, kind person" who had been raised genteelly, and then had married a man who could take off on a whim for the Klondike. (Her name was Emma Soule, a surname she shared with John Babsone Lane Soule, the author of the maxim often attributed to Horace Greeley, "Go west, young man, and grow up with the country.")

Emma stayed with Allen "because she was really in love with him," Mrs. Swain said, and although she did not go with him to Dawson, they were reunited later in Nome—after she had lost all her dowry and furniture, washed over the side of the ship. She returned to Seattle a few months later for her daughter's birth.

Allen was a friend of the mystery writer Rex Beach and always hoped that Beach would write his biography, his daughter said. He had kept a diary of his *Nugget* years, and it was still extant in 1935 when Russell A. Bankson quoted extensively from it in a book about the newspaper. But a fire later destroyed the printing plates for the book, and the diary itself disappeared. After his wife's death, Allen lived with a woman who said she had gotten rid of his "black book" with accounts of his Klondike experiences. Mrs. Swain thought it might still exist somewhere—she had a name or two that could be checked—but the time when she might have asked about it had passed.

What I drew most from my afternoon's conversation with her was her affection and admiration for an often absentee father. This was the first time in years, she said, that she had sat and talked about him. Earlier visitors, I gathered, had wanted to talk mainly about the *Nugget.*

The *Nugget* expired with its issue of July 14, 1903, after many vicissitudes. One later researcher, using microfilm, questioned Pierre Berton's assertion that it was printed for a time on butcher's paper. But I looked at the actual issues in the library of the University of Washington, and butcher's paper they are.

Like the newspaper, Allen's career fluctuated, his daughter said. After the *Nugget*, he tried an express business, which failed. Then he worked for papers in Nome and Teller, Alaska, before returning to his brother Pliny's printing business in Seattle. Later he was with papers in Valdez and Cordova, Alaska, as well as Wallace, Idaho, and Spokane, Washington. For a time, he ran a theater (or perhaps it was a movie house) in Saskatoon. Then he came back to the printing business in Seattle, where in 1935 he re-established the Seattle Press Club, disbanded during the Depression. He took charge of arrangements for its re-opening banquet, and persuaded Vice President John Nance Garner to be the speaker. Both Garner and Allen played chess, and a match was arranged for the night before the banquet. As the Vice President entered the room, Allen rose to greet him—and fell dead of a heart attack.

[2007]

DAWSON, YUKON TERRITORY, TUESDAY, MARCH 19, 1901.

"A lane to make one's heart rejoice, it was so very Cornish."
—A.L Rowse

CORNISH COMPANIONS

I HAVE JUST READ, for perhaps the tenth time, a little book called *West-Country Stories*, by A.L. Rowse. Sometimes I jump around in it, but this time I read the 21 essays straight through, from "The Wicked Vicar of Lansillian" to a commemoration of Rowse's friend, the Cornish historian Charles Henderson.

Why some books speak to our hearts is a mystery. My wife picked up *West-Country Stories* years ago in Amsterdam, and we have both read it with pleasure. But for me there is something deeper than enjoyment. When it's a dismal 3 a.m. in my soul, I turn to Rowse's little book for solace. It was with me at the start of a year's work in Taiwan, when I was wondering if it had been a terrible mistake to go 8,000 miles from home and family. Rowse's stories consoled a sleepless night, and I faced the new day feeling I had communed with an old and dear friend.

And yet the book doesn't immediately announce itself as a companion. Even the title is slightly misleading. Rowse justifies it by invoking a medieval definition of "stories" as narratives both of fact and faction. But he has really just swept together some occasional pieces, written between 1927, when he was 24, and World War II. There are several ghost stories, a little Cornish history, some portraits of interesting Cornishmen (and women), and a few personal fragments and travel pieces. What pervades them all is his deep love of Cornwall and the Cornish. My own roots are elsewhere, but I recognize the impulse, and in a profound way Rowse takes me home, too.

Some pieces speak to me more than others. The ghost stories are fine in their way, but it's only when I reach "Restinnes?

Restinnes?" that I am fully engaged, captured by Rowse's opening line: "It happened to me the other day—what I had often
hoped for in vain before—to be lost within a few miles of my
home." What an interesting and unusual hope! There follows a
remarkable paragraph in which he reproduces the sensation of
being "pisky-laden"—bewitched by the daemon of the place and
sent stumbling around an enclosure with no apparent exit, until he
trips and goes sprawling on his back. Then the daemon relents,
and

> I found that my mind, no longer agitated with the problem
> of finding a way out, was only concerned with bringing to
> the surface a once-known, half-guessed name: the name of a
> farm. A whisper seemed to come up from the withies of the
> wilderness, bearing a name which strangely I had had in my
> mind before finding myself there: "Is it Restinnes? Is it
> Restinnes?" it said. "Restinnes? Restinnes?" it echoed in the
> contented chambers of my mind.

Rowse is a master at describing the Cornish countryside. He
had approached Restinnes by way of "the little valleys through
which the china-clay streams run off their refuse sand to the
sea—had passed through the evangelical village of Bethel, up the
valley through Tregrehan Mills, and into that savage and desolate
region which so expresses itself in its name, Garker." From there
he took a more pleasant path to the farm itself: "It was a lane to
make one's heart rejoice, it was so very Cornish." Elsewhere, he
writes of "the characteristic groups of tiny Cornish elms, the
hedges in early summer coloured with purple vetch and crows-
foot, the first foxgloves and pink campion. And over all these is
the rumour, the magic presence, of the sea, invisible yet always
there."

But Rowse also knows when to forgo color and get straight to
the point. "Have you heard how Dick Stephens fought the bear?"
he begins another essay, about an aged farmer whose life reached

its zenith in a youthful triumph at a traveling fair. Rowse meets the old man in a lane and persuades him to tell his story—to act out, really, his throwing of the bear. He finishes, and Rowse writes:

> The sun was going down behind the woods of Penrice, as the sun was going down, gently, evenly, hardly perceptibly for him. The mellow notes of the bell struck 10. It was time to part and go home our respective ways. "Yes," he said, "it must 'ave been fifty-one or fifty-two years ago." And a dark shadow, the shadow of time, came into his eyes.

I can read quickly through Rowse's script for the pageant celebrating Plymouth's 500th anniversary, but not without stopping to smile again at Sir Francis Drake's words to his partner when news of the Spanish Armada broke in on their game of bowls: "My Lord, you shall not escape so easily. There's time to finish this game and to thrash the Spaniards, too." Then come several fine essays on Cornish history, and an explanation of the difference between Cornwall as a modern shire, and the Duchy of Cornwall, a vast landed estate belonging to the sovereign's eldest son or, absent a son, "lying dormant in the crown." When Rowse describes Cornwall's role in the English civil war of the 1640s, one feels he was there, knew the combatants, and perhaps was with King Charles at Boconnoc on the night "when, frightened of conspiracy, he slept in his coach in the park, surrounded by his guards."

Coming to more recent times, Rowse takes the reader on a walking visit to the Harmony Cot birthplace of the Cornish painter John Opie, whose work I later discovered for myself in a Scottish castle. He reviews the diaries of the Rev. Francis Kilvert, who visited Cornwall in the 1870s and left a vivid record of the country and of his hosts, the Hockins. The young parson lost his heart to the enchanting Mrs. Hockin, and those who have experienced something similar will appreciate Rowse's comment on the aftermath:

> The passion that once was so intense as hardly to be bearable, so absorbing as to exclude everything and give one the illusion of being eternal, is transmuted by time into something gentler—and one finds that it is to the memory that one is being faithful.

There are other treasures. Perhaps the best is Rowse's tribute to his friend, Charles Henderson, who died while still young, in the midst of a brilliant career. But here I stop; the reader can easily find *West-Country Stories* and much else by Rowse.

Affection for his book was one reason that drew my wife and me to Cornwall in August, 1997. Another was my interest in the poems of W.S. Graham, a Scotsman who lived and wrote in Cornwall. (He and his wife, Nessie, supported themselves at times by raising and selling violets—a perfect occupation for a poet!) Both interests were well repaid. In Penzance I found a bookstore with a clerk, Richard Ogden, who had known Graham and still visited Nessie. He put me in touch with Graham's literary executors, Michael and Margaret Snow, with whom I still correspond. Karen and I tracked down place names in Graham's poems—those hard, sharp Cornish names like Botallack, Gurnard's Head, and Zennor.

Graham had had a strong influence on me when I began writing poetry, because his early poems—which I encountered first—pushed at the limits of comprehension. What to make of lines like:

Here next the chair I was when winter went
Down looking for distant bothies of love
And met birch-bright and by the blows of March
The farm bolder under and the din of burning.

And that was one of his more accessible poems! Later he would write with great clarity about the difficulties of communication, and of the artist's task:

The poet or painter steers his life to maim

Himself somehow for the job. His job is Love
Imagined into words or paint to make
An object that will stand and will not move.

Karen and I took, at least in fancy, what Graham called "the track the tin singers made." We walked a mile to an abandoned tin mine in the area of Cornwall called Levant. Miners there—all members of Wesleyan chapels and fine choristers—used to sing out hymns during the ride up and down on a beam-engine elevator. (This was an ingenious device, like a dumb waiter, which raised or lowered each miner a few feet with each swing of the beam. The miner stepped off onto a platform at the end of each stroke, then stepped back on at the next stroke to be carried a few feet further. It was a long process that left plenty of time for song.) Eventually, I wrote my own poem:

A mile out
under the Atlantic
they groped for tin.
The air rotted. They stuck
candles on felt hats,
could hear storms
roll boulders overhead.

Finishing, they rode
the beam engine's
rocking stair to grass,
A seam of singing men

153

who made the shaft
one mighty tremolo.
"Lord of the World-Bright Tin,"
they sang, and "Strong to Save."

The years broke them
like pit ponies,
but not their song.
I hear it on Levant's
ruined shore
this morning,
over the wasted shafts.

While in Cornwall, we also visited the Scilly Isles and saw from a distance the island for which another writer, Bryher (Annie Winifred Ellerman), had named herself. And back on the mainland, we explored the castle reputed to be the home of the giant slain by Jack. It was an echo from childhood and the *English Fairy Tales* of Flora Annie Steel, illustrated by Arthur Rackham:

Here's the valiant Cornishman,
Who slew the giant Cormoran.

A guide told us the bones of a man nearly eight feet tall had been found behind a long-sealed door. Maybe the old story was true after all!

From Penzance, we took a train to St. Austell, about which Rowse had written lovingly. We inspected the cathedral sculptures he admired, then visited his "little quayside" at Lostwithiel and ate wonderful apple-blackberry pie at the Tawny Owl. We climbed a hill in the rain to Restormel Castle. At a distance, from the bus, we saw the granite tower of Luxulyan church, another of Rowse's favorites.

One day I went alone to the Heligan Gardens and then missed my return ride. An attendant suggested hiking a back road into Mevagissey to catch the bus for St. Austell. The road was one of Rowse's Cornish lanes—I had to climb over a stile—and like him I found my heart rejoicing.

I didn't know until I got home to Indiana that I had passed within a mile or two of Rowse's home in the village of Tregarren. He was 93 and died several months later—but it pleases me that we were near each other briefly in his beloved Cornwall.

I also didn't know, until a friend sent me a long obituary, what a distinguished scholar and prolific author Rowse had been. He was a towering authority on Shakespeare, and had tracked down the likely identity of the "dark lady" of the *Sonnets*. But then he spoiled his triumph, the obituary writer said, by arrogance and a refusal to concede anything to critics. The last of his 105 books, written when he was 90, is a dismissal of historians with whom he disagreed.

Even the Cornish didn't always take kindly to this china-clay worker's son who became an Oxford don. I have a copy of Rowse's *Tudor Cornwall* that was originally presented to a scholar named E.G.R. Hooper "for his services in the study of the Cornish language." At one point in the book, Rowse writes of "the now-forgotten Cornish language," and Hooper has scribbled in the margin: "Since *I* don't remember it, it's forgotten!"

But there is no such acerbity in *West-Country Stories*, which has a sweetness of temper not always found in literature. Whatever passions Rowse stirred, however he may have failed, his love for his Cornish home and its people saved him here. To me it is a book without a single wrong note.

[2005]

The west entrance to Chartres Cathedral, 1958

A PILGRIMAGE TO CHARTRES

TRYING TO REMEMBER why one did something 50 years ago, in distant youth, is an exercise of ingenuity at best, and at worst of fabrication.

All I really know is that on a September day in 1958, I boarded a train in Würzburg, Germany, and went to Chartres in central France, where I spent the better part of two days in and around the famous cathedral, reading and photographing, before going on to tour the Loire Valley by bicycle. Of the trip across Germany and France, I remember almost nothing, except that I blew by Paris completely, arriving at the Gare du Nord and leaving for Chartres from the old Gare Montparnasse, as quickly as I could get across town. Whether I accomplished this by Metro or taxi I don't recall, and it doesn't matter. I didn't even see the Eiffel Tower, or want to.

My fellow passengers saw a skinny, gangling American, happy in "civvies," and carrying in one satchel everything for a 10-day furlough. The satchel contained a copy of *Mont-Saint-Michel and Chartres* by Henry Adams, an ancient Argus C-3 camera (35mm), and a pair of gray biking shorts. (I had the shorts until a few years ago—they never quite got clean again.) Beyond that, I can assume a change or two of underwear, socks, maybe a sports shirt, and a raincoat. In fact, I can vouch for the raincoat because it performed an important function later in the trip. I think I had some twine for tying the satchel on the back of the bike, but may have bought that along the way.

In a pocket were my wallet, well lined with soldier's pay, a card identifying me as draftee No. US52451237 (assigned to the 3rd Infantry Division information office in Würzburg), and my youth hostel card, obtained for the trip.

The proximate reason for going to France was to get away from the Army after six months in Germany, editing the division's weekly newspaper. It was not a job that required, or welcomed, much imagination. (The paper's name had just been changed from *The Rock of the Marne* to *The Marne Rock*, after a division-wide contest.) I was also getting away from Maj. Arch Roberts, our spit-and-polish CO, who was hounding me about my dirty fingernails. I could have realized my aims more cheaply and closer to Würzburg, as I did later in Munich. If I'd wanted a longer trip, I could actually have *seen* Paris.

But Chartres beckoned on two counts. My Uncle Stephen was a renowned designer of stained-glass windows, and Chartres had the world's finest. Stephen hadn't touted me on Chartres, however. The compelling reason for going was Henry Adams, dean of historians, grandson of a president, who had died in 1918. Adams is not much read by 20-somethings today, although he might be with profit. But I was an oddity even in 1958. The draft had yanked me from graduate school, but I had a caterpillar hope that I might emerge from the Army as something gorgeous. I had read not only *Mont-Saint-Michel and Chartres*, but also *The Education of Henry Adams* and a new Adams biography by Elizabeth Stevenson. In short, I had overdosed. Adams had fallen in love with Chartres and the Middle Ages. *Post hoc, ergo propter hoc*. If I followed him to Chartres, I would become wise, write brilliantly, and speak in Latin. I would begin by re-reading Adams's lyric descriptions while sitting in the cathedral itself. At 23, this seemed a perfectly natural thing to do.

The train trip from Paris southwest into the plain of the Beauce took only an hour or so. It was much easier than the pilgrimage, in 1582, of the last Valois king and his queen, who, Adams said, had walked the 50 miles to Chartres "in the dead of winter, in robes of penitents, over the roughest roads" to beseech the Virgin for an heir, and then walked back again to Paris. And did this annually for seven years, without result. I got to Chartres in mid-day and went straight to  the cathedral for a quick look, before hunting up a cheap hotel down the hill behind it (see right). Despite knowing almost no French, I managed to negotiate a room for the night and to order breakfast the next morning. And to eat it, while wondering whether I was supposed to lift my bowl of café au lait and drink it, or use a spoon. Have I mentioned that I was a bit innocent in the ways of the world? Another diner solved my problem by lifting his bowl.

But that was on the second day in Chartres. On the first day, after finding a room, I hiked back up the hill to where the cathedral hung like a vast upturned keel over the city. (It's visible, I'm told, for miles across the Beauce, but I left Chartres at night and didn't get to see.) I don't recall being awestruck as I got down to the business of inspecting the cathedral's famous west front, the towers and porches, and the statuary that Adams had rhapsodized over. I remember (or think I do) that the great church seemed unusually clean in the sunshine, without the soot of a large city. "For a first visit to Chartres," Adams had written, "choose some pleasant morning when the lights are soft, for one wants to be welcome, and the cathedral has moods, at times severe." I had chosen well.

159

The south tower ("the most perfect piece of architecture in the world," according to Adams) was scrunched against the newer central façade, just as he had complained. Had I not "read up," I would have had every tourist's first response to the cathedral—the towers don't match! The south tower vaults skyward from the earth in one clean spring, disguising with high gables the point at

which the square base turns into the octagonal *fléche*—and I need to stop here and say that you should know at least two words of French before reading Adams. One is *fléche*, an arrow or spire. The other is *parvis*, the space in front of a church entrance. (*Parvis* comes distantly from "paradise"—St. Peter's Square in Rome was once known as "the paradise.") The north tower of Chartres doesn't begin its *fléche* until it has cleared the façade. It's also likely to strike the tourist as architecturally fussier than the "old tower."

Not long ago, I re-read *Mont-Saint-Michel and Chartres*, the *Education*, and Stevenson's biography of Adams. They provided some clues to how I spent my time in Chartres, and why. Clearly, I spent that first day photographing the west front and the north and south porches, because Adams had said that all French sculpture originated in the elongated, Byzantine figures surrounding the entrances. They looked sadly worn and disfigured to me, but Adams could not err. I took photos to consult when my own knowledge and perception should have matured. (Re-reading Adams also cleared up a minor mystery from a slightly later trip, to Geneva. Why had I located and visited the room where the "Alabama" privateering claims were settled after the Civil War? Simple. Adams's father, Charles Francis Adams, had been the U.S. negotiator with Great Britain, and I had Adamses on the brain.)

Inside Chartres, I spent part of the second day sitting in a corner and re-reading Adams, or walking around the cathedral with *Mont-Saint-Michel and Chartres* in hand like a guidebook, which it is—an indispensable one for any tourist striving to put himself into the 13th century, if only distantly and for a moment. I was having a wonderful time. Adams knew all that non-antiquarians need to know about medieval French religion, art, and politics. He wrote about it in a lively style, and knew when to wind up a learned exposition on statuary and exclaim, "Now let's go inside!" *Mont-Saint-Michel and Chartres* was his hymn to a vanished unity, just as his later *Education* describes the centrifugal shattering of modern life. It is far from a religious book, but it makes its main point time and again—that the vast outpouring of labor, wealth, and love on Gothic cathedrals was not an affair of conventional religion or even the established Church. It happened because people knew that Mary, Queen of Heaven, was actually *there* in the cathedral, and deserved no less than their best. And that her infinite mercy and love were their only hedge against the implacable judgments of the Trinity.

And that, as Adams might say, is enough religion for the tourist. Let's look at the glass!

Artisans were just starting to make stained glass when the fenêtrage (another lovely Adams word) of Chartres was being planned. The new cathedral presented problems. The windows were of an astonishing height. To make them as large as possible (which the Virgin wanted), the builders had to devise vaulting that was both light and strong, supported by "flying buttresses" that would carry the stress out and away until the last support "touches ground at a distance, as a bird would alight," Adams said. Working for love of the Virgin, without thought of self and ignorant as yet of how to economize, the glassmakers produced windows that have never been surpassed. The world's masters have come here

161

to be instructed. My brother Steve told me recently that he had just read a monumental treatise on stained glass by Charles Connick (who gave our Uncle Stephen his first job). Connick told of visiting Chartres and listening as a guide talked nonsense to tourists. Connick knew everything, of course, but refrained from interrupting.

I also avoided the guide, not because I knew everything (or anything), but because Adams was with me. Mostly I bathed in the astounding light and color. The great western rose did not strike me as forcibly then as it did later. More captivating was the north rose, given by Blanche of Castile—a medallion of vivid colors and lozenges that reminds me irresistibly of a box of candied fruit. "Whatever Chartres may be now," Adams said, "when young it was a smile." The southern rose—more militant, more masculine—was given by Pierre Mauclerc, Count of Dreux, who was Blanche's great antagonist. Their windows gaze at each other across the center of the church and unite their quarrelling sponsors in adoration of the Virgin.

Letting my eyes fall from the windows, I loitered over the floor worn by the feet of pilgrims for nearly 800 years. Neither Adams nor I seem to have noticed the meditation labyrinth, which, I'm told, is built into the stones of the floor.

There are no pews in Chartres, only chairs and benches, because it was designed for throngs—10,000 could gather in it easily and 15,000 when necessary, Adams said. The cathedral seemed immensely old to me, and organic, as though the stones had grown up out of the earth. In summer and fall, it is blessedly cool after the heat outside. No doubt in winter it is simply cold. Henry of Valois and his queen wouldn't have warmed themselves much after their January walk from Paris.

Immensely old it certainly was, but Adams caught something else about it when he wrote that "its youth is so young, its age so old, and its youthful yearning for old thought is so disconcerting" that it resembles the premature agedness of a baby. I, too, knew

162

something about being young and enticed by the gleam of age and wisdom.

I went on from Chartres to Tours, farther to the southwest. I have a dim memory of waking at midnight to change trains. In Tours, I trotted out my poor stock of French—"Je veux louer une bicyclette"—and acquired a rental bicycle, which I rode around the Loire Valley for the next week, visiting chateaus. I remember the chateaus, but not much of the territory between, just a few dim images of country lanes bordered by poplars. It was a Monet landscape. At one chateau town, my guidebook promised a "son et lumiére" performance, a sound and light show. At lunch I asked the *garçon* what time the show started. He drew himself up with Gallic hauteur and exclaimed, "M'sieur, nevair!" Oh, well, perhaps at the next chateau. I cycled on. Twenty-five years later I told the story to a French professor, who began laughing. "Bill!" she said. "He was telling you the time! *Neuf heure*, nine o'clock!"

I stayed at hostels part of the time, but while my cohorts were munching apples and cheese, I was spending my francs on good meals in French restaurants. One country inn served delectable potato puffs; eating one was like biting into a small, fragrant cloud. When no hostels were handy, I slept rough—in a cave one night, and (at Azay-le-Rideau) in an open field, with my raincoat propped on sticks to shelter my head. As a result I went back to the barracks with walking pneumonia.

Sixteen years later, in 1974, my family and I went to Europe. This time I saw Paris, and then we took the train to Chartres for an afternoon. It was all as it had been, except that the rather bare *parvis* before the church now rioted with flowers. The towers were as mismatched and as marvellous as ever. My wife remembers organ music falling down through the arches of the nave, and the striking blue of the windows. She was in perfect accord on this with Adams, who devotes considerable time to the blue glass of Chartres, and to how other colors, especially green, are used with stunning effect against it.

I had learned a little more about stained glass, Gothic architecture, and life since 1958. This time I paid more attention to the great western rose and the lancets that Adams loved almost beyond reason (well, certainly beyond *reason*). When I re-read *Mont-Saint-Michel and Chartres* a few days ago, I marked his description of how the border of one lancet has been compressed and filled with ornament to disguise how the window was narrowed to fit the space. The designer succeeded, Adams commented casually, "since no one has ever noted the difficulty or the device." No one?

When we came home, I wrote a poem about Chartres, but it was a failure. In 1982, I returned to it and made some changes, which helped a little but not much. While writing this sketch, I got it out and tried again, this time without striving and with a small prayer to the Virgin. It went better, but still is inadequate. Maybe if I go back to Chartres in extreme old age, I'll find the right word, as Nono, Tennessee Williams's 100-year-old poet, does at the end of *Night of the Iguana*.

Meanwhile, all tourists and writers must live in the glory and shadow of Henry Adams's summation of the Gothic age, at the end of *Mont-Saint-Michel and Chartres*:

> *The delight of its aspirations is flung up to the sky. The pathos of its self-distrust and anguish is buried in the earth as its last secret. You can read out of it whatever else pleases your youth and confidence; to me, this is all.*

[2007]

CHERRY DELIGHT

IT IS A LATE SUMMER MORNING in McCordsville, Indiana, and Carol McVay is arranging a vase of home-grown flowers on her new dining-room table. The table is the glowing, rosy brown of new cherry; in a few years it will darken to the rich red of old cherry and be a much-loved and polished heirloom.

* * *

In the main saw building at Foley Hardwoods in Bargersville, a 16-foot-long cherry log meets the "head saw." It is a violent and noisy encounter, but a precise one. The saw, a continuous steel belt with two-inch teeth on both sides, passes back and forth along the log, slicing inch-thick planks as easily as a cheese wire through cheddar.

* * *

At the Sampler furniture mill in Homer, Jim Krammes is hand-sanding a cherry board. He has been sanding boards and fashioning fine cherry furniture since coming here in 1953 as a two-week "fill-in." But he is a newcomer next to sales manager Emmett Newkirk, who arrived in 1947. When customers hear Newkirk's Hoosier twang on the phone, they don't think "salesman." They think, "Why, it's Emmett!"

* * *

Out in Larry McVay's woods along White River, an American black, or wild, cherry tree is getting bigger. In a few years, Larry will harvest it. The log will go to a sawmill like Foley's,

165

and then very possibly to Homer and to a dining room where someone will arrange flowers as Larry's wife, Carol, is doing this fine summer morning.

* * *

Encyclopedia item: "The American wild cherry, *Prunus serotina,* is much sought after, its wood being compact, fine-grained, not liable to warp, and susceptible of receiving a brilliant polish."

Bruce Levi, who manages the Sampler cherry-furniture mill in Homer, is less literary about it. "Furniture salesmen tell me it isn't practical to build from solid wood—they're right," he says. "But you're not going to get the warmth and beauty of cherry from anything else."

In quantity, cherry is a minor player on the Indiana hardwood scene. But in quality it is a prima donna, with the fire and temperament to match. During last year's wet spring, the diva took a lot of deft management. Furniture has to be built tighter in damp weather, Levi explains, because it shrinks and loosens as it dries. You live with the fact that beautiful hardwoods expand and contract.

"Plywood is always the same," Levi says, contemptuously.

The Sampler showroom is at 1 West Railroad Street in downtown Homer. It almost *is* downtown Homer, a hamlet with 235 people at last count. The furniture mill is a long block away, in a former cannery built of tiles manufactured just across the road. Open windows are the air-conditioning.

Steve Brown, assistant manager, leads visitors through what is essentially an old-time carpenter's shop. He shows how a piece of raw cherry is fed through a jointer to square up all its sides. He points out a machine in one corner that cuts "dovetails," the interlocking teeth that hold a drawer together. A plate says the machine was patented June 1, 1887, by the A. Dobbs company of Grand Rapids, Michigan. Brown wants to show some of its special knives. "They're in the coffee can," a millworker says.

CHERRY DELIGHT

The McVay table began here in the mill as boards and leg "squares" stacked in racks on the second floor. The legs were then roped—incised by machines with a graceful spiral pattern. The boards chosen for the top were glued together and put in clamps on a revolving rack that can hold up to 18 table tops.

Then sanding began. The mill has more machines for sanding than for anything else, Brown says, adding, "We spend a lot of time making dust."

After the legs and the top were joined—and after more sanding—the McVay table got a coat of tung oil finish, which penetrated deep into the wood but left its natural color and pattern intact. The Sampler will darken cherry with stain on request, but it clearly feels this is a step toward plywood. Victorian woodworkers used mahogany stain to cover up the grain patterns and sap streaks of cherry; now these are regarded as the wood's character.

The Sampler advertises its work as "Midwest cabinetmaker's style," which Bruce Levi describes with a smile as "what we make." Pressed, he says, "We design from older pieces made in this part of the country. Good solid joinery. Doors that fit. Drawers that operate smoothly."

A Sampler sales brochure calls it "not far-out, not fattening, not free." The mill makes about 50 dining-room tables a year and sells them for up to $1,840 each. It also makes beds, chests, secretaries, desks, chairs, rockers, cupboards, dictionary stands, armoires, commodes, and about any other piece of cherry furniture you can name. But only cherry.

* * *

You smell the sawdust at Foley Hardwoods, but you don't see it because it has been sold and trucked away. A semi-trailer load of dust, bark, and other scraps goes out every seven hours.

Cherry is only about 1 percent of the 6 million board feet that pass through the Foley saws each year. Red oak makes up nearly a third, and hickory and poplar about a fifth each, followed by smaller amounts of white oak, ash, walnut, elm, basswood, and sassafras.

Hickory is a specialty, co-owner Don Foley says, even though "it's just a bearcat. It fights you all the way from the tree to the saw."

Walking around logs piled in the yard, Foley points out defects visible in the butt ends—lines or "seams" caused by lightning, surface checking, and cracks due to "wind shake." He indicates a spot that he calls "doty," a term used by timbermen since at least 1420 to mean punky or rotten.

These are big logs but not giants. "We don't like great big old trees," Foley said. "A tree's like a stalk of corn; when it reaches maturity, it's got to be harvested."

A cherry log, straight and unblemished, is marked "1/84" on the end, meaning it contains an estimated 84 board feet of top-grade "face" lumber. (A board foot is a piece of wood a foot long, a foot wide, and an inch thick.) At perhaps 85 cents a board foot, this log cost Foley a little over $70. The same pile includes other logs graded 1 through 4. Anything below that goes to another pile destined to become crating. Even a layman can see that some of it is doty.

* * *

Sign in the Foley sawhouse: "Knowledge and timber shouldn't be much used until they are seasoned."—Oliver Wendell Holmes.

After the Foley saws have turned logs into boards, these go into special stacks for kiln-drying. Some woods can dry together, others can't. Too much heat on oak "and you can crush it with your hand," Foley says.

It takes 15 to 17 days to cook the water out of a one-inch cherry board. Thirty to 35 stacks of lumber go into the kiln's six chambers at a time—more than 300,000 board feet. A glance inside an access door steams one's glasses instantly in the 165-

degree heat. Workmen don't go in for more than a brief period, or alone. "You'd dehydrate in a hurry," Foley says.

When the lumber is down to about 6 percent moisture, it moves on to the grading shed, where a grader stands above a moving stream of boards and punches a keypad to spray each with a dye code.

A totally finished, kiln-dried board may sell to a lumber dealer for $2.30 a board foot. The dealer may resell it to a home handyman for $4 to $5. Prices vary with customer demand, Foley notes. "It's like the shoe business."

* * *

"We want a long-term forest that will always be there."
—Don Foley

The old logger's maxim was "Cut the best and leave the rest," but those days are gone, Foley says. He preaches good forest management to the private landowners who control nearly 90 percent of Indiana's timberland. He also requires his loggers to take training and encourages them to play "the Game of Logging," an annual competition for the state's best loggers—ones who "can split a hair with a chain saw."

Foley also urges landowners to make their woodlands "classified forests," which means no clear-cutting, a tax break, and periodic inspections by the Indiana Department of Natural Resources.

Landowners "are getting smarter," he says, then corrects himself. "Not smarter, more educated."

All this is far from the minds of Larry and Carol McVay as they plan a dinner for friends to christen their new cherry table. Fresh flowers are on the table; bratwurst, corn on the cob, and tomatoes are on the menu.

Larry, who runs a construction business out of their home, mentions in passing that he has 125 acres of classified forest in Morgan County—walnut, red oak, ash, and "20 or 30 nice cherry trees." In fact, he adds, a fellow named Don Foley has just written him to ask about possible logging.

But the forest was harvested about 25 years ago. "I think I'll wait a few more years," he says.

[1996]

A head-saw blade at Foley's

THE FIRST AMERICANS

'SLEEPER' AND HIS PEOPLE

THE BOY WOKE SLOWLY, the last as usual to return from the country of dreams. For this they called him Sleeper and sometimes played tricks on him. But this morning the others, already busy over last night's kill, left him alone. He kept his eyes nearly closed to watch his older brothers dress the deer carcass with stone knives, while his mother and sister spread strips of flesh to dry on a rack of sticks. The air had changed since yesterday; this morning Sleeper could feel the cold time coming. And after the cold, the People would meet again for the days of magic and marrying, of exchanges and story-telling. But he did not think about that for long. Hunger and the tasks of the morning called him, and he sprang up into the fresh day, the newest day, a day on the very spearpoint of time.

Time. We talk much about the Millennium, but millennia have been common in the long sweep of history. Sleeper would not have had our notion of them, any more than he would understand our putting a name to a single bright morning—say, the first of September in the year 8000 B.C. But if we could time-travel there, he might see us as some part of the People, and we might recognize the nearby trees as familiar oak and hickory, the trails into the forest as manmade, and the fast-flowing river below as what our ancestors called La Belle Riviere, the Beautiful River, the Ohio.

"There are millions of prehistoric sites in the state," says Rick Jones, Indiana's state archaeologist. That sounds unscientific, until you realize it must be literally true. Europeans have been here for barely 500 years, the earlier inhabitants for more than 12,000. Indiana is old, old ground, scarred by human settlements as permanent as cities and as fleeting as the campsites of solitary hunters. In studying such sites, archaeologists differ about many things, but not about the deep humanity of those whose history they seek to retrieve.

"They were people of tremendous imagination and innovation, not primitives or savages," says Jim Mohow, an archaeologist with the state's Division of Historic Preservation and Archaeology. He describes how the Smithsonian tested the power of an atlatl, a spear-throwing tool. Its projectile destroyed a target with the force of a .357 Magnum. Power like that was needed to bring down big game, which would have been merely annoyed by a hand-thrown spear.

"And it's not good to annoy a mammoth," Mohow says.

Linking atlatls to mammoth hunting is conjectural, but the first Hoosiers did hunt mammoths successfully. These were Paleoindians, Sleeper's ancestors and the first humans to see the land between the River and the Lakes. They came here some 12,000 years ago, the descendants of Siberian hunters who had crossed the Bering land bridge into Alaska.

There were only a few of them, and they kept on the move, following game and eating wild plants to survive. They made excellent spearpoints from chert, a fine-grained rock that flakes when struck with a rock or a piece of deer antler. They occupied Indiana for more than two millennia, "a thin scatter of humans," archaeologist Brian Fagan has written. They left almost nothing behind.

If you look at Indiana's unrecorded past as a drama, the Paleoindians are a short first act of some 2,500 years. The next seven millennia, from 8000 to 1000 B.C., are a very long second act, which archaeologists call the Archaic. It lasted as long as all recorded history, from the invention of writing in ancient Sumer

172

until today, and it would not have made especially good theater. The changes from beginning to end were critical, but their importance might have escaped us as casual time travelers. If we had left during the second act, though, we would have missed a brilliant finale.

That finale was the 2,500 years before European contact, during which Native America came into its own as a manufacturing, trading, and agricultural civilization. It was not to last, but reminders of its people are everywhere in the state today.

"There are times when I've looked out over the sites of their lodges and campfires and just for a split second I've seen them," Mohow says.

> *Here, reader, you should pause and reflect that what you have read so far is a great simplification. The dates are not this exact, the history not this linear. Antiquity is a vast patchwork quilt. "It's best to think of it as a cultural continuum that becomes more elaborate through time," says Bob McCullough, also an archaeologist with the state's Division of Historic Preservation and Archaeology.*

The people of prehistory inhabited an Indiana much different from ours. Sleeper, in 8000 B.C., would have found the climate cooler, although the boreal forests of jack pine and spruce had already moved north with the retreating glaciers. Great hardwood forests mixed with prairies and swamps covered the state. Rivers were cleaner and stars brighter in the clear air. In that immense landscape, the number of humans was very small.

"You could have walked for a long time before you ran into a group of people," says Rick Jones. "There would have been camps and fires burning. People would have been wearing skin clothing, pendants, decorations."

Early Archaic people traveled in small bands across Indiana, probably coming together for rituals, for trade, and to find mates. They were smaller than we are but perhaps in better shape, even though injuries and diseases like TB and pneumonia made 35 or 40 years an exceptionally long life.

"Some were probably walking around for years with low- to mid-grade fevers, and that can kill you eventually," Jones said. Broken bones sometimes healed crookedly. Teeth wore down early, but as with us it took the introduction of sugar and starch to make cavities a serious problem.

By 6000 B.C. they were burying their dead. No one knows just when they began to live in "houses," although there are hints of postholes in deeply buried Archaic sites. When they did, these were probably conical huts or simply saplings tied together and covered with hides.

They had dogs.

They spoke, as far as we know, languages as complex as our own. No researcher has ever found a primitive language, and it seems likely that Sleeper and his band could converse in words as adequate to their needs as any modern family's.

They had music. Later cultures had copper-covered reed flutes, Jones says, and maracas made from turtle shells and quartz crystals. There could have been drums even in the Early Archaic, although none have been found. "It wouldn't surprise me if there were music all the way back to the beginning of human occupation in Indiana," Jones says.

An archaeologist always sees a partial picture. For each stone tool found, there may have been three wooden or bone ones and half a dozen more delicate ones used for basketry or leatherwork. All we know comes from those artifacts that survive and what specialists in disciplines like paleobotany and ancient weather can tell us.

"A word or the motion of a human arm 6,000 years ago is not recorded," Mohow says.

But there is no lack of archeological sites. Some 47,000 have been identified in the one or two percent of Indiana that has been professionally evaluated. Of these, fewer than two percent will ever be seriously studied. The sites are disappearing rapidly to development and looters, although the latter have been restrained somewhat by laws passed in the 1970s. But even as sites vanish, they yield priceless information.

In 1995, diggers at Bartholomew County Site 1036 unearthed what may be the largest Early Archaic cemetery in the eastern United States, with 19 burials in 10 locations. Site 1036 is now "inaccessible" beneath a housing development, but state archaeologists rescued a wealth of information before it disappeared.

In the long second act of the Archaic, researchers date change by differences in stone projectile points, shifts in burial customs, the appearance of new trade goods. They trace the gradual growth of population and the change from small wandering bands to larger ones that spent more time in the same places each year. They plot the movement from early egalitarian societies to more socially stratified ones, and from hunter/gatherers to the first tentative farmers.

But the changes, enormously important, cover an expanse of time that defies our eager notions of progress. Not until some three millennia ago did the action quicken. Around 1000 B.C., the last stage of the Archaic passed into the Woodland epoch, with a succession of cultures including those now known as Adena, Hopewell, and Mississippian. The rise of agriculture allowed populations to grow and to stay put. Heavy pottery, hard to carry from place to place, began appearing. Maize agriculture—corn— had arrived in the state by 700 A.D. , although the first ears were tiny, "not like the nice big famous Indiana ones," Jones says.

Adena people of the Early Woodland period lived in settlements as large as a dozen houses and buried their dead, sprinkled with red ochre, in log tombs beneath mounds. They made pottery and grew gourds and sunflowers. Their culture gave way after a few centuries to that of the Hopewell people, whom we might have recognized as tribes. They buried their dead elaborately and thus helped fuel the 19th Century myth of a single ancient race of moundbuilders. They were skilled in art and trade, with networks that brought copper from Minnesota, shells from the Gulf, obsidian from Yellowstone. They and the Adena built earthworks, like those in Mounds State Park at Anderson, aligned to observe the sun and stars.

"Some people have called them the Greeks of North America" or even "the overachievers of pre-history," Jones says. "They were just dramatic in their complexity."

But by about 500 A.D. Hopewell culture had faded, to be followed in time by what Brian Fagan has called "one of North America's most brilliant achievements, the Mississippian tradition," a patchwork of large and small chiefdoms scattered over the southeast quarter of the present United States.

The best-known Mississippian site in Indiana is Angel Mounds, now a state historic site on the Ohio River at Evansville. Eight hundred years ago, it was a town of 1,000 to 3,000 people living within a palisade more than a mile long and surrounded by prosperous farmsteads. The town was abandoned before European contact, no one is sure why.

Europe presented Native America, in Indiana as elsewhere, with a challenge for which it was unprepared. The diseases of the invaders—notably smallpox—preceded them, decimating native populations and creating the myth that the new settlers had entered a nearly virgin land.

The effort of Indiana's first people to hold their lands, and their persistence down to the present, is another story. But the epitaph of prehistory might be in words from the Walum Olum—the "Red Record," found in Indiana by the frontier scholar Constantine Rafinesque. Largely discounted today by archaeologists, it tells in pictographs the migration history of the Delaware people. At its end, a narrator sights Europeans approaching the Atlantic coast and asks, "Friendly people in great ships; who are they?"

Native America was about to find out.

BEING MIAMI

THE MIAMI NEVER WANTED to leave Indiana.

Neither did the Potawatomi, the Wea, the Piankeshaw, the Delaware, the Wyandotte, the Shawnee, the Kickapoo, the Mascouten—all those "first peoples" for whom the land between the Ohio and the Lakes was a last stronghold against the invading Europeans. "Indiana" is more than a name. It is a distant echo of what the namers knew—that this was the homeland of other nations.

One by one, most of those nations left, were driven out, or became indistinguishable. But Native Americans are still here. The figures for populations four centuries ago are unreliable, but one writer believes the Miami may have numbered 12,000 then. The 1990 U.S. census tallied about the same number of Indiana residents who consider themselves Native Americans.

Census takers don't distinguish among tribes, but the Indiana Miami carry some 3,200 on their tribal rolls. The Pokagon Band of Potawatomi, divided between Michigan and Indiana, numbers about 2,900. A state Native American Council deals with issues affecting the state's first residents, but half of those on the 1990 census roles have little official visibility.

Nevertheless, they are here.

The Miami lost their federal recognition in 1897 and are still trying to get it back. The Pokagon Band of Potawatomi lost recognition in 1937 but regained it in 1994; the band covers six Indiana and four Michigan counties but is considered a Michigan tribe because its headquarters is there.

"How long have you been in the area?" John Warren, the band's cultural coordinator, is asked. "Eight hundred years, maybe a thousand," he replies.

* * *

The Miami never wanted to leave Indiana, but circumstances sometimes forced them to.

The French first met them as refugees from the Iroquois, near Green Bay, Wisconsin, in 1654. As French power grew, the Miami moved back toward their origins, the legendary "coming-out place" near South Bend.

Later they occupied Kekionga, the "glorious gate" between north- and south-flowing rivers where Ft. Wayne now stands. Other Miami-speakers, the Piankeshaw and Wea, settled on the lower and middle Wabash, while the Potawatomi occupied the future state's northwest. New refugees, including Shawnee and Delaware, found homes along the Wabash. Except for the Potawatomi, those nations are gone from the state today or exist only as remnants. But some Miami never left.

It was not for lack of pressure. The Miami have fought for their home ground against invasion, cultural warfare, and "Indian removal." Their present chief, Paul Strack, talks about "removal" with the gravity a Mayflower descendant might devote to Plymouth Rock, but his tone is different.

Such tenacity would seem to require a long past. Archaeologists lack proof, but the Miami believe they have always been here, trading between east and west, fishing, hunting, and raising their famous soft white corn. Ray Gonyea, curator of native art and culture at the Eiteljorg Museum in Indianapolis, also believes they have been here for hundreds, perhaps thousands, of years. The fur trade with the whites, he says, "was simply the latest new product."

The recorded part of that history can be viewed as a century of accommodation with the French, a short and unhappy interlude with the British, a desperate struggle with the new United States, and a long twilight behind the receding frontier. Modern Miami hope they are in a fifth era, when they will have both their own culture and recognition of it by others. "We're here today," their chief says. "You don't have to go to someone else's museum to see and hear about us."

To explain their determination, it helps to know some history, starting with the fragile balance of the 1700s, when the French wanted furs and Native Americans wanted European guns and goods. That balance began failing with the British defeat of the French in 1763 and vanished with the American Revolution and the War of 1812. There would be no Indian barrier state in the Old Northwest. Only a name, Indiana, would hint at the lost possibility.

But other dramas would play out. Refugee Shawnee and Delaware would tumble into the Miami homeland. The Miami would find a superb leader, Little Turtle, who in 1790 crushed nearly the entire U.S. standing army near Kekionga. Four years later, "Mad Anthony" Wayne reversed that defeat at the Battle of Fallen Timbers, near what is now Toledo. There is a postage stamp for Fallen Timbers, none for Little Turtle's triumph.

The Greenville Treaty of 1795 dispersed the Miami from Ft. Wayne to the Upper Wabash, Eel, and Mississinewa rivers. At Greenville, Little Turtle claimed all of Indiana and western Ohio for the Miami. Events overwhelmed his dream, but in a neck pouch the present chief carries stones from the four corners of that domain.

The new United States wanted all the land. In 1803, President Thomas Jefferson wrote William Henry Harrison, governor of the Indiana Territory, that "we shall push our trading houses, and be glad to see the good & influential citizens among them [the Indians] run in debt, because we observe that when these debts get beyond what the individuals can pay, they become willing to lop th[em off] by a cession of lands."

Harrison soon made treaties securing the southern third of Indiana, for a few cents an acre. The pan-Indian revolt of the Shawnee brothers, Tecumseh and the Prophet, flared briefly, but again Harrison was the nemesis, defeating the Prophet at Tippe-

179

canoe in 1811 and Tecumseh and the British in southern Canada two years later. By 1816, native power was broken, and all major tribes but the Miami and Potawatomi had left Indiana.

Then began 30 years in which the Potawatomi lost their three million acres in northwest Indiana and the Miami nearly all their 900,000 acres, most of it in the Miami National Reserve east of Kokomo. The tool was Jefferson's formula, to which traders added the alcohol that fostered violence, shrank population, and ruined pride. Strack describes that time, grimly, as "the years of debauchery in Ft. Wayne."

An 1818 treaty obtained most of central Indiana for the new state. More was annexed in 1826 and in 1834, when the Miami ceded nearly a third of their national reserve for a dollar an acre. By now, a parasitic bond had formed between Native Americans and the Hoosier entrepreneurs who dealt in land, tribal annuities, and—soon—removal contracts.

Those contracts posed a dilemma, since the financiers could not both remove Native Americans and continue exploiting them. But settlers were rushing in, hungry for land, and removal began. The Potawatomi were expelled in 1838, many walking "the trail of tears" to new homes beyond the Mississippi. The Miami drove a somewhat better bargain, accepting the idea of removal but undermining it through exemptions, "family reserves," and creation of a 10-square-mile communal reserve along the Mississinewa. They also got control of tribal membership, crucial in determining their future.

In 1840 they agreed to removal in five years and ceded the rest of their national reserve. But only in 1846, after a last brisk business in sale of the removal contracts, did canal boats with nearly 330 Miami set off for Kansas. Those who were removed eventually were pushed further south into Oklahoma, and today they are recognized as the Miami Tribe of Oklahoma.

Others simply did not leave Indiana. Some were exempt and remained on the tiny reserves held by families or the tribe. Some hid when removal agents came. Some returned from Kansas. One owner of a removal contract attributed Miami resistance to a rather simple reason: "They dreaded the idea of leaving that splendid Indian country where they had lived all their lives."

The Miami history of the last 150 years has been told in other places, including a recent book, "The Miami Indians of Indiana: A Persistent People," by Stewart Rafert. The story involves the final loss of most tribal land and the withdrawal of tribal recognition in 1897 by an assistant U.S. attorney general—an order the Miami are still trying to reverse through legal action. In the 20th Century, the Indiana Miami pursued financial claims against the federal government and won many of them. When Peru became a center for the circus industry, some Miami became circus workers. Already poverty-stricken, tribal members were hit doubly hard by the Depression. But in the most difficult times, they maintained their identity and tribal organization. The persistence of this "functional tribal government," says the Eiteljorg's Ray Gonyea, is the best proof that Miami history has never lapsed.

* * *

The Miami never wanted to leave Indiana, and they are incorporated today as the Miami Nation of Indiana, with their headquarters in the former high school at Peru, Indiana. The building houses the offices where they conduct all tribal matters. There are a shelter for battered women, AA programs, a day-care center, and bulletin boards with notices of Native American events and programs. Miami population is concentrated in Miami, Wabash, Grant, Huntington, and Allen counties. But without tribal recognition, the Miami cannot participate in federal job-training and educational programs, or market their craftwork as "made by Native Americans." The Pokagon Band of Potawatomi offers these benefits to its members in St. Joseph, Elkhart, Marshall, LaPorte, Kosciusko, and LaGrange counties. It also offers extensive social services, including health care for the diabetes that afflicts an un-usually high percentage of the tribe.

But recognition is also a matter of pride.

"Without some sort of recognized government relationship we're not able to hold a position with our brother tribes," Paul Strack, the Miami chief, says. "For us to be dismissed and spoken of in the past tense, in the history books and so forth, is not a good thing for our people. We're here today."

"Being Miami" has always been more a matter of history and culture than blood percentage, and today the Miami are reviving parts of their culture that were almost lost. They are again making the ribbon-work clothing for which they were known. They have a tribal drum and singers who accompany dancers at ceremonies and pow-wows. They are working to revive the Miami language. For the last four summers, a week-long language camp has been held on 33 acres of Miami land reacquired near "the Seven Pil-lars," a limestone formation sacred to the tribe, on the Missis-sinewa River.

Among those leading the language effort is Daryl Baldwin, who is finishing a master's degree in linguistics at the University of Montana and working on a dictionary of the Miami language.

The last conversationally fluent speaker died in 1962 or '63, he says. But the Miami have continued to give their children tradi-tional names and to preserve songs and prayers—basic keys to reclaiming the language.

At Columbia City, the Miami hold an annual two-day pow-wow named for Little Turtle, or Mihsihkinaahkwa (Mish-i-kin-NA-kwa). It features dances, ceremonies, Native American food, and bus tours of historic landmarks, including the spot where the great chief lived in retirement.

Such programs help the Miami reinforce their ties as a tribe and make their presence known to the state. Their visibility was raised in recent months when the Eiteljorg Museum sponsored an extensive exhibit, with artifacts and an interactive computer program on the tribe's history. (A computer CD is available from the museum.)

A more tangible part of Miami history is a one-room school which the tribe will restore at a new site in the Meshingomesia cemetery near Peru, using money from the state and the tribe. A ceremony honoring the building's donor took place in September; it's hoped the school will become a center for tribal events.

The Miami have other goals. The case for regaining federal recognition is still in court, despite setbacks in recent months. Paul Strack acknowledges a concern by some that the Miami might use recognition to sponsor casino gambling, even though the tribe's governing body has disclaimed any such intention. The Miami also seek recognition by the Indiana General Assembly, which would allow tribal members some educational benefits, permit the marketing of crafts, and help build a tribal identity of people and place.

"This is our historic homeland," Strack says, "and we need to act like it."

* * *

It is late June, under a sky piled with sun-shot clouds. The Mississinewa River is running bank high past the Seven Pillars and the brick home of Chief Richardville, who once guided the Miami in peace as Little Turtle had in war. Over the back roads, the woods and cornfields lies a deep quiet. It is "that splendid Indian country." The Miami never wanted to leave it, and some of them never have.

[1998]

Since these stories were written, the Miami have lost their federal lawsuit for restoration of their official tribal designation. Efforts to achieve that continue, and in recent months the tribe was invited to send observers to a meeting of the United Nations Working Group on Indigenous Peoples. The

Miami have also received a gift of 150 acres in northern Indiana, on which they hope to build a museum and "living village."

These two stories were commissioned by Outdoor Indiana *magazine, and were researched and written by my wife, Karen Petersen Bridges, and me. The first appeared in the magazine's issue of November-December, 1998. The second was rejected as being too supportive of Miami claims to be published in a state-sponsored magazine. We declined to re-write, and the story is published here for the first time.*

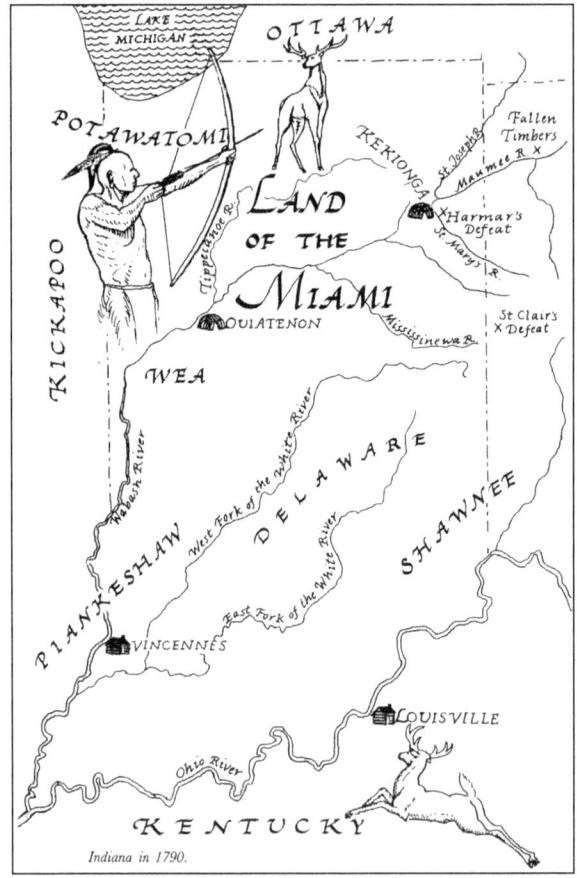

From *The Miamis!* by Betty Niblack Baxter
Map used by permission of the artist, Richard Day

PLACES
&stories

WILLIAM BRIDGES

OF SHORT (AND SHORTER) FICTION

There are stories *about* some of the stories that follow. "Dragon's Dilemma" grew out of an agreement with two friends to exchange fairy tales. I wrote one story, one writer dropped out, the third wrote two books and is working on a third. "Death Sentence" was written for the Edward Bulwer-Lytton contest, which annually seeks the worst possible beginning for a novel. ("Death Sentence" didn't win, which makes it either better or worse than the winner.) "Murder in the *OED*" also was written for a contest. It didn't win either, but I got so involved in it that I created an entire genealogy for the main character. And finally, in "Flash Fiction," I kept trying to get closer to Hemingway's purported six-word masterpiece, but could get down only to 100 words. (A reviewer for an on-line flash fiction site complained that one of these stories "lacked character development." You can't have everything.) At least one writer, Duane Ackerson, has surpassed Hemingway. His title and three-word story in full are:

SIGN AT THE END OF THE UNIVERSE

This end up.

Who cares about character development, that's genius!

THOSE WHO CAN LIVE LONG ENOUGH

GRACE MORGAN WAS ABOUT 50 and might have weighed 100 pounds in her shift. A wiry hill woman. She was cross-eyed, she wore the same shapeless gray house dress in all seasons, and she loved me.

That was why, when Grace asked to take me from Indiana to visit her folks in North Carolina, my mother delayed, made excuses, thought no, and finally said yes. Had the word babysitter existed then, with its connotations of temporary and untrained care, she probably would have balked. Or if the newspapers had been full of stories about child abductions. But Grace had helped raise me from birth to my current age of seven. And she loved me.

The Depression, still with us though in retreat, was pushing our family toward the lower middle class, perhaps even lower. My father complained about the cost of domestic help (*i.e.,* Grace, who cleaned, washed, ironed, and did child care so my mother could teach at the local college). There were harsh words and tears late at night, and then my father was gone, looking for work in another state, I was told. My mother was tense and snappish, with my baby sister still waking her at 2 a.m., and I reacted as always to her moods, coiling like an overwound clock spring and losing weight.

"I'll take good care of him, missus," Grace said. "We'll be back in six or eight weeks, before school takes up again."

A few days later, on the Fourth of July, Grace's brother Rolly arrived in an ancient Ford V-8, into which we stepped cautiously, since many of the floorboards were gone. I remember the view underfoot on that three-day trip from Indiana to the Smokies—the road flying by beneath us, "tarvy" usually, but sometimes gravel or the sudden purling of water as we forded a stream. That and dim memories of visits to "relations" in Kentucky and Tennessee, of sandwiches eaten out of oily paper sacks, and of stops at Tydol stations where gasoline flowed down from glass reservoirs into the car. We traveled late and early to avoid the mid-day heat. I remember the cigarette burn on the worn velour of the back seat, next to my face as I drifted off to sleep. And somewhere late at night, through a corner of the rear window, a star.

Grace's folks, it turned out, lived in a log cabin, with no road. Rolly abandoned the car in a ruined tobacco barn at the foot of a hill, and we walked for nearly a mile up a dry creek bed, over-hung in July with ash, hickory, and sassafras. Standing in the cabin door was the oldest woman I had ever seen, gaunter even than Grace, her scant gray hairs pulled back in a knot, and her toothless mouth caved in like a sinkhole in a plowed field. Her birdlike blue eyes looked straight at me, not blinking.

"Gracie, you're here, and young Billy with you," she said, her voice cracked and reedy. Behind her a thin man in overalls emerged from the shadows but said nothing.

"Oh, Lord, Gracie, but ain't we had troubles since Rolly went to fetch you! Come in, come in, let Pa and me look at you. And you, too, Rolly, you need to hear."

After the bright yard, entering the cabin was like falling down a well. It took a few moments to see the interior—one large room with a loft, the walls insulated with old newspapers, and a wood stove in a corner next to an oilcloth-covered table. There were several chairs, a broken-down sofa, and a washstand with a pitcher, basin, and a bar of black Lava pumice soap. On the back of the door, years of calendars hung from a peg. A door in the op-posite wall led into what was perhaps a bedroom; from it now ap-peared a lean man with shaggy black hair, a beard, and intense blue eyes.

"Samuel," the old woman said, "this is Billy. Take him outside and show him the farm, while we have some words with your sister and brother."

Samuel laid a broad hand on my shoulder and propelled me outside. "Fish?" he asked. I shook my head. "Won't learn no younger," he said, picking up two sticks from which dangled strings and hooks. Then he shouldered a mysterious bucket and strode off into the woods, leaving me to keep up the best I could.

Two hours later, with only a few more words and no fish, we returned, and Samuel disappeared again into the back room. Later that day, Grace gathered me to her lap on the heavy board swing in the yard. After we had swung and cozied for a while, she said, "Billy, it's a strange world, and sometimes you just have to see things and not say anything." We swung a little longer, and Grace continued, "There may be people coming, asking questions. Ma and I will answer them. You must not say anything, promise me, cross your heart?" I promised and crossed. "Now," Grace said, "it's Saturday night and we'll be going down to the spring to get water for your bath."

In the days that followed, I became a little mountaineer, with a pair of cutdown overalls, an old blue shirt, and my bare feet blessedly free of store shoes. I lived much of the time in the woods, often following Samuel, who continued teaching me to fish and also to use a squirrel rifle. He showed me where to find paw-paws and how to lie so quietly in the leaves that sometimes a rabbit or raccoon would come almost within reach before scampering away. And once I saw Samuel's hand dart out and catch a rabbit by the neck, then let it go.

Samuel was the quietest person I had ever known, if one could claim to know someone who rarely spoke and about whom one knew next to nothing. No one ever mentioned him in front of me. He never ate with us and seemed to inhabit the back room only, alone except at night when Ma and Pa retired there while Grace and I climbed to bed in the loft. Once I saw him coming across a field when I knew he had not come out the cabin door. I had seen him go in, and had been sitting in the yard swing ever since, with the door in plain sight. There was something unaccountable about Samuel.

Meanwhile, I began to lose some of the tension wound into me at home and started putting on weight. It would have been hard not to, when the day's eating began with a breakfast of ham, eggs, grits, biscuits and gravy, coffee, and apple pie, then picked up steam as the day went along, ending at night with chicken and dumplings, roasting ears, green and lima beans, yams, more biscuits and gravy, more coffee, and more pie. I learned to drink coffee "saucered and blowed" by Grace or Ma, then poured back into my cup.

When not tramping the woods alone or with Samuel, I followed Pa as he fed the chickens, slopped the pigs, or cultivated his tiny fields of corn and tobacco. I was not allowed to follow him over the big hill, from behind which strange pungent smells sometimes drifted. He didn't talk much more than Samuel, but seemed quite willing for me to tag along after him and even to ride Grover, the mule. On rainy days, I curled up on a rag carpet in the cabin and listened to Grace and her mother as they cooked, washed up, sewed, or ironed the men's shirts, with actual "irons" heated on the stove. They ironed facing each other as they worked their way on opposite sides of a shirt, from the broad to the narrow end of the board.

Ma's real name was Molly, I had learned. She accompanied her ironing with occasional remarks and bits of hill wisdom: "Even a blind sow will find an acorn in the woods now and then" (stroke, stroke); "What can't be cured must be endured" (stroke, stroke); "Everything comes out all right, if you can live long enough" (stroke, stroke). Once I surprised her sewing extra pockets into a pair of Samuel's overalls. "What are you making, Ma?" I asked. "Layovers to catch meddlers," she replied, turning away.

I think we might have gone on like that forever, or at least for a few more weeks, but one August night as we sat down to supper there was a loud knock. Ma opened the door to a heavyset man carrying a rifle. Behind him were two more men, also armed.

"We'd like to talk to Samuel," the big man said.

"He ain't here," Ma said. "Ain't been here since the Fourth of July, as you know very well, Nathan Jones."

The man's big face relaxed slightly, with the hint in his eyes of a smile that stopped short of his mouth.

"Now, Molly, we know he's here somewhere. We've been looking for him, and it ain't as if he can't be seen. Fact is, we saw him come in here an hour ago and he ain't come out. There's one door to this cabin. The law has to be satisfied, Molly—so if you don't mind, we'll just come in and look around."

"Suit yourself, sheriff," Ma said, "but he ain't here, ain't been, ain't going to be. If it's the law you're so concerned about, maybe you should be talking to the Carters, about why our cousin is lying all cold and still over in Amity burying ground, and nobody arrested."

"Molly, Molly," Nathan said, more gently. "You know the Carters run things hereabouts, and they won't let it end. The judge says we have to do our duty. So now we'll just come in and look around a little."

It's surprising how long three men can take to search a two-room cabin. They lingered a long time in the front room, checked the loft, and talked more loudly than seemed strictly necessary. When they finally pulled open the door to the back room, I noticed that the pants with the extra pockets were no longer hanging from a peg on the door.

When the men came out again, the two deputies went into the yard, but the sheriff stayed behind.

"You know, Molly," he said, "if Samuel *was* here—which he plainly ain't—you ought to be telling him to go to Cordell Springs or someplace further on, out of the jurisdiction. That's the only way it will end."

"He's my last son, Nathan," Ma replied, looking straight at him, not blinking. "But if he *was* here—which he plainly ain't—I know that's what I'd have to be telling him."

We saw no more of Samuel, and his name was not mentioned again. A few days later, Rolly came walking up the creek bed. I put my store shoes back on, painfully, and my Indiana pants, which no longer fit so well around the waist. For three days we journeyed, with the road unfurling beneath the rotting floorboards. At home, my father had found a new job in our town. My baby sister was thriving and sleeping through the night. I built a house in the backyard tree-of-heaven, with a trapdoor in the floor.

My mother seemed happier and less nervous than I remembered. She and Grace Morgan did the ironing, facing each other, on either side of the board.

"Well, missus," Grace said (stroke, stroke), "everything comes out all right, if you can live long enough."

[2002]

WILLIE & WALTER

(A PEN-PAL STORY)

ONCE UPON A TIME (as the best stories always begin), a brand-new fountain pen lay in a shop window on St. Catherine Street in Montreal. It was a Waterman (the very best pen), with a gold clip and a barrel of rippled blue, like water running over stones.

"I wonder who will buy me?" it thought. "Maybe it will be a Great Writer or a World-Famous Musician! I will help him write the World's Best Novel . . . or she will use me to write The Symphony That Made People Forget Beethoven!" (The little pen thought a lot in capital letters.)

One day a woman stopped at the window and saw the little pen.

"My husband is a teacher," she said to herself, "and has to grade many papers. That blue pen will be just the Christmas present for him, back in Indiana."

"Oh, no," thought the little pen. "I'm going to be a Hopeless Drudge. And Indiana does not sound like a place where anyone ever wrote a great symphony—or even listened to one."

A tiny, inky tear dribbled down his point.

But the woman bought the pen, and because she liked naming things said, "I will call you Willie—Willie Waterman."

"This is the last straw," thought the little pen. "Not only am I going to live in the land of pigs and corn—I will have a goofy name, too."

But he knew his duty, and on Christmas morning the woman's husband smiled happily.

"I have always wanted a Waterman pen, and this must be the most beautiful one ever made," he said.

The little pen began to feel slightly better.

Over the years, Willie went everywhere with his new owner. He did grade freshman papers, and for a while he got to work on ones by an exchange student from his Canadian homeland.

"Now this is more like it," he thought.

The teacher was definitely not a Great Writer, but he did write poems for obscure magazines, and many letters, including some to the Canadian student, who had returned to the Great White North and was having adventures of her own.

"Life is certainly not all capital letters," Willie thought, "but this is really not so bad."

After a while, the teacher discovered faculty grants and began to travel—sometimes alone, but sometimes with his wife or students. Willie went along—to Germany, to Australia, to an ancient Inca city in Peru. Once he even went back to Montreal, where the teacher (an incurable romantic) took him to visit the shop on St. Catherine Street where he had started out so long before. For a year he lived in a Chinese city and learned a great many strange new letters, like 紙 for paper and 筆 for pen. And once he went to a desert island!

Sometimes the teacher wrote on a typewriter or computer. But when it was a fairy tale or a poem, or when the Canadian student needed a letter from an island or an airplane, Willie got the job.

"I have not written a novel or a symphony," he thought, "but I have Seen Life."

Time passed, however, as it does even in fairy tales, and Willie began to look old and worn. He did not always write smoothly, and patches of brass began to show through his beautiful blue barrel. One day the teacher said, "Willie, you must go back to the Waterman factory for repairs. But I will write a letter to go with you."

Now the teacher was not a Great Writer (have I made that clear?), but he knew how to make a pitch. He wrote to the Waterman factory about what a good pen Willie was, and how he had traveled to all the countries of the world. He told about the poems and letters Willie had written, including the ones to the Canadian student. And he even quoted scripture.

"I love Willie more than apples of gold in pictures of silver (Proverbs 25:11)," he wrote.

At the Waterman factory, the Senior Pen Repair Person read the letter, looked at Willie, and stroked his long white beard thoughtfully.

"I know that parts are no longer made for you," he said, "and I cannot make your beautiful blue barrel new again. But the Waterman company is A Company With A Heart, and when we say 'lifetime guarantee,' we mean it.

"I will clean you carefully and send you back to the teacher, but I will also send along a brand-new Waterman—deep blue, like a sky with moonclouds—and there will be no charge."

So he did. And when the teacher and his wife opened the package, they found two beautiful fountain pens, filled with ink and words.

"You will always be Willie," the wife said to the old pen. "And you are Walter," she told the new one.

The teacher smiled happily.

"Willie," he said, "you will not have to grade freshman papers anymore. You will live on my desk in the penholder with the Chinese characters for 'patience.' And when there is a special poem or story to be written, we will write it together.

"And now, Walter," he said, "it's time for you to get to work. The Canadian student is far away in Victoria, learning frightening things like 'stakeholder relations' and 'risk management.' She will need a story to cheer her up, and we are going to write it for her."

And they did.

[1998]

Rubber-stamp carving by Dianne Jenkins

Dragon's Dilemma

(A Chinese Fairy Tale)

SAM WAS A DRAGON—green, scaly, about 35 feet long when fully extended, of hideous mien. He lived on Yangmingshan, a mountain overlooking the city of Taipei on the island of Taiwan, or Formosa, the Beautiful Island, as the Portuguese explorers called it.

Sam wasn't his real name, of course. All Chinese, including dragons, adopt English names for dealing with the West. Sam's real name was Hwo-gwo, or Fire Pot, after the delicious wintertime stew that is served everywhere in Taiwan, but most especially at one stall on the mezzanine of the Taipei Railway Station.

Up on Yangmingshan, there still are woods and ravines and bosky dells where a dragon—a rather shy dragon—can hide or come out to frolic in the moonlight. For Sam, despite his ferocious appearance, had the heart of a toasted marshmallow. In fact, he loved marshmallows, which he toasted by putting them on the tip of his tail and breathing on them.

But of course a dragon's life isn't all moonlight and marshmallows. There is a tradition to be upheld, and it has to do with Maidens in Distress and Knights in Shining Armor. And fairies. Sam's own special fairy was Mei-hwa, Beautiful Flower, who lived under a toadstool beneath the third cinnamon camphor tree from the right in the deepest, darkest dell on Yangmingshan. Mei-hwa was Sam's special friend, the one he could tell all his troubles to. And he had one big trouble.

197

It had to do with the tradition, you see. The maidens of Yangmingshan expected, indeed demanded, that Sam carry them off, with appropriate roarings and fire-breathings, so that their boyfriends could rescue them and they could live happily ever after. This was the Knight in Shining Armor part.

All would have gone well had Sam not been so tender-hearted. When he carried off a maiden, she would begin to wail and lament to attract her boyfriend. And her appeals would be so heart-rending that Sam would begin to cry. Not puny little tear-droplets, but great dragon dollops of salt water that poured down his scaly cheeks and into his nose and mouth, where they promptly put out his fire.

You can imagine what a disappointment this was to the maidens. It's one thing to be rescued from a roaring, fire-breathing dragon, but quite another to have one's Knight in Shining Armor confront only a sniveling, sobbing, faintly smoking hulk of green misery.

"Well, I *would* have rescued you," the boy would say. "Oh, of course, you say that *now*," the maiden would reply. "But if you had had to fight a *real* dragon for me, I'll bet you would have run away. Yang Ming-yuan now, he would have fought a *real* dragon for me."

They would walk away arguing, and Sam would cry all the harder, because he really wanted to be a good dragon and bring the young people together with the proper amount of romance.

"What am I going to do?" he moaned to Mei-hwa. "I know the maidens are just pretending, bless their hearts, but they're so pretty and they look so terrified that I can't help crying."

Sam and Mei-hwa tried everything they could think of, from self-help books to hypnotism. Mei-hwa would dart back and forth in front of Sam until his eyes went glassy. Then she would say, "You are a big, ferocious dragon who *loves* to devour maidens, and next time you will not cry." But nothing worked, for the very next time Sam gazed into the terrified eyes of a maiden, his tear ducts would open and put out his fire.

This was not even the worst of it. A dragon can relight his fire only from the sacred dragon hearth on the top of the highest mountain in the Most Remote Chinese Province of Sinkiang. Once, Sam had been able to fly there in a few hours, but now the Chinese Communists—who believe dragons and fairies are secret agents of the evil capitalist government on Taiwan—refused to let him enter their air space. So Sam had to take a fishing boat across the Taiwan Strait and then travel to Sinkiang by fourth-class railway carriage. In fact, he had to buy tickets for a whole carriage, since a 35-foot-long dragon leaves very little room for ordinary passengers.

Mei-hwa always went along, to cheer him up and bewitch any border guards who might be inclined to ask for his papers. The trip back was easier, since Sam could work his train passage by breathing into the boiler to keep the steam up.

But as soon as the next maiden needed rescuing, the same sad story would begin again. Sam began hiding even deeper in the dell to avoid the maidens. He hardly talked to Mei-hwa, and even when she brought him marshmallows he could get up only enough fire to turn them a pale tan. After the last maiden, he didn't even bother making the trip to Sinkiang to relight his fire. He was a seriously depressed dragon.

Now at the top of Yangmingshan there lived an old hermit. He could remember everything that had happened for at least 100 years, and many other things that had never happened at all. One day Mei-hwa flew to his cave and told him about Sam's terrible problem.

"Hmmmm," the hermit said, clearing his throat. "Hmmmm," he said several more times. Then he sat very quietly for nearly an hour, until Mei-hwa began to be afraid that he had gone to sleep with his eyes open.

But just as she was about to fly away, the hermit spoke, in a grumble that reverberated down the length of the cave.

"When the dragon will not come to the mountain," he said, "the mountain must come to the dragon."

Then he was silent for another hour. Finally he spoke again.

"A dragon without a fire is like a rhinoceros without a horn," he said, "and they must help each other."

Hermits always talk in a way that nobody understands, which is why they seem so wise, and are never wrong about anything. Those who hear them have to figure out for themselves what the words mean.

Mei-hwa flew home, thinking about dragons and mountains and rhinoceroses. Then she remembered that she had heard Old Wu complain that he could no longer buy rhinoceros-horn powder from Yu Chan at the village medicine shop. Rhinoceroses were now an endangered species, Yu Chan had told him, and selling their horns for powder was against the law.

This was a great sadness to the old men of the village, who thought the powder would make them feel younger and able to start rescuing maidens again. (It had no effect whatever, but they *thought* it did, which was the important thing.)

Mei-hwa flew back to the deepest, darkest dell and had a long talk with Sam. What she told him made him so happy that he wept tears of joy, which Mei-hwa carefully caught in a big glass bottle with a round stopper.

Then she took the bottle to Yu Chan's medicine shop and talked to him. The next day, when Old Wu came into the shop, there was a new bottle on the shelf labeled "Dragon's Tears."

"You should try them, Old Wu," Yu Chan said. "They're much more effective than rhinoceros-horn powder. Old Chao tried them just last week, and he has already rescued a maiden and married her. A very pretty maiden, too."

After that, Yu Chan could hardly keep dragon's tears in stock.

Meanwhile, Mei-hwa flew to the tallest mountain in the Most Remote Chinese Province of Sinkiang and broke off two pieces of flint from the sacred dragon hearth.

Now when Sam is called on to carry off a maiden, he still cannot help crying. But Mei-hwa quickly collects his tears and then strikes the two pieces of flint together in front of his nostrils. The sparks relight his fire, and this makes him so happy that he forgets to cry.

By the time the maiden's boyfriend arrives, Sam is roaring and flaming, and the maiden is wailing and lamenting. The boyfriend shakes his fist at Sam and tells him that he had better turn loose of that maiden *right now*, or he is going to get *what-for*. And of course Sam turns her loose.

It's a very happy time now on Yangmingshan. Sam and Mei-hwa are happy, the maidens and their boyfriends are happy, the old men of the village are happy. Yu Chan is happy and has grown so rich that he is thinking of starting a chain of medicine shops in Taipei. The International Committee for the Protection of Endangered Species is happy, because no one wants to kill rhinoceroses any more for their horns.

At the very top of Yangmingshan, the old hermit is also happy. He has a new wife, and Sam flies to his cave once a week to weep dragon's tears especially for him.

"The virtuous shall not go unrewarded among the four seas of the Middle Kingdom," the hermit says. Which means whatever you want it to mean.

[1993]

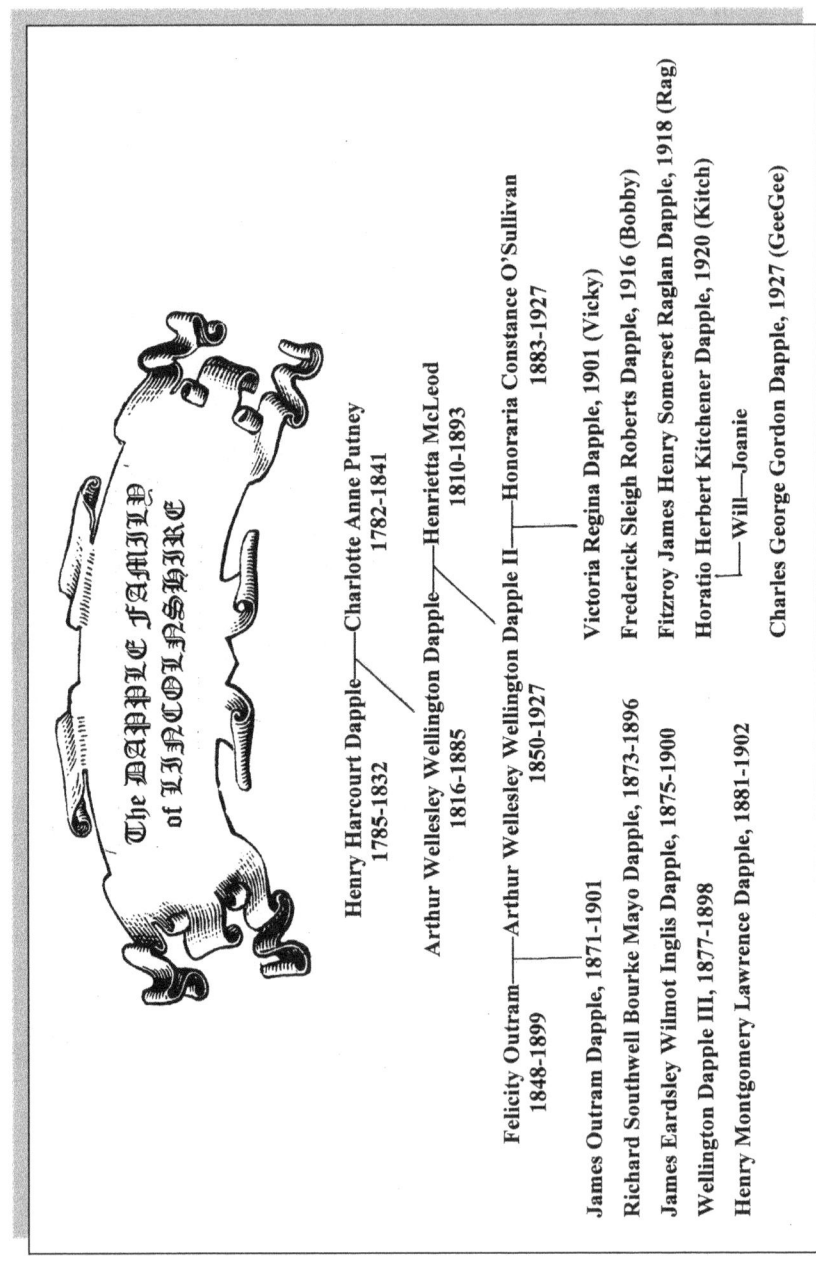

The DAPPLE FAMILY
of LINCOLNSHIRE

Henry Harcourt Dapple——Charlotte Anne Putney
1785-1832   1782-1841

Arthur Wellesley Wellington Dapple——Henrietta McLeod
1816-1885   1810-1893

Arthur Wellesley Wellington Dapple II——Honoraria Constance O'Sullivan
1850-1927   1883-1927

Felicity Outram——Arthur Wellesley Wellington Dapple II
1848-1899

James Outram Dapple, 1871-1901   Victoria Regina Dapple, 1901 (Vicky)

Richard Southwell Bourke Mayo Dapple, 1873-1896   Frederick Sleigh Roberts Dapple, 1916 (Bobby)

James Eardsley Wilmot Inglis Dapple, 1875-1900   Fitzroy James Henry Somerset Raglan Dapple, 1918 (Rag)

Wellington Dapple III, 1877-1898   Horatio Herbert Kitchener Dapple, 1920 (Kitch)

Henry Montgomery Lawrence Dapple, 1881-1902   ┌── Will──Joanie

                                                  Charles George Gordon Dapple, 1927 (GeeGee)

A NOTE ON THE DAPPLE FAMILY OF LINCOLNSHIRE, TO WHICH IS APPENDED THE INTRIGUING MYSTERY OF 'MURDER IN THE *OXFORD ENGLISH DICTIONARY*.'

READERS OF THE LINCOLNSHIRE *REFLECTOR* will be quite familiar with the name and family connections of the newspaper's editor emeritus, Charles George Gordon Dapple (known to his friends as "GeeGee"). The name will also sound a martial note for students of British military history. But for readers elsewhere the following brief sketch is provided.

The founder of the Dapple family's military fortunes was "GeeGee" Dapple's great-grandfather, Henry Harcourt Dapple, who fought in the infantry under Wellington at the Battle of Waterloo in 1814. He named his first child (born 1816) Arthur Wellesley Wellington Dapple, in honor of the Iron Duke. Wellington, as he was known, fathered Arthur Wellesley Wellington Dapple II in 1850—this was GeeGee's father. The long period of time involved will be explained.

Wellington Dapple II continued staunchly in the family's military tradition, entering the enlisted ranks and marrying (in 1870) Felicity Outram, a distant cousin of General Sir James Outram, whose slab in Westminster Abbey bears the sobriquet, "The Bayard of India." Wellington was posted to India in 1870, shortly after his marriage, and Felicity was able to use her connections to accompany him. Their first child, born in India in 1871, was named (not surprisingly) James Outram Dapple.

There followed four more sons—Richard Southwell Bourke Mayo Dapple (1873), named for the martyred viceroy under whom the Dapples had come to India; James Eardley Wilmot Inglis Dapple (1875), named for the defender of Lucknow during the Mutiny; Wellington Dapple III (1877); and Henry Montgomery Lawrence Dapple (1881), whose name commemorated another hero of Lucknow, "the noblest man who has lived and died for the good of India."

All five sons entered the military and by 1902 all were dead, without issue—fallen in famous battles or obscure skirmishes on two continents. These vanished half-brothers would always be to GeeGee heroic and shadowy figures known only from sepia photographs—dashing and doomed young men, forever waving goodbye from the decks of ships and the windows of dusty troop transports.

Meanwhile, their father, Wellington II, was advancing in the ranks, eventually reaching sergeant-major and taking part in the now-forgotten Asiatic scuffles of the late 19th century. He was in the honor guard at the 1879 durbar marking the investiture of Queen Victoria as Empress of India, on the famous "Ridge" overlooking the Mogul capital of Delhi. In 1885 he fought honorably in the 3rd Burmese War. Then in July, 1897, during a minor clash with natives in Swat, his kneecap was shattered by a minie ball, and he was invalided back to England and eventually out of the service.

He and Felicity looked forward to a long, sunny retirement in Sleaford, Lincolnshire, but this was not to be. Influenza carried off Felicity in the winter of 1899, leaving Wellington Dapple a vigorous if limping man of 49. Within a few months he was married again—to a red-haired colleen of 17 named Honoraria Constance O'Sullivan, who had come from County Cork to work as a maid in Sleaford. Wellington immediately got down to the serious business of adding more men to the military might of England—

although it may well be that Mrs. Dapple, being Irish, was less interested in strengthening that might.

At any rate, Wellington's intention to continue the Dapple tradition of producing males with appropriately resounding military names was frustrated almost immediately. To his enormous surprise and momentary consternation, the first arrival (on April 1, 1901), was a red-haired girl. But in a nation mourning the loss of its longest-reigning sovereign, a name was no problem; the new arrival honored the nation's ultimate commander, Victoria Regina—and became Vicky then and ever after in the Dapple household.

Although Wellington seems to have loved this surprising daughter, he may also have felt a bit disconcerted by such an interruption in the male line. For whatever reason, 15 years elapsed with no further additions to the Dapple menage. Then in 1916, perhaps in response to the Great War, the military march resumed with the birth of Frederick Sleigh Roberts Dapple, named in honor of Lord Roberts, under whose command two half-brothers had been killed in the Anglo-Boer War. "Bobby" was followed in 1918 by Fitzroy James Henry Somerset Raglan Dapple, named for the great general of the Crimean War and the eponymous inspirer of the raglan coat and sleeve. "Rag" Dapple soon gave up youngest-son honors to Horatio Herbert Kitchener Dapple or "Kitch." Then the Dapple energies seemed to flag again, and seven years went by before the birth, on Jan. 28, 1927, of a fourth son. Retired Sergeant-Major Arthur Wellesley Wellington Dapple II, now 77, held the gawky, red-haired bundle in his arms and declared that since Jan. 28 was also the birthday of the Hero of Khartoum, the new arrival would be named Charles George Gordon Dapple.

Two days later, Wellington suffered a stroke and died. Less than a year later, Honoraria Constance O'Sullivan Dapple was struck by a lorry and killed as she stepped off a curb in Sleaford. Suddenly, Vicky, 27, an unmarried milliner's apprentice, was mother to four boys, aged 12, 10, 8, and 1. She rose to the task with all the energy, devotion, spirit, and determination of both her parents. From that day until the last of the four Dapple boys was reared, educated, and safely embarked on a career, Vicky made sure they were fed, bathed, read to, comforted when necessary, and sternly disciplined when that was required—which was often. She fended off all efforts by community do-gooders to break up the family and farm the boys out to other households. She worked in Sleaford shops, made hats at home in the evenings, and with a modest amount of insurance money "got by"—barely.

The result was that more than half a century later, all the Dapples had done well—exceedingly well—in their chosen fields. Under Vicky's influence also, none of them became soldiers unless absolutely required to in a time of dire national emergency, and then for as brief periods as possible. Vicky decided early that the Dapples had done enough for England on the field of battle. Once the boys were reared, Vicky took the small inheritance remaining from her parents, opened a preparatory school, and served as its headmistress for 30 years. She and the boys retired in good season, and in 1990 (when the story accompanying this takes place) they were all vigorous, possessed of all their faculties, and in GeeGee's case bored out of his mind with retirement.

Vicky at 89 remains the matriarch of the family, beloved and still depended upon for the final word in matters of faith, duty, and morals. Bobby is 74, retired as Regius Professor of History at Oxford, Rag, 72, is retired as chief of an export-import business with worldwide connections. Kitch, 70, closest both in age and interests to GeeGee, is a noted archaeologist. GeeGee, who took early retirement in 1987 at 60 as editor of the Lincolnshire *Reflector* because of his wife's failing health (she died within a year), is the baby of the family and is well known as a leading provincial journalist and amateur lexicographer. (It is not as well know that he is an aspiring and chronically frustrated poet.)

Great height is a family characteristic, and GeeGee shares this, being 6-foot-4. Until recent years he was ramrod straight, and walked as if there were a march playing somewhere. Now he moves a bit—but only a bit—more slowly and stoops a little. He is still as lean and lanky as the infant his father briefly held, and his shock of unruly hair is a distinguished salt-and-pepper with a faint tinge of red.

The Dapples have not been as prolific as old Wellington II. GeeGee is childless, but has various nieces, nephews, and "grands" scattered about England. He is closest to his brother Kitch's son, Will (whose name actually is Arthur Wellesley Wellington Dapple IV). Part of the attraction is propinquity (Will lives in the next village) and part is Will's wife, Joanie, a dear girl. Will is 24, the child of Kitch's late second marriage—the Dapples continue to stretch out the generations more than would at first seem possible.

It is 1990, as our story opens . . . .

MURDER IN THE *OED*

CHARLES "GEEGEE" DAPPLE emptied his letterbox and, because it was a sunny Tuesday morning in June, stepped outside to glance at the two bills, a letter from his nephew, Monday's Lincolnshire *Reflector*, and the inevitable rejection slip from *Speckled Pheasant, A Magazine of the Poetic Arts*.

He knew it was a rejection slip because it always was, and because he had learned to gauge precisely the weight of his returning poems. Only when he had finished doing so did he notice the Jenny Haniver in a small wicker basket on the cottage doorstep, six inches from his left shoe.

It was a rather frightening Jenny Haniver, at least what he could see of it, which was mostly two gray, leathery horns and a cyclops eye peering out over a scrap of blue and white blanket. There was no note, and as GeeGee picked up the creature he saw that it was only an ordinary skate, or small marine ray, anamorphosed by someone with a sharp knife and needle into the dried

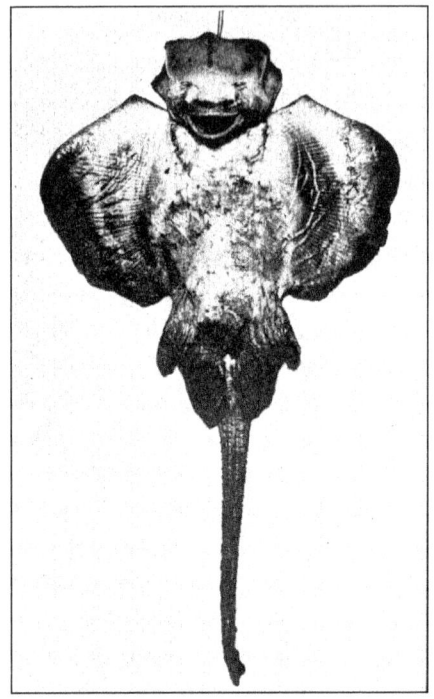

and wrinkled doll that now grinned satanically up at him. It was not, as he had hoped for a breathless moment, a true *Myliobatis noctula*.

"Anamorphosed." Gee-Gee smiled at having thought of the precise word. Once an editor, always an editor. Then the smile faded, as the word and the doll reminded him of a minor disappointment; his brand-new Second Edition of the great *Oxford English Dictionary* had come the week before, and it had not contained the citation he had submitted, three years earlier, to the *OED*'s editors at The Clarendon Press, Oxford. He had written the citation in the dictionary's compact style:

> "1934 E.W. Gudger, Scientific Monthly, XXXVIII. 511 I explained to him that this was a Jenny Haniver, made of a ray transformed by hand and dried into this mythological monster."

Or at least GeeGee thought he had submitted the citation. He certainly remembered discussing it with his nephew Will and Will's delightful wife, Joanie, and he remembered putting the letter into an envelope, along with a copy of Dr. Gudger's article: "Jenny Hanivers, Dragons, and Basilisks in the Old Natural History Books and in Modern Times." The article, more than a half-century old, had been the prize of a two-day orgy in London's second-hand bookshops.

But he could not actually remember putting the envelope in the postbox; it might still be somewhere in the chaos of his post-editorial retirement to this comfortable but lonely cottage in Silk Willoughby, Lincolnshire. The cottage was near the Silk end, which was short for Silkby, an SMV or shrunken medieval village. He felt decidedly shrunken and medieval himself on many days.

Not having a secretary to post letters and keep your office in trim was only one of the melancholy things about retiring from a busy newspaper life. Another was standing on your cottage door-step, fretting about dictionary citations, because nobody was calling to say that your mid-morning tea was going cold in the kitchen, and that you had best hurry in. Three years a pensioner, two years a widower. GeeGee went back to the kitchen and decided to think instead about the morning post and why someone would leave a deformed marine animal on his doorstep.

He threw the bills in the direction of the worktop. Will's message was brief, part of a continuing postal exchange between ex-editor uncle and would-be-writer nephew: "Four English words end in 'gry'—three of them are hungry, angry, and (if you'll accept the variant spelling) puggry. What's the fourth?" GeeGee wrote the answer at the bottom, put the note in a new envelope, and addressed it to Will. He enjoyed the exchange by post, even though Will and Joanie lived just a village away.

Then he thought for a while about the Jenny Haniver that was still malevolently sharing his tea table. The *Reflector* had been printing stories about the appearance of satanic cults in Lincoln-shire—perhaps he had been chosen for a visit by cultists seeking to intimidate the newspaper through its retired editor. But this, while possibly flattering, seemed unlikely.

Monday's *Reflector* was no help on satanism, but a front-page headline just below the splash took his mind off the subject. "Employee Murdered in Newspaper's Library," it read. GeeGee saw with a shock that the victim was young Geoffrey Hardcastle, an assistant in the *Reflector* library.

Recently he had been working to move the paper's antiquated cutting files onto a computer database. Geoffrey had been a sharp lad and often helpful, GeeGee recalled, when he had needed some bit of esoterica on deadline. The boy had been found stabbed to death, the paper said, across a volume of the *Oxford English Dictionary*, which was lying open on a table in the library. "A man is assisting police with their inquiries," the article concluded.

GeeGee could visualize the scene in the musty basement archive, sandwiched between the newspaper's press-hall and the pressmen's shower and reached by an ancient iron staircase. He could see the table covered in green oilcloth, and the three rickety stools around it.

Damn, he thought. In what volume of the *OED* had Geoff been looking? Did anyone know what he was trying to find? Did anyone even ask such questions, now that GeeGee Dapple and his fabled curiosity were out to grass? And what a terrible thing. Poor Geoff, and poor Geoff's wife and young son, if he remembered correctly.

"Was the post late? You took just a half hour longer to ring up than I thought you would." Harold Stimson, the *Reflector*'s current editor, came on the line, after GeeGee had struggled successfully to identify himself to a new secretary. Sic transit gloria, he thought—here today, Helpringham tomorrow. "And before you even ask," Harold continued, "it was the A-B volume of the *OED*. Is there anything else I can help you with, my inquisitive friend?"

There was quite a lot, in fact. In the next few minutes, GeeGee learned that Geoff Hardcastle had been stabbed in the back with a company letter opener, and that he had died instantly, between 9 and 9:30 a.m. on Monday, after slumping forward on his stool and spewing a great deal of blood across the library table and a lesser amount across pages 306 and 307 of the dictionary.

And no, nobody knew what word among the "As" he had been looking up.

While the police were being publicly silent, the *Reflector*'s enterprising reporter had learned that the fingerprints on the letter opener matched those of Howard Robbins, Geoff's co-worker on the computerization project. Rumors were flying of an affair between Robbins and that young wife of Geoff's. All this, in short, was why someone whom the newspaper could not name was now assisting police with their inquiries.

"Thank you, Harold," GeeGee said. "It looks as if they've got the beggar, and all you senior editors can stop watching each other like basilisks." There was a moment of aggrieved silence before Harold answered. "Really, GeeGee," he said, "an editor who would stab a colleague in the back? Where would the police start?"

"By the way," GeeGee said as he prepared to hang up, "someone left a Jenny Haniver on my doorstep this morning."

"We all have our crosses, old son," Harold said. "Don't feed it and perhaps it will go away."

In the afternoon, GeeGee learned a few more things. A call to Wilfrid Crabbe, a Lincoln police inspector and old friend, confirmed that Howard Robbins was the leading, in fact the only, suspect. But, off the record, several things puzzled the police. The killer would have had to be well-versed in anatomy, or eerily lucky, to have killed Geoff instantly with one thrust of the letter opener. Also, there was blood on the table under the *OED* as well as on the opened volume.

Crabbe confided that Howard Robbins appeared devastated by the murder and was firmly protesting his innocence. He and Madeleine Hardcastle were indeed in love, but murder as an outgrowth of adultery seemed out of the question. Geoff had known all about the affair, and matters were proceeding in a civilized fashion toward divorce. No reason to hurry Geoff's exit. Meanwhile, Howard and Geoff had been working together, using an optical scanner to computerize the newspaper's cutting files, so that the cabinets full of mouldering envelopes could be discarded.

Crabbe knew a little about satanic cults in the county, and he remembered that Howard and Geoff had been nearly to that point in computerizing the "C" files. The inspector seemed puzzled by his friend's interest in the occult, and GeeGee had to explain about the Jenny Haniver and the fears of an aging Former Editorial Person in isolated Silk Willoughby. Crabbe spoke soothingly and promised to come round if any more dolls should surface, made from former marine animals.

On Wednesday morning, the letterbox contained three bills and a rejection slip from *Poetry Unchained*, a free-verse publication that had no interest in GeeGee's meticulously rhymed and metered lines. He supposed he should study marketing a bit, instead of picking intriguing names at random from his directory of little magazines. But it was, after all, just a way of getting through retirement.

There were no more nasty surprises on his doorstep. GeeGee spent the morning browsing in his old and new sets of the *OED*.

On Wednesday afternoon, he rang Harold Stimson again to ask if he was sure no one except Howard Robbins had been in the newspaper library during the critical half hour.

"As a matter of fact," I never said there weren't others," Harold replied. "You assumed that—you really are getting rusty out there, you know. Besides young Robbins (who says he was out of the room most of the time), two reporters went down together for a moment to look at a cutting. The char passed through and saw both of them, and they saw her. None of them had bloody hands. Jimmy McGregor was there—he's always there. He didn't have bloody hands, either. Anyway, he's deaf as a post and was reading or asleep in a far corner behind the shelves. He told the police he didn't see or hear a thing. Would you like me to find out what he was reading?"

"Thanks, Harold, but no," GeeGee replied. "Even my curiosity has its limits, difficult as that may be to believe."

"Thank God," Harold said. "It's nuisance enough having that superannuated fool of a retired librarian underfoot, without having to interview him about his reading habits."

"Poor Jimmy—forgotten but not gone," GeeGee said with a chuckle. "At least you said superannuated fool, singular."

"Don't press your luck," Harold said.

On Thursday morning, GeeGee's doorstep was still free of monstrous objects. In the letterbox were four bills, no rejection slips, and a note from Will asking if he knew the world's longest palindrome. He did. Will was due to come up with something more challenging, and GeeGee hoped it would be soon.

After perusing the post, GeeGee called a neighbor who drove him to the Britrail station in Sleaford just in time to catch the 11:20 "Sprinter" to Lincoln. He spent the 35-minute journey contemplating clouds above a pastoral landscape dotted with the sheep that Joanie liked to describe as "maggots on a hillside." Descending at Lincoln Central, he walked past Brayford Pool and up Newland Street to the *Reflector*, where it took a flourish of his gold "editor emeritus" card and a brief exercise of his full editorial glare to persuade a flustered personnel clerk that she really should bring him James A.H.M. McGregor's personnel file from the pensioners' cabinet.

He read it carefully, then popped round to the library to look at the file on Cults, Satanic, Lincolnshire. He chatted with the char sweeping the floor between the filing cabinets. He looked at the 11 volumes of the *OED* in their familiar, shabby dust jackets and noted that a twelfth volume, A-B, was missing. Then he left the *Reflector*, walked round the corner, and drank a pint of Ruddles County at his old table in the Wig & Whistle. After that, he walked back to the station, caught the 4:19 to Sleaford, and rang up his neighbor to fetch him home to Silk Willoughby.

On Friday morning, both his doorstep and letterbox were empty. He phoned Harold Stimson, who was mildly miffed that GeeGee hadn't stopped by to see him. "And incidentally," he said, "there's a new order in Personnel that no one, especially no one waving a gold card of any sort, is to be permitted access to confidential employee files. Hell's bells, what were you up to anyway?"

GeeGee told him, and Harold listened very quietly. Then he hung up and told his secretary to get the chief inspector on the line.

GeeGee told the rest of the story on Sunday night to Will and Joanie over glasses of Famous Grouse in his nephew's back parlor.

"It had to be Jimmy McGregor, the old librarian," he said, "and he didn't argue at all when the police began questioning him. He'd been stealing cuttings and books from the newspaper and public libraries for years, and sending citations to the *OED*. His flat was stacked with purloined items. He couldn't stand the idea of all his precious print being turned into blips on a computer screen. Plus, he apparently was afraid that Geoff was onto him and that he'd never be allowed inside a library again. He stole Howard's letter opener, with his fingerprints, and moved Geoff's opener—they're identical—to Howard's desk. He was shrewd enough to wear gloves, but totally mad."

"Sort of like that old fellow who sent James A.H. Murray all the *OED* citations from Broadmoor Criminal Lunatic Asylum," Will interjected.

"Something like that," GeeGee said, "and Jimmy will probably be remanded to the same sort of place."

"But how could a doddering old man stab someone in the back vigorously and accurately enough to kill him?" Joanie asked.

"Jimmy retired from the *Reflector* the same year I did," Gee-Gee said, with only a hint of frost in his voice. "He just didn't leave. Don't forget that Jimmy worked on newspapers for 40 years, and we get to know a lot of things, even anatomy. And also don't forget that when you carry books like the *OED* around for years, you develop strong arm muscles.

"In fact, it was the *OED* that put me onto him. It had clearly been placed under young Geoffrey after the stabbing, and there had to be some reason for that. A message of some sort, maybe. But the page numbers confused me at first, until I realized that Geoff was bleeding onto pages 306-307 in the 1961 reprint of the First Edition, not the 1989 Second Edition. What I wanted was on page 436 of my new Second Edition.

Will was watching him narrowly. "All right, Uncle GeeGee," he said, "are you going to explain, or do we have to take the Dapple course in comparative lexicography?"

"Well, you see, it was a signature," GeeGee replied, "a sort of byline. Something newspaper librarians never get. Page 306 in the old volume contains one of the very few citations from his own writing that James Augustus Henry Murray put into his great dictionary—it's one of the few places where he let his own name appear side by side with those of his other quoted authors. And something about that appealed to Jimmy—James Augustus Henry Murray McGregor.

"I can understand a little how he felt," GeeGee added. "Jimmy's parents seem to have gone in for famous lexicographers the way mine went in for famous generals."

"So what word of his own devising did old James A.H. Murray put into the *OED*, on whatever page it was?" Will asked.

"Anamorphose," GeeGee said. "A rare verb meaning to deform something monstrously. Strangely enough, something deformed that I found on my doorstep Tuesday morning put me in mind of it."

GeeGee sipped reflectively at his scotch and watched his nephew and niece. Joanie began to giggle.

"Will said it would make your life in Silk Willoughby more interesting," she said. "We found it in a curio shop in London. I wouldn't let him buy the other thing we found."

"But you would have loved it, Uncle GeeGee," Will said. "It was a Victorian picture frame, encrusted with shells, and inside it was a real fish's skeleton superimposed on a piece of dried pork skin. The title was 'Bony Part Crossing the Rind.'"

"Anyway," Will added, "I hope the Jenny Haniver didn't give you too much of a turn."

"Not at all," GeeGee said with a smile. He was thinking about the copy of a novel, *Elizabeth Appleton*, by John O'Hara, that he had arranged to have recommended to Will by the Sleaford librarian. On page 32, John Appleton observes that facetious "is the only word I know of that contains all the vowels and in the proper order." But in the margin someone had added, very lightly with an editor's soft pencil, "I know two others."

[1990]

Anamorphose (ænămṓˑɹfoᵘs, -ŏs), *v. rare.* [f. next (or its Gr. elements) on model of METAMOR-PHOSE.] To represent by anamorphosis; to distort into a monstrous projection.

1876 J. A. H. MURRAY in *Mill Hill Mag.* IV. 79 Shakspere might have seen this very picture, or, if not, some other in which a skull was thus anamorphosed; in which 'looking awry,' a 'shape of grief' was found. [Cf. *Rich. II*, ii. ii. 22.]

216

I THINK I SEE MY TRUE LOVE COMING

ROBERT ISN'T SURE why the painting attracts him so much. It's a fine painting, certainly, with much to say about color and composition, but far more representational than his own work. The title is "Girl With Plant." Richard Diebenkorn. 1960.

Only after he has looked at it for a long time does the plant begin to seem like an alien being, gesticulating or perhaps entreating, its hands stretched toward the girl in the red chair like glove puppets, like fantastic green macaws.

The plant seems to have drained the girl of her vigor. She rests quietly, her right arm extended on the table beside her, as she appears to listen to the plant. Its abundant green foliage balances the dark of her dress and of her hair, beside which the barest sliver of flesh tone suggests her averted face. Something about the plant's energy and the passivity of the girl interests Robert, or are they aspects of the same thing, he wonders? Diebenkorn cannot answer; he has died since the beginning of the year, a card next to the painting says.

The Phillips Collection is nearly deserted this summer Saturday morning. Only a few art-loving tourists have found their way to this remote corner of Washington, far from the White House and the Lincoln Memorial. Robert, whose apartment/studio is around the corner, moves past them to look again at his favorite pictures—the Vuillards, the room of Pierre Bonnards with their human figures curiously abstracted against the depths of landscape, Seurat's "The Stonebreaker," nearly lost in the candied glow of Renoir. Robert stops, for perhaps the tenth time, before

217

"The Watering Place," Picasso's faint drypoint of 1905 (No. 1432 in the Phillips catalogue). A friend's line of verse comes to mind: "A prospect of smoke and horses." The drawing is strong as steel and frail as smoke.

Robert's own work is going badly, if it can be said to be going at all. "Technically proficient" is a term he hears too often these days, with its suggestion of something closely held and limited, a dryness. He has been painting his precise silhouetted shapes for months now, trying to follow the lead of Myron Stout, his major influence, and to paint what Stout called "every bloody atom" individually. But it isn't working; the shapes lie dead on the canvas.

Robert, who is 23, has begun to fear the loss of his gift, and this makes him think of the fairy tale about the girl who loses her golden ball. "And now, lass, you must die," the hangman says, with a matter-of-factness that Robert found horrible even as a child. He remembers the agony of waiting for the girl's father, mother, brother, and sister to arrive—each without the golden ball, each eager to see her hanged. Only her true love's perseverance saves her: "And I have brought your golden ball and come to set you free. I have not come to see you hanged upon this gallows tree."

Robert has a true love, but Lucy is not helping to set him free or to find the lost golden ball of his artist's first vision. In fact, she is annoyed with him much of the time. His artistic difficulties are an old woe by now, and she has her own problems, which have to do with the solid-waste management survey she's conducting on contract for the Environmental Protection Agency. Also, Robert has been unkind about the flowered paper she hung on one wall of the studio, wasting one of her valuable days off. Their evenings have been less satisfactory, and shorter.

"I sell myself nothing," Picasso said, and Robert thinks of that when he looks at the mounting number of canvasses, unsold either to himself or to anyone else. He feels up against some barrier that he can't get over or even fully comprehend. The fine fresh mornings of two springs ago, when he was working well, are a distant memory, and now he is repeating himself, trying to recapture whatever it was that informed those earlier paintings.

"Pardon me, young man, do you have the time?"

The voice at his shoulder is harsh and old. The woman to whom it belongs is at least 75, maybe 80—of indeterminate age really, an old woman in a black dress, with gray hair pulled back and a pale gold chain at her throat. He tells her the time, but instead of moving away she remains next to him, looking at Picasso's horses and riders.

"He did it with almost nothing, didn't he?" she says. "It's just barely there, isn't it?"

Robert smiles. "That struck you, too. Yes, it seems like such a fragile sketch, but a line doesn't have to be heavy to be a line, does it? And he could do more with a line than anyone else."

"I supposed you were an artist," she replies. "You've been standing there for 20 minutes, and it's almost the last day of the exhibition, and everybody has to go around you. If you'll let me buy you coffee downstairs and tell me what you see in the Picasso, I'll consider it my contribution for the day to other art lovers."

Being picked up in a gallery by someone older than his grandmother is so unexpected that Robert can't think of anything to do but agree. In a few moments they are seated in cane-backed chairs in the Phillips's tiny coffee shop, and he is telling her about the Picasso and why he can't stop trying to get his mind around those drypoint lines that are so nearly not there, so faint that it seems a flash of sunlight could make them vanish forever into the paper.

Anna—he has gotten that much of her name—listens and asks about other artworks he likes. Her eyebrows lift slightly when he mentions the girl with the plant.

"Yes," she says, "I've always thought I could have posed for Diebenkorn, if it had been 30 years earlier. I was that girl, all

219

proper and quiet and dark, and arguing with this great green thing that only came out when I was writing something and getting it right, and feeling like the top of my head was coming off—as they say."

Anna goes on talking about writing, about editors and rejection slips. Robert's curiosity grows, and when the conversation swings back to him, he says, "Excuse me, but I can't help wondering. You're not *that* Anna, are you—the one who won the Pulitzer or a National Book Award?

"Oh, no!" Anna replies, with a brief laugh. "You wouldn't want my autograph. I tried hard, but I'm an artist with the art left out—and even that's not original.

"If you want the truth, I was 'on' about half the time—not enough for the Pulitzer committee, but I cut quite a swath through the literatii on R Street."

"But didn't it drive you crazy?" Robert asks. "Wanting to do something big, the top of your head coming off and all that, and not being able to command it at will?"

"Of course it did—does," she answers. "That's why I'm a cracked old woman who talks to young artists in galleries." And then, more seriously: "But I had to throw myself in and find out. And I've written some good things, and I might really have had it, you know."

She pauses for a moment, and then says, "It's my true love. So what if I'm not all that good at it?"

Robert is laughing by this time, happily and loudly enough that the counterman is looking at them curiously.

"I never thought of it that way before," he says. "Maybe when you see your true love coming, it isn't a person at all, but just a different way of looking at things."

"Well," Anna says, "isn't that what a true love usually is—just someone ordinary you looked at differently one day."

I THINK I SEE MY TRUE LOVE COMING

That evening, in his studio, it occurs to Robert that the silhouettes don't matter anymore—they were a way of seeing, but not his way, a path followed to a necessary end and now ready to be abandoned.

He picks up a bucket of bright paint and a brush and begins to draw lines across the flowered paper of the studio wall, thinking as he does so that Lucy will be furious, and that she will be right to be, and that he will know what to do about it.

He paints a long curving line, then another and another, as the ball of the evening sun washes the room with its golden light.

[1993]

Illustration by Arthur Rackham for *English Fairy Tales*, 1918
Reprinted by the kind permission of the Rackham family

Death Sentence

IN THE FIRST ARDOR OF COMPOSITION, Percy resolved to write one sentence of such a delicious and bewildering convolution, of such ripe and orotund sonority, that the reader, entirely seduced by its music and wandering dream-lost through the sinuous pathways and green pergolas of an involvement no less complex, lozenged, or like a casket of scented dainties than the great north window of Chartres, would, long before he reached what he had imagined might be the end, be beguiled instead into a faery landscape, so charming in its indolence, so redolent of endless summer days in woods and water-meadows, so bewitchingly furnished with pleasaunces, bosky resting places, and vistas half-seen through the boughs of flowering trees, that whatever goal he might have set for himself, whether this was simply to emerge at last into the clear sun of simple syntax or to reach that evanescent edifice of conclusion whose turrets and machicolations, as coruscated and glittering in the last light of comprehension as Ruskin's vision of St. Mark's, seemed to grow ever more distant as he pressed toward them, he would have eventually forgotten both his starting place and his destination and, having for escape surrendered even the faintest velleity, would be content to wander forever at the writer's will; but this was not to be, for, before Percy had fairly embarked upon the floodtide of his consummate sentence and even before he had been compelled to his first semicolon, he was found dead in the library, bludgeoned savagely with the one-volume edition of *Recherche du Temps Perdu*.

FLASH FICTION

*For a while, I was writing "flash fiction," stories that try to
pack their action into as few words as possible. I kept trying
to whittle them down still more, and finally reached just under 100 words in "Sticker Shocker"—still far short, or long,
of Hemingway.*

HEART

TWENTY-TWO YEARS OLD, in New York, with a dicey heart.

Florence took an elevator the dozen floors down from Dr.
Muzillo's office, then crossed the lobby to Starbucks, where she
ordered a large house blend, regular, and lit a cigarette. In old
movies, she thought, they always give you a cigarette before the
firing squad goes to work.

"Dicey," Dr. Muzillo had said. A funny, old-fashioned word,
evoking images of crapshooters in alleys. "What's happened to
you is serious," he went on. "We could operate, but it's not always successful. Best thing for now is take medicine, stop smoking, drink decaf. Watch your diet. Avoid excitement and see me
again in a month."

"So could I, like, drop dead tomorrow?" she asked him, hoping for a good bedside manner. "Sure you could—but then so
could I," the doctor said cheerfully. "With care, you could live a
long time. You just need to be very cautious."

"Oh, that's me," she thought now, stirring sugar into her coffee. "Florence Cautious Graham." Coming to New York had been
the big gamble of her life, spurred by a scholarship and the chance

to study with real physicists. And her plan was working, right down to the two-room walk-up in Brooklyn, the old-movie houses, the temp-service jobs, the wonderful grind of graduate physics. She even had the grind's T-shirt, "Guilt Without Sex," which she was working to change. What hadn't been in the plan was a death sentence.

"Miss, you can't smoke in here," a pimply Starbucks attendant was saying.

"I've just been told I'm dying," Florence said, making her voice go raspy, like the movies. "This is the last cigarette of my life, and I'm entitled to it. Leave me alone."

The attendant fell back, wide-eyed, and scuttled for what Florence assumed was management country. She dropped the cigarette in her cup and walked out into the sunshine. At a pharmacy down the block, she got her prescription filled. ("My life from now on?" she wondered.)

On the subway to Brooklyn, she reviewed the facts. These included assurances over the years by her hometown doctor that she had only a slight heart murmur. "You'll probably grow out of it," he had said, with a much better bedside manner than Dr. Muzillo, who was a specialist and told her exactly what "slight murmur" meant in her case—a highly unusual arrhythmia, getting worse, treatable to an extent with medicine but curable only with last-ditch surgery. "You're a really rare bird," he said happily. "One for the medical journals." She would have to tell her parents, who would want her at home so they could help her live cautiously for whatever time she had left. She thought that perhaps she would not tell them just yet.

By the time her stop arrived, she had reached the bargaining stage in the grief process. "I won't smoke anymore," she promised. "I'll cut down on the coffee—but please, God, not all decaf. I'll never make it to class."

To fulfill this partial pledge, she stopped at a C-Town market and picked up a can of green-label Melitta. She was on her way to checkout when she saw the woman and little boy in the candy aisle. The woman—bloated, low-browed—was addressing the boy in a voice guttural with menace. The boy, four at the most, was cowering in his shopping-cart seat. "Joey, you little bastard," the woman was saying, "if you take another piece of candy off the shelf, I'll kill you, so help me God." Joey opened his mouth, and she backhanded him, then slapped him hard on the return swing, suppressing the start of a wail.

Florence's heart did a little quick-step. Farther down the aisle two shoppers disappeared into Produce. In that moment, it occurred to Florence that, given her circumstances, she was free to do anything she wanted, and that she had no reason not to. It also occurred to her that she was angry. She marched up the aisle and into the face of the furious woman.

"Do that again and you're dead meat," Florence said.

"And who the fuck do you think *you* are?" the woman exploded, reaching for the nearest shopping-cart weapon, a stalk of celery.

"I know perfectly well who I am," Florence said, quiet but steely, her best old-movie voice. "I'm Officer Florence C. Graham of Child Protective Services. I'm on the undercover detail, and I will spend every minute of my time putting you in jail if you ever strike that child again. I'll be watching you. And drop that stupid celery."

Her heart went hopskip again, and there was a soft thud on the floor. Florence turned to the boy, now snuffling and wiping his nose with a sleeve. "Joey, if she ever hits you like that again, call 911 and ask for Officer Graham in Protective Services. Or talk to whoever answers. And learn your address so you can tell the officer how to get to your house."

Then Florence turned on her heel and got the hell out of there, past the crowded checkout lanes, onto the street. She was half a block away before she realized that she had shoplifted the can of coffee. Her pulse was steady—a little fast maybe, but steady. She suddenly knew, beyond any shadow of diagnosis, that she had the heart of a lion.

LIES AND HALLUCINATIONS

DAVID AND I GRADUATED first and second in our class at theological seminary, and in the same sequence lost our faith. Then we were out of touch for 20 years, until we ran into each other late one afternoon at Florian's in Venice. There was an instant of uncertainty, then delighted recognition and a quick catch-up on our lives, careers, marriages (divorce for him, my wife's death—coming to Venice was my effort to find Sophie again, in a place where we'd been happy).

Inevitably, we got into theology, an obsession that had survived our apostasy. David is still the one person I know who can reliably explain the difference between *homoousios* and *homoiousios*. And I found myself telling him about the Chinese Christian I had met in Taipei who "blessed God" aloud—night after night, sitting in his darkened apartment, looking out at the polluted sky. And how one night he felt a hand on his shoulder, turned, and looked up into the face of Christ.

David laughed. "The hand is a special effect," he said. "For the rest, well, it's a continuum. At one end, lies and hallucinations. At the other, maybe, a genuine mystical experience. Mother Church would send a prelate to investigate."

We sat in easy silence for a minute or two, looking out across the Piazza to the church of San Marco, a miracle in its own way, adorned with the pillaged treasures of a thousand years. At the other end of the Piazza, over San Geminiano, a rain shower and the westering sun had painted a pale rainbow.

David said, "Did you know there are people who pray for God? I'm not sure just whom they pray *to,* but they ask help for God, because He carries such heavy burdens. Maybe your Chi-

226

nese friend was one of those. If he was, then what happened to him could have been genuine, and extremely rare."

Our talk turned to friends from seminary and then to Venice. David seemed to have church-crawled through every *chiesa* in the city, including the deconsecrated ones now turned into movie houses. "See the Tiepolos at Sant' Alvise," he told me. "Most tourists never make it that far." As we parted, he said, "I've got a serious decision coming up. Can't tell you about it, but if you can still say a prayer for me, I'd appreciate it."

Back home, I realized I hadn't gotten his address or e-mail, so I called the seminary alumni office and asked for Marge Hallett, the secretary, whom I'd dated briefly. "I shouldn't go into this," she said, but since it's you . . . . David had a total breakdown about five years ago. Decided one day that he was the fourth person of the Trinity. He's in a sanitarium upstate. I understand he's gotten loose a time or two, but they've managed to bring him back before he could hurt himself—or anyone else."

'FOR SALE. BABY SHOES. NEVER USED'

SHE DIDN'T HAVE A BABY and he couldn't play the guitar. So there they were, walking through the park, laughing at each other.

They had met at the garden center up the street, where he'd jumped out of the passenger side of a truck delivering 40-pound sacks of wood chips from Indianapolis.

"Why the guitar?" she asked. "It helps me get rides," he replied. And pointing to the empty stroller next to her, "Why no baby?"

"It's my sister's," she said. "She was pregnant, but the baby didn't make it. So I brought it down here to give to LuAnn, but they just took her to the hospital. I guess I'll have to leave it."

"So, you want to go for a walk?" he said, giving the guitar an off-key wallop that caused an old woman to look up from the bed of nasturtiums she was inspecting.

Now they were walking through the park, telling their stories. She told him her name was Annie, and he said his was Fred. She told him she was a creative-writing student at the local college and liked Hemingway. He told her he was a college student in Indianapolis and *loved* Hemingway, especially his six-word short story: "For sale. Baby shoes. Never used."

"I liked that, too," she said.

She asked why he was hitchhiking. He said it was because a friend had borrowed his car and he had to get here to visit his grandmother, who was really sick.

"Your grandmother!" She began laughing. "None of this is true, is it?"

"Only the bit about Hemingway. Who did the stroller belong to?"

"I don't know. It was just parked there. I think the kid had been stolen."

He looked at her for a long moment.

"So, you want a cup of coffee, Annie?"

"That would be nice, Fred."

STICKER SHOCKER

HE BEGAN LIVING his life by the advice on bumper stickers. He thought globally, acted locally. He didn't love Jesus but honked anyway, just in case. Then one day he saw a girl getting out of a car with a sticker that read, "Wrangler butts drive me nuts." He was wearing Wranglers, so he acted locally, but she got honked and called a cop, who threw his butt in jail. "Bad cop, no doughnut," he pleaded. But the judge, who also read bumper stickers, said, "Don't blame me, I voted for Kerry," and gave him 30 days.

WHAT DREAMS MAY COME

EDWARD WOKE FROM HIS OLD MAN'S NAP with the strong feeling that he had an appointment with someone and was about to miss it.

He had missed one early in the term—the forgetfulness of a scholar in his 80s—and now he was careful to mark his engagements in a pocket datebook. In fact this was what made his dream puzzling—he had seen, with the clarity of complete wakefulness, today's line in the datebook: "A.—7 p.m., library."

When he got the book from his desk, there was no such entry, but the vividness nagged at him. Could one of his graduate students, Aileen Evans perhaps, be walking to the library even now to meet him?

He had fallen asleep fully dressed. Now he slipped on a coat and stepped out into the snow for the quick stroll to the library. When he reached it, the lounge was empty, but a gas log was burning brightly. He slumped into an easy chair, breathing a little heavily from his brisk walk through the snow. If Aileen was coming, she would want to talk about her research into the work of her famous relative, the discoverer of the Minoan Linear B script. Edward was an authority on the Minoans and still saw serious students.

But Aileen wasn't coming—his dreaming mind had played a trick on him. He would rest a few minutes, get warm, and walk home. His head drooped, and he passed into a dreamless sleep.

* * *

Artiane entered the room exactly on time, sat down on a wooden chair before the fire, and waited for Reg, who was late as usual. The fire and the cold through which she had walked made her drowsy, and she was already beginning a scrap of dream when she heard footsteps on the stones. She woke to see Reg approaching her, his arms spread wide.

"Darling, you're late," she said. "The dance will have started."

"Do you really care?" he asked, laughing and gathering her into his embrace. "We could stay here, all alone."

"Oh, come on, let's go," she said, laughing now herself. "We can come back here later and still be alone—there won't be anybody in the library tonight."

They linked arms and walked out into the snow. The scrap of dream—there had been an old man in it, vivid, oddly familiar—faded from her mind. It was a "bright night" with Xylos making a full disc overhead and the thin crescent of Aöthes near the horizon.

From the lighted pavilion just ahead come the graceful music of the Long Dance, and they hurried toward it.

[2006]

ACKNOWLEDGMENTS

MY FIRST AND DEEPEST DEBT is to my wife, Karen Petersen Bridges, for a lifetime of encouragement, editing, and wise counsel. I have learned that when she says, "You need to work on this some more," she's nearly always right. Thanks go also to Susanna Rich, Mike O'Connor, Ann and Edwin Wakeling, and Marvin Sosna, who reviewed parts of the manuscript.

I am grateful to the following for permission to use the materials noted: Trustees of Columbia University, lines from poems by William Bronk; Keith and Judy Ford at the Paragon Speedway, the track's logo; Susanna Rich, the story *Willie & Walter*, first printed in her book, *The Flexible Writer*; Michael and Margaret Snow, literary executors of W.S. Graham, lines from his poems; the family of Arthur Rackham, his drawing from *English Fairy Tales*, by Flora Annie Steel; Richard Day, map of the Miami Indian territory; Duane Ackerson, "Sign at the End of the Universe." Most photographs in the book are mine, but I am happy to credit the New York Zoological Society for the photo of my Uncle Bill in Africa. Bill took the picture of the ABC Hotel and also drew the "colophant" on the final page. Two other small pictures are from old postcards and brochures, the originals of which I have been unable to trace. Dianne Jenkins, a good friend and wonderful rubber-stamp artist, carved the picture of Sam the Dragon, exactly as I pictured him. Some of the information in "Murder in the *OED*" as well as the picture of a Jenny Haniver are from a 1934 article in the *Scientific Monthly*, "Jenny Hanivers, Dragons, and Basilisks in the Old Natural History Books and in Modern Times," by Dr. E.W. Gudger. I am indebted to *Wandering Ghost* by Jonathan Cott for background on Lafcadio Hearn. The picture of Henry N. Dick is from the *Vincennes* (Ind.) *Sun-Commercial*.

Steve Johnson, manager of the Bronx Zoo library, was especially helpful in supplying my uncle's *Animal Kingdom* articles from the Congo, as well as tracking down additional information on elephants. Dennis Cripe of the Franklin College faculty performed prodigies in rescuing good photos from old snapshots. Lindsay Hadley and Tim Lisko did their usual fine cover job. Others who helped in various ways (sometimes without knowing it) were the staffs of the Knox County Public Library and the Johnson County Museum of History, Ivan Lancaster, Betty Legan Smith, Simone Pilon, Karl and Colin Bridges, Mary Alice Lecclier, Candace Moseley, and David Carlson.

www.ingramcontent.com/pod-product-compliance
Lightning Source LLC
Chambersburg PA
CBHW070059260626
47160CB00004B/1252